Pierre moaned  s
up Odette's c e
knickers and pull them down swiftly. He had them
round her ankles and she opened her knees to let him
catch his first glimpse between her legs.

While he stared at the delight he had uncovered, she
prised her knickers off one foot with the toes of the other
and spread her legs.

'You are very beautiful,' he said in a whisper.

'I know,' she replied, 'and I'm not just for looking at
either . . .'

Also available from Headline

Amour Amour
Amour Encore
Amour Toujours

Love Italian Style
Ecstasy Italian Style
Rapture Italian Style

The Pleasures of Women
The Secrets of Women
The Delights of Women

The Royal Scandal
The Girls's Boarding School

Bonjour Amour

Marie-Claire Villefranche

Copyright © 1995 Marie-Claire Villefranche

The right of Marie-Claire Villefranche to be identified as the Author of
the Work has been asserted by her in accordance with the
Copyright, Designs and Patents Act 1988.

First published in Great Britain in 1994
by HEADLINE BOOK PUBLISHING

A HEADLINE DELTA paperback

10 9 8 7 6 5 4 3 2 1

All rights reserved. No part of this publication may be
reproduced, stored in a retrieval system, or transmitted,
in any form or by any means without the prior written
permission of the publisher, nor be otherwise circulated
in any form of binding or cover other than that in which
it is published and without a similar condition being
imposed on the subsequent purchaser.

All characters in this publication are fictitious
and any resemblance to real persons, living or dead,
is purely coincidental.

ISBN 0 7472 4803 6

Typeset by CBS, Felixstowe, Suffolk

Printed and bound in Great Britain by
Cox & Wyman Ltd, Reading, Berks

HEADLINE BOOK PUBLISHING
A division of Hodder Headline PLC
338 Euston Road
London NW1 3BH

Bonjour Amour

Odette Begins A New Career

Laurent Breville's studio was a large and pleasant room, a part of his comfortable apartment on the Boulevard Edgar-Quinet. On the walls were cork boards to which were pinned examples of his work for fashion magazines. They were watercolours in a sketchy and impressionist technique of women in stylish lingerie. There was no other subject on view, just underwear. Bras and knickers and slips. Matt or shiny. Frilly or minimal. The man must be a monomaniac.

In studying the sketches round the walls Odette saw that the artist paid no attention at all to the models' faces. Just a dab of red for the mouth and two dots for nostrils, two dashes for the eyes. Whether his models were pretty or plain, nineteen or forty, there was no way to tell from his pictures. On the other hand, the styling and colour of the hair were carefully painted and formed an important part of the overall effect – and that very clearly was to focus the onlooker's eye on the garments, not the model.

Does he really need living models for this sort of painting? Odette asked herself. It would be easier and cheaper and surely more convenient if he bought a shop-window mannequin – not just the old-fashioned rigid dummy, but the latest type with movable arms and wigs to change. He could pull frilly silk knickers up its long legs to cover the blank space between the thighs. And slip the matching petticoat over its expressionless head, and pull it down to cover breasts as unyielding as wood.

As for the hair, he could select from a dozen blonde and brunette wigs to complete the ensemble.

Evidently this Breville wanted real women in his studio, real bottoms inside the stylish knickers and real *nichons* inside the beautiful bras and slips. Perhaps it inspired him, to look at a woman in silk underwear and know there was warm soft flesh in those thin almost-transparent little nothings of lingerie – and a pretty *joujou* inside the flimsy knickers. Certainly Breville produced marvellous colour sketches for fashion magazines.

But should a commercial artist be dependent on inspiration? His job was to draw clothes, underwear, whatever. Even if they were on a hanger, what difference did that make? No, there was a little more to Monsieur Breville's habit of wanting models to wear the garments he drew, Odette concluded. Men were like that – everyone knew it. Whatever the occasion, if a woman was there on her own, a man would always try to . . .

At this point Odette's thought was interrupted by the sudden entrance of Laurent Breville into the studio.

'*Bonjour*, Mademoiselle,' he said briefly.

He was not at all what she had expected. Though she was not sure what she expected of a magazine artist. Madame Drouet, who ran the model agency, had hinted very discreetly that he was not the easiest of her clients to please. Something in the way she said that, and something about her pursed lips when she was speaking of Breville, had given Odette a vague impression that he was a degenerate, a middle-aged pervert.

BONJOUR AMOUR

She had pictured him in her mind as a forty-year-old voyeur with little piggy eyes and hot hands and almost no hair on his head. In short, a monster drooling over pretty young models who were paid to pose for him in Givenchy knickers.

But now she saw him, her picture had been entirely wrong. He was no more than thirty, this Laurent Breville, a tall slender man with a faintly sulky expression. And he dressed well to work, not in the least sloppily. He was wearing an expensive pullover with a pink silk scarf knotted loosely round his neck and tucked down inside. His elegant trousers were dove-grey. His shoes had gold buckles and were of soft glowing leather, as fine as gloves.

His appearance indicated a man doing well in his profession, not a struggling bohemian in a miserable attic, living on bread and cheap red wine. Laurent Breville evidently had money in the bank. And investments, no doubt.

He looked Odette up and down in a calculating way.

'You've got the body and legs of a usable model,' he said at last, 'neat backside, not too much bosom. You'll do for now – I have to finish this job by tomorrow midday so I can't waste any time selecting models. It's for *Vogue*.'

It was not the most flattering greeting Odette had heard, but at least it meant she was working again. She asked Breville if he did much for *Vogue*. 'Naturally,' he said, and he waved a hand at the water-colour sketches pinned round the studio. 'And also for *Harper's Bazaar*,' he added to impress her. 'My work appears in all the important magazines.'

'I thought they used photos,' said Odette.

'Yes, photographs cost a lot to set up,' he said impatiently, as if everyone knew that. 'And the camera lens is merciless. It shows every small imperfection. If it is a question of a range of garments like underwear, it is more effective to commission me to produce colour sketches.'

'Then you are an expert on women's underwear?' Odette asked, trying not to grin in case she offended him.

'I am the only expert,' he answered with great pride, 'I may say without fear of contradiction that I am regarded as the top artist for underwear. The great designers and makers turn to me for beautiful pictures of their latest creations.'

Odette thought he was about to give her a tirade in praise of his own genius at sketching knickers but he glanced at his gold wristwatch, shook his arm and looked at the dial again. He said the morning was half over, there was no time for conversation – that was not what he was paying her for.

Odette nodded and asked how he wanted to begin.

'The garments arrived yesterday,' he said. 'They are there on the chaise-longue. I'll start with the slip. Undress behind the screen and put it on. Carefully, no creases. And please hurry.'

The chaise-longue was an elaborate piece of furniture, gilded and carved, all pale pink velvet and richly polished dark wood. The sort of thing that was far too fancy for the house of anyone but the mistress of a vulgar scrap-metal millionaire. But right for a film-set or as a prop for fashion sketches.

On it, in layers of rustling tissue-paper, lay matching sets of underwear in different colours; slips, knickers, brassières. Odette asked which he wanted her to wear first and he said the blue. She carried all the garments behind the screen and began to undress.

The screen was another extraordinary piece of furniture, made of red leather, mother-of-pearl and polished brass, adorned with hand-painted peacocks. No expert could have put a date and place of manufacture to it because it was a fake antique, theatrical and absurd, made for show. In Breville's studio it looked right.

Behind the magnificent screen was a small gilt chair on which Odette draped her clothes as she removed them. She was not sure what was usual on these occasions, having never posed before in underwear. She called to the artist over the screen.

'Do you want me to keep my own things on under the slip or am I to wear the whole set that goes with it?'

'The set, of course,' he said crossly. 'I've no time to waste while you keep darting behind the screen to change knickers.'

Odette shrugged and stripped naked. Breville was a difficult person to work for, it seemed. She put on the set he had called blue – the word surely didn't do it justice. It was an intense sapphire-blue, it made her skin glow like alabaster.

The slip was high-waisted and knee-length, lace edging at the hem and bust-line. The knickers that went with it were chic and flimsy, with more lace, and the brassière was a wisp of silk-satin in the same astonishing sapphire-blue.

Odette ran a comb through her walnut-brown hair and checked her lipstick in a tiny round mirror from her handbag. Breville wouldn't care if she had make-up or not, as he ignored faces in his work, but she felt better when she looked good. She stepped from behind the screen and the uncovered wooden floor felt hard beneath her bare feet.

Laurent Breville sat upon a high stool behind a drawing-board that swivelled from upright to horizontal. His feet were on the stool cross-stave, with his knees up, and the board was set at the angle he wanted. It sloped down to his lap – but not too steeply, for water colours run easily. From where Odette stood she could see only his head and shoulders above the top edge of the drawing-board, and his feet below the bottom edge.

'Stand sideways to me,' he said, staring at her, 'feet apart, as if you are walking toward the door over there. Now half turn to me, keeping your feet where they are. A little more. Now put your arms up as if you are brushing your hair. That's it! Stay like that.'

He wants me standing like this to make my *nichons* stick out, Odette said to herself. If he wanted big ones, he ought to have asked Madame Drouet for a different girl, not for me. Mine are a nice average size, not the great big pink balloons that drive some men crazy.

Breville worked quickly, dashing down an outline in charcoal, then dragging brushfuls of water-colour across the thick paper. In twenty-five minutes he made five sketches of Odette wearing the sapphire-blue slip. Four standing, to show the slip's long graceful line, then for the other he had her sit on the chaise longue sideways, her knees up and her arms round them.

He worked in silence. Odette spent the time admiring herself. The blue slip was precisely the sort of thing she should wear every day, she decided – it represented the chic and luxury she knew she deserved.

Her skin looked gorgeous beside it. And the way it hugged the line of her thighs was very flattering. What she needed was to make the acquaintance of a man able to give her the clothes and jewels that would set off her looks. A rich and charming man to take her to all the fashionable restaurants. And to install her in an apartment in a stylish part of Paris.

Odette was twenty-two. She had a good figure and pale green eyes. The men she knew expected her to go to their apartment after they'd paid for dinner in even a cheap restaurant. And get into their bed for the night. As for clothes, they thought themselves very generous if they bought her a pair of silk stockings.

It was necessary to meet a different type of man, she knew. A man who would adore her and cherish her and give her everything without wishing to own her completely. Not easy to find.

Breville's work at the drawing-board was going well, his mood was greatly improved. He smiled at his work, though not at his model. At least he sounded affable when he said he was ready to start the next drawing and asked her to take off the slip.

Odette didn't go behind the screen for this, not after he had complained earlier about wasting time. She eased the slip over her head and draped it over the screen. She shook out her hair and turned to face him, wearing only the sapphire-blue knickers and brassière.

'Shall I stand or sit?' she asked.

Breville was occupied with drawing-pins and sheets of paper – he spoke without looking at her.

'Start on the chaise-longue,' he said, 'one elbow on the back and one knee up – a very casual pose.'

Odette did as he asked. She rested easily on the pink velvet, radiating charm. After five minutes she turned her head toward Breville to see if he was ready for a change of pose yet. Over the top of the drawing-board he was staring fixedly at her, his face flushed, his eyes glazed as if in a trance.

'Monsieur Breville?' she said. 'Shall I move round?'

There was no answer from him. And she realised where his gaze was fixed, between her thighs, where little curls of dark-brown hair showed past the lace edging of the blue knickers. For her it was totally natural, the riotous brown thatch between her legs, but she knew what the effect on men was.

'I forgot,' she said, 'I hope you don't think it displeasing. I've never posed for underwear before.'

Breville became even redder in the face when he realised that it was no secret where he was looking. His eyes were fixed on the brown fleece that grew down the inside of Odette's shapely thighs, he made gurgling sounds as he struggled to recover the power of rational speech.

'I don't understand,' he said faintly, 'you shave under your arms. But this . . .'

As he said, her armpits were smooth and her face was made up with skill, her toe-nails painted, her skin sleek and perfect. Only one part of her slender body remained in the state Nature intended. The fleece between her legs was thick and untamed, as if she despised the sophistication of bare tidy groins.

'Ah, my little fur coat,' she said, moving her thighs further apart, 'some men find it *sauvage*, but I prefer it like this.'

'But this is impossible,' Breville said hoarsely, crimson of face as he stared at the nut-brown thatch that spread three or four centimetres down the insides of her thighs. From where he sat he could know nothing of the delicate and expensive perfume by Lanvin with which those curls were sprayed. A pity for him.

'Where is the problem?' Odette asked. 'You can leave it out, just as you leave out my face from your drawings. I'm sure that fashion magazines don't want pictures of hair between a woman's legs, or even under her arms. The pictures they print show women looking as waxed and unreal as dummies in a dress shop window.'

Breville said nothing, he continued to stare at her, his eyes almost popping from his face. Odette decided his attitude was offensive. She had already reached the conclusion that Breville took young men to bed, not women. To annoy him she leaned upon the velvet-upholstered back of the chaise-longue and spread her legs, to display more of her curly brown fleece.

Still Breville said nothing – although his cheeks were purple and his eyes insane. Odette found the situation amusing. On a sudden impulse she jumped up and took three long strides towards him. Till then his hands had been hidden from sight by the tilt of the drawing-board, but now she stood beside it she saw that he had undone his trousers. His stiff part was out and he held it tightly in his fist.

'*Oh la la*, Monsieur!' said Odette. 'So this is how you treat your models.'

This must be what Madame Drouet at the agency had hinted at – her best client had the habit of giving himself secret little thrills while looking at women in silk underwear! Well, Odette thought, it was tame really, compared with some of the oddities she met modelling clothes for wholesale garment manufacturers in the show-rooms of their factories. Mostly they were twenty years older than Breville and by no means as good-looking.

Breville tried to stuff his stiff part back into his trousers out of sight. Odette put her hand on his wrist to prevent this shame-faced cover-up.

'Let me see,' she said, and he blushed hotly.

The *savoir-faire* of his fashion work for chic magazines,

the studied sophistication of his expensive clothes from the rue du Faubourg Saint Honore – the glossy veneer vanished in an instant and he was pink-faced with shame and remorse. He begged Odette not to say a word about his momentary weakness. Surely she must see that it was an unfortunate and unaccountable lapse, nothing more than that.

Odette was completely convinced now that Breville played with himself every time he had a pretty model posing for him in silk underwear. Catching him at it was fortunate – she could ask him for double the normal modelling fee, in return for keeping her mouth shut. She was thinking about this and hardly listening to his absurd babbling when he said something that astonished her. He said he had become engaged to be married only a week ago.

'Truly?' said Odette, smiling doubtfully. 'But surely your interests lie elsewhere. Why else should the sight of a woman's body upset you?'

He understood her meaning and assured her she was wrong about him. He was not left-handed, he maintained, not in the least! On the contrary, he had become engaged to a most charming lady. And with some pride he added that her name was Marie-Louise de Beaucourt-Villiers.

Odette was an intelligent person, said Breville, and charming too in her own way. She surely understood that if a hint of his momentary folly reached Mademoiselle de Beaucourt-Villiers the engagement would be broken off. Especially if her parents heard about it.

'I understand,' said Odette.

Indeed she did. Laurent Breville was trying to wiggle his way into the upper crust. He wanted *cachet*, this sketcher of knickers and bras. And that raised possibilities in Odette's agile mind. Nothing so criminal as blackmail, but perhaps a little discreet persuasion.

'I'm sure that Mademoiselle de Beaucourt-Villiers is a proud fiancée,' said Odette in an amiable manner. 'She understands that an artist for important magazines has models in his studio – girls stripped down to their underwear. Naturally, she trusts you not to exploit these situations, as some men would.'

'I am utterly faithful to her,' Breville said very earnestly, 'but to be frank, Mademoiselle Charron, I fear she has a rather suspicious nature. She asks me the same questions every time we meet – who has been to model for me, how much of their body did they reveal, did I see their breasts, their thighs? And did I become sexually excited while I was sketching.'

'She asks you questions like that?' said Odette with a smile as her eyebrows arched upwards. 'Well, well!'

'It is an obsession,' Breville said, nodding his head sadly. 'She needs constant reassurance from me. I find it embarrassing to be accused in this way, but I love her.'

'Poor man,' said Odette, her busy mind examining the ways of benefiting from what she was hearing.

It seemed clear to her that Breville's fiancée must be plain, if she were permanently worried about models posing in knickers. After all, if Mademoiselle de Whatever was young and pretty and rich as well as of good birth, why would she marry a commercial artist – however successful he was?

On reflection, Odette considered it unlikely Mademoiselle the Fiancée was either beautiful, rich or young. It explained a lot about Breville, if he planned to marry a plain woman older than himself because of her name and family.

Odette smiled at him in a sympathetic way to calm his

evident agitation. He smiled back warily – then his smile vanished when she undid his belt and pulled up the front of his shirt.

'What are you doing?' he gasped.

While they had been talking his upright part had drooped. He sighed a feeble word of protest when Odette's hand encircled it – a half-hearted *No* that means the reverse. And she grasped his slackening flesh with a firm touch to restore it to stiffness.

'Explain to me why fashion magazine pictures show women like dummies in a window,' she said.

His only reply was a gasp of guilty pleasure.

'Then I will tell you,' she said, while she handled him with a light touch that made him sigh. 'The purpose of these magazines is to show beautiful clothes. The reason women wear beautiful clothes is to enchant men. And the reason for that is obvious: the men go stiff in their trousers, off comes the couture frock and the silk knickers – everything your drawings ignore is laid bare to eye and hand. *Et voila*!'

'It is very uncivilised to be so direct,' Breville murmured.

Odette stroked up and down firmly. He was fully stiff and her fingertips slid on the smooth skin and over the purple head. He squirmed on his stool, his nerves set on fire by the caress.

'In your sketches you eliminate everything that interests men seriously,' she said, 'but when you catch a glimpse inside the silk knickers you are aroused – you become so uncivilised that you pull *this* out behind your drawing-board and play with it.'

'Oh no, no . . .' he was sighing faintly.

'Ah but yes, my poor Laurent,' she said, awarding herself

the intimacy of using his first name, 'the moment you laid eyes on my little fur coat you wanted to stroke it.'

'No,' he murmured, hardly able to speak, 'it is not pretty to be so hairy. It would be much better trimmed . . .'

Odette chuckled to feel the tautness and strength she held. A scheme was formulating itself in her head, but it required some care. So far all was proceeding well, Breville was staring down into his lap, fascinated by what she was doing to him. His eyes were wide and his mouth hung open.

She reached up with her left hand to push her forefinger into his open mouth. His lips closed on it and he began to suck, as if at her breast.

'You are a strange man, my poor Laurent,' she murmured. 'I've never heard of anyone being so faithful to a fiancée before, as you claim to be. You must be truly and desperately in love with her. That's very romantic. You've only been engaged for a week, you said. Yet when you almost saw what is between my thighs you opened your trousers and touched yourself and stroked yourself. In another minute you'd have spurted on your sketch and ruined it – even though you say I am hairy and ugly.'

Breville stared at her with bewilderment in his eyes. He was unable to answer with her finger in his mouth, even if he had anything rational to say. While she smiled into his eyes he put his hand on her bare thigh below the sapphire-blue knickers and stroked her smooth flesh.

It was a strangely furtive stroking. Odette knew he wanted to feel the thick dark-brown hair between her thighs but dare not, in case he lost control of himself and did what he might regret afterwards.

'Your fiancée must be very beautiful,' she said, her voice

as tantalising as she could make it. 'When you make love to her it is marvellous – yes?'

Her finger in his mouth gagged his reply. He nodded his head, his eyes fixed on her face, his hand not quite slipping up the lace-edged leg of the blue silk knickers.

'I'm sure you make love to her often,' Odette went on, 'very, very often. Every day. Twice every day? Nod your head if I am correct. Ah, I guessed so.'

She didn't believe him for an instant, but it was part of her developing scheme to gain the ascendancy.

'Does she come to the studio and undress?' she asked softly. 'Does she lie on the chaise-longue and part her legs? Does she shriek at the climax or is she a silent one?'

Laurent moaned lightly and took hold of her wrist to pull her blocking finger out of his mouth.

'You mustn't speak of her like that,' he said, hardly able to speak himself, his breath ragged in his throat.

'Then I won't speak of her at all,' said Odette as the rhythm of her fingers on his stiff flesh sent tremors of pleasure like electric shocks through his body, 'but I know she comes here to lie on the chaise-longue by the screen, you cannot deny it. How hairy is she between the legs? Like me? Or thin and patchy?'

'No, no, she is beautiful...' Laurent sighed, very nearly at the end of his tether.

Odette bent down to take his jerking hardness into her mouth. He gasped and squirmed on his stool as her wet tongue flickered over the smooth purple head. She straightened her back and took him in her hand again.

'Is your fiancée coming this afternoon to lie down for you on the chaise-longue, Laurent? If so, we must stop doing this or you won't be able to make love to her. What would she think if she stroked *this* and it wouldn't go hard enough to get up her? She'd suspect you'd deceived her with another woman. Though you hadn't, of course. But only you and I would know that.'

The sensations gripping Laurent Breville had carried him far beyond all possibility of rational speech. He stared blankly at Odette, his mouth open, cheeks flushed dark red. His whole body shook, his loins were jibbing forward.

Odette took his hand and pushed it into the lace-edged leg of the sapphire-blue knickers. His open palm trembled over her thatch of walnut-brown hair, his twitching fingers explored its texture. He touched the soft lips concealed in it.

It was time to finish him, Odette decided. Her hand beat fast on his jerking flesh, he wailed like a tomcat on a rooftop by night, his passion spurted furiously. He twitched and moaned as spurt after spurt spattered across the sketch of her in blue silk knickers on his drawing-board.

Laurent Loses His Independence

The little sketch was ruined – Laurent was wailing and spurting to the beat of Odette's hand on his jerking flesh, spraying his passion across the tilted drawing-board. The bright blue water-colour ran and spread on the thick paper, the elegant knickers he had sketched were splotched and spoiled, the outline face he had drawn merged into a blob of mixed reds of lips and black of eyes, a surrealist anarchy.

His feet had slipped from the cross-bar of his high stool and hung loosely just above the polished floor, his legs were apart and twitching, his elegant dove-grey trousers wide open for his hard-swollen part to strain furiously upwards. Odette smiled in her heart as well as with her lips – she was confident that she had taken a first and most important step toward a new ambition and a brighter prospect.

When Laurent was calm again she winked at him and tucked away his shrinking part and fastened his trousers.

'Not a word to anyone,' she said, before he could recover the power of rational speech and say the same words to her, as she was sure he would. 'This is our secret. Not that you have been unfaithful in any way to your fiancée – no one could accuse you of that, no more than if it was your own hand made you spurt.'

Laurent's mouth opened in an O of surprise at her words.

'It would have been your own hand,' Odette said with a shrug, 'if I had not come round the drawing-board to see what you were doing. I am sure you have given yourself this thrill many times while pretty models stood over there by the screen wearing just the expensive silk knickers you draw. Perhaps you do this every day – and why not if it amuses you? And in your mind there is no question of being unfaithful to Mademoiselle Marie-Louise.'

Laurent nodded his agreement, though shyly.

'Exactly,' said Odette, nodding her own head in sympathy with him, 'but in spite of that, a certain prudence is necessary in matters to do with fiancées. Don't you think so?'

'Ah, but you are a very intelligent woman,' he said, sounding surprised and yet much friendlier now than half an hour before. Then he qualified his praise by adding, 'for a model.'

We'll see about that, Odette said to herself. Aloud she said, 'Except for one thing, apparently. You told me that it is not pretty to be hairy. This has never bothered me before, in fact it pleased me. But naturally, I must listen seriously to advice from an important artist like you.'

'For underwear work, and for swimsuits and beach-wear, it is essential no hair is visible on any part of the body except for the head,' Laurent told her, sounding slightly pompous.

It made him feel superior to give professional advice of this type to a very attractive young woman. It restored his feeling of being in command, a feeling which had been lost the instant she looked round his drawing-board and caught him stroking his stiff part. He wasn't really back in command of the situation, of course, the feeling was mere self-deception, but it suited Odette's purpose to let him believe so.

'You said it would be better trimmed,' she reminded him, 'but I don't understand what you mean. Clipped very short all over – or reduced in extent, perhaps. You must explain to me what you think I should do to improve my appearance.'

While she was chattering away she pulled aside one leg of the expensive sapphire-blue knickers and let him see this nut-brown thatch that had attracted his comment. He stared in fascination and his lower lip hung slightly open – just as he had the first time he saw it. Evidently he had never seen a woman who could match Odette's luxuriance.

'But trimmed how?' Odette prompted him. 'I don't know how to go about it. How shall I trim it? You are the expert here.'

Laurent liked being thought an expert. He was very willing to give advice and they discussed the question for a while. In the course of his explanation of what would look best and most chic he found it necessary to run his fingertips briskly through the thick-growing curls. He clasped Odette's *joujou* in the palm of his hand to demonstrate how really extensive her fleece was. He stroked the soft lips up and down to show that they were hidden most of the time under her curls.

'But is that bad?' Odette asked, standing with her feet well apart so that he could play with her all he liked. She knew she had him hooked now – but she must reel him in carefully to make sure he didn't escape at the last moment.

His golden-brown eyes were close to hers and his face serious while he explained his artistic theories of how the female body should look to conform with the canons of good taste. This took some time – a time of touching and stroking between her legs to illustrate his point, or so he made out. He became increasingly enthusiastic as he talked, eventually he came to the conclusion that a practical demonstration was necessary.

'I can draw what I mean, if you prefer,' he said, although it was clear he would much rather demonstrate on her body than on mere paper. Odette encouraged the thought that an actual true-life demonstration was more enlightening than a hundred little drawings or a thousand words.

What followed was entirely to be expected – he led her to his bedroom to show her what he meant by *trimming*.

First she had to take off the expensive underwear sent to him for magazine illustrations. She did this without hesitation, she was proud of her body and pleased to show all of herself to the man she was planning to blackmail by means of her body. No, *blackmail* was too ugly a word for what she planned. Enticement, that was a better description.

She followed him naked through the apartment, from the studio to his bedroom, carrying her own clothes over her arm. Laurent kept turning round to look at her, and she was worth looking at as her bare breasts bobbed up and down to her step and her hips swayed. As he tried to walk half backwards and half sideways he tripped over his own feet and fell on his backside. The look on his face showed such bewilderment that Odette couldn't help laughing.

She stopped instantly when she saw him blush for shame at his own clumsiness. This could ruin everything – this sudden impact on the floor and the shock to his nervous system! Suppose he'd bruised himself painfully – in his mortification he might tell her to get dressed and go. Then all would be for nothing.

Instantly Odette dropped her armful of clothes and went down on her knees beside him as he struggled to a sitting position, his face red and his mouth set tight. She put her hands lightly on his shoulders and pressed him down again.

'Wait,' she said, 'we must not take chances. Let me make sure nothing is broken before you get to your feet, Laurent. Does it hurt badly anywhere?'

He lay back while she ran her hands along his arms from wrist to shoulder. She held his chin in her palm and rolled his head gently from side to side. She gave the impression that she was checking for sprains and strains, although he would surely have to be completely dazed by the fall to be deceived – her fingers were too caressing, her touch too deliberately exciting.

While she was touching him she was murmuring: *Does that hurt, my poor Laurent, do you feel any pain when I do that? Or that. Once more . . .*

When they were both reassured his upper body had sustained no harm, Odette ran her hands up his legs from ankle to knee, then raised each leg in turn to flex the knee a few times, murmuring all the while, *Any pain there, is that all right, does that give you any discomfort at all? Do not attempt to be brave, my poor Laurent, be absolutely honest.* And when she was certain no shin bone was broken and no knee-joint strained, she used both hands on each thigh in turn, feeling upward – almost stroking through his thin trousers – right up into his groin.

'Nothing is broken there, thank heaven,' she said with a tiny smile of encouragement. 'A final check to make sure there is no internal damage . . . Lie still for just another moment . . .'

Laurent closed his eyes and sighed as she undid his belt and his trousers and slipped a hand under his shirt. She felt along his belly carefully, her hand cool on his skin, up to his chest and her fingertips played over his flat nipples. He shook with momentary pleasure. She noted that and did it to him again and smiled to herself to see his pleasurable shudders.

Her flat hand pressed down hard on his belly, palpating liver and lights and whatever else was to be found in there. Her palm caressed round his belly-button in a rotating movement that set all his nerves twitching in delighted anticipation. If only she would keep on doing that . . .

Her hand slid smoothly down into his underwear. He sighed yet again as her fingertips explored his hot groin. *No strain here* she asked him, pressing lightly, *no stretched ligaments or torn muscle from your fall? Tell me if there is the least pain, you must be completely frank about it.*

Laurent turned his head from side to side to indicate he felt nothing. Well, no pain, at least. A long quiver ran through his body from toes to head when he felt her clasp his hairy pompoms in her hand.

'No problem here, my poor Laurent?' she asked. 'These are so fragile they can be damaged very easily. With terrible results. Is there any ache or twinge?'

'No,' he breathed, 'nothing, I assure you.'

He gasped softly as she released his precious parts and felt her hand trailing over his limpness.

'All is well,' she informed him, 'as far as I can tell, there is no injury. You are very fortunate.'

Laurent stared up into her green eyes with interest. His gaze flickered from her elegant bare breasts down to the dark-brown muff between her slender legs. And under her trailing fingers she could feel he was losing his limpness. It was time to bring this little comedy to an end before he tried to pull her down on the floor and get on top. She withdrew her hand slowly from his underwear and stood up.

With some reluctance he took the hand she held out to him and got to his feet. She asked where the bedroom was, and he showed her the door and opened it for her. He told her to go in and he would be with her in a moment when he'd collected the things he needed for the trimming demonstration. It was a large, pleasant bedroom, Odette saw, one she would be happy to have for her own when her luck changed for the better.

Laurent had furnished it in *Vogue* magazine taste. There was a broad and low bed with a silk coverlet in cream and pale blue over it. And square matching cushions propped up at the head to give an air of casual opulence. On the bedside table there was a long-stemmed pink rose in a tall crystal vase. Just one rose. And three books, the latest novels all intelligent people were reading that month.

On the wall opposite the window there was a large and restful water-colour in a thin black frame. It was a country landscape with poplar trees and a river-bank. Was it Laurent's work, she wondered? There was no way to tell, it was unsigned. Which probably meant it was not his – he was too vain a man to remain anonymous.

While Odette was examining the bedroom fittings, Laurent came in with the necessities for what he planned. He carried a large fluffy towel which he spread on the bedside after turning down the coverlet.

'Lie on that,' he said, 'while I show you what can be done.'

She arranged herself as he asked, her feet on the thick woven carpet, her back on the bed, her shoulders propped on two down-filled cushions to see what he had in mind. If he had been the man she was living with there would have been no question about what he would do, not for a moment! Robert would simply wrench his trousers open and hurl himself on her naked body. But this wasn't Robert staring down at her as she lay with her legs open wide, it was Laurent Breville, the fashion artist. And he was a very different proposition.

It amused Odette to see how very seriously Laurent took this little comedy. There was a frown of concentration on his face as he knelt down between her thighs with a pair of scissors in his hand. On the floor he had a copper bowl of warm water, his shaving-brush and a safety-razor.

But it is too ridiculous, Odette told herself, struggling not to laugh and spoil the moment. How intent he is, how determined – he is completely captivated. He will be a marionette to dance to my tune very soon now.

Laurent combed out her fleece, a pleasant sensation, and this grooming made it look even larger. When he'd finished, the thick brown curls seemed to stretch a long way down the insides of her thighs and almost up to her dimple of a belly-button. He stared at it thoughtfully for some time, as if considering this possibility and that possibility. He spread his fingers as wide as they would go to measure Odette's fur coat from the top edge to where it came to a point and vanished between her thighs.

He measured across the widest extent of curls with his spanned fingers, he compared breadth and length, he thought more – and eventually he went to work with the scissors. First he snipped round the edges of her curly thatch to reduce the size.

Between her feet, on the fluffy white towel, little commas of hair were accumulating. Most of the Lanvin perfume she used for effect was not lost in the shearing. When Laurent thought he'd trimmed away enough, he took the shaving-brush and he lathered round the edges of her fleece, across her belly and down inside her legs. The soft sweep of the brush on her skin was curiously arousing. Odette closed her eyes and sighed a little, enjoying the touch.

He was adept with the razor, gliding it over her skin without a scratch or a nick, a consideration of supreme importance when the blade was so close to her most intimate parts. She felt the kiss of the sharp steel on her flesh and became so excited she dug her fingers into the bed to stop herself trembling.

Laurent was too preoccupied with his close shaving to notice her heightened emotions. He washed off the last trace of creamy lather with warm water, took his scissors to clip a stray hair or two, and rocked back on his heels to inspect his work, head turned a little to one side. When he was satisfied with what he had achieved he raised his eyes to her face – the first time in ten minutes.

'There!' he said proudly. 'What do you think of that?'

She opened her eyes and looked down to see the result of so much concentration and barbering. He had tamed her wild and exciting thicket, he had reduced it to a small and well-clipped heart shape that fitted neatly between her slender thighs – and left her belly bare almost down to her pink lips. For Odette it was no great improvement on her natural state. On the contrary, she thought her new look was uninteresting.

Certainly, it made her *joujou* much more prominent now that it was exposed. And it was an interesting shape, the long curve of the mound that now had only a thin veil of brown curls over it instead of the old thicket she'd been proud of.

The soft and pinkish lips protruded as if to kiss any male part coming within reach.

No doubt about it, the shearing of her *joujou* produced a very sexy effect – for a man. For herself, Odette was not impressed. Whenever in the past she had looked at herself in a long mirror she'd always found the sight of her thick dark-brown bush exciting – it concealed so much, it suggested a certain modesty, instantly dispelled when a finger parted it to show the soft lips beneath the curls. It was like a second undressing – first the knickers and then the rich brown veil of hair.

But that was her own private opinion. Laurent was so absurdly pleased with his handiwork that she humoured him as part of the process of reeling him in. She praised his taste and his talent as an artist. She ran her fingers over the short-clipped heart and said how witty and chic it was, a true inspiration! And by praising his skill she drew his eyes away from her face to her shorn charm. It was time to strike the hook in and catch him.

Laurent was still down on his knees. His hands on her thighs to support himself while he stared at what he had achieved. The effect on him was satisfactory, Odette thought, his face became flushed and there was a long bulge in his elegant trousers.

'Am I pretty now you have trimmed me?' Odette asked. 'Please be completely candid. No compliments, just the simple truth.'

'You are beautiful,' he murmured in an abstracted way, as if his thoughts were too deep to be disturbed by conversation.

Odette spread her thighs a little wider. Laurent moaned as he unbuckled his alligator-skin belt and opened his trousers.

Out jumped his stiff length, nodding rhythmically like a mechanical toy. He held it to keep it still and he stared doubtfully at it and then even more doubtfully from it to her *little heart*. She spread her legs another centimetre or two and Laurent was lost.

With a stifled cry he lay forward on her bare belly, wriggled twice and pushed his engorged part deep into her. Odette closed her eyes and smiled secretly to herself.

'What am I doing?' Laurent gasped as he thrust in and out to a rapid rhythm. 'This is terrible, I love Marie-Louise – I must not betray her! Save me, Odette, before it's too late!'

'My poor Laurent, I won't let you betray her,' she said while she locked her legs over his back to hold him close and prevent him from withdrawing if his foolish conscience gained control. She jerked her belly up at him to urge him on.

'But I love her,' he moaned, 'what am I doing?'

'I know you love her, Laurent,' said Odette calmly, 'you love and adore your fiancée. You can never, never betray her, that is completely understood. What is happening here has nothing to do with her, nothing at all. Trust me.'

'I can't help myself,' he moaned, 'I am the victim of my own talent – when I looked at that beautiful *little heart* I created between your thighs I wanted to possess it. Unless you help me, Odette, I shall be unfaithful to Marie-Louise!'

'But of course I'll help you,' she said, feeling how strongly he was driving into her, his hard flesh filling her completely, stretching her, carrying them both on towards the crisis.

'Do not despair,' she sighed, 'I will help you, Laurent!'

His hands were under her bottom, grasping the taut cheeks and holding her tight while he drove into her. His flushed face was just above hers, his eyes open and bemused. Odette slipped his pink silk scarf out of the top of his fine pullover and held on to the ends. She used the scarf to drag his head down, staring into his eyes all the time.

She almost laughed to see his curious expression of not quite understanding what was happening to him, perhaps not wishing to understand. She pulled his mouth down on to hers in a kiss that cut off his nonsensical babble of words.

And not only words – the long kiss did away with the pangs of conscience that troubled him. His mouth on hers and his tongue pressing in between her parted lips, Laurent thrust like a wild beast until he spurted his passion into her. Odette gasped and bucked under him as a fierce orgasm gripped her.

When the ecstatic sensations began to fade, she congratulated herself on her achievement that morning. From now on she would insist on being Laurent's regular model. It would be impossible for him to refuse because he would forever be afraid she might say something to Mademoiselle Marie-Louise de Wherever to ruin his engagement.

There was no question of blackmail, of course, there was only an arrangement of benefit to both parties. If Laurent wanted to take out his pride and stroke it behind his drawing-board, then Odette would undress and pose for him in silk knickers for as long as he liked. She intended to keep him happily dependent on her. Four or five sessions a week ought to do it, she considered. He would be personally responsible for the regular trimming of her *little heart* – she was confident he would play Cupid and pierce it with his arrow every time he clipped the curls.

That would conveniently stir up feelings of bad faith towards his silly fiancée and keep his conscience in a turmoil. Much to the advantage of Odette. His uncomfortable emotions ensured she had the upper hand in their dealings. From now on she intended to be in charge of a vital part of his anatomy.

Naturally, he would pay her the top model rate. And she would insist he introduced her to other fashion artists he knew – and recommend her. She was convinced she was at the beginning of a new career, a fascinating new career. Who could say – perhaps the catwalk at Dior was not out of her reach when she began to meet the right people and make the right contacts.

'Laurent,' she murmured, pressing her cheek close to his and holding him close to her with her legs, 'you did that well.'

'But I shouldn't have done it,' he said mournfully.

His brown eyes were dull, his voice heavy with useless self-recrimination.

'What nonsense,' she said, very satisfied with this immediate manifestation of uneasy conscience. 'There is no reason to feel guilty. Set your mind at rest, my poor Laurent. Lie here on the bed beside me and I will explain it to you again.'

'Odette,' he said, with gratitude in his voice.

'There is no question of unfaithfulness to your fiancée, the idea simply does not arise,' she said, 'and for a very obvious reason.'

'What reason is that?' he asked curiously. She had unlocked her legs from around his waist and he got up from her belly. He lifted her legs and arranged her lengthways on the bed, and lay down beside her. His hand was on her belly, not doing anything, but he was enjoying the touch of her body.

'Tell me the reason,' he said, starting to sound pleading.

Odette was thinking fast. She needed a form of words that would reassure this idiot Laurent enough for him to want to do it to her again and keep on doing it to her in the future. Only not so reassuring that he slipped off the barbed hook she had planted in his conscience.

'Consider this,' she said carefully, 'you adore Mademoiselle de Beaucourt-Villiers and you are engaged to be married to her. You take her to a party, a grand affair, in the chateau of some of her friends, perhaps. The ladies are in beautiful ball-gowns and the men are elegant in dinner-jackets. There is champagne, music, you dance with your fiancée and you murmur you love her. As indeed you do, to distraction.'

'Yes, yes!' said Laurent, seeming to recognise the scene.

'While your fiancée is chatting to old friends you dance with another lady,' said Odette, 'and she too is very beautiful. You admire her, you respect her. You take her out on to the terrace for a breath of cool air. There is a big golden moon in the sky and suddenly the lady is in your arms and you are kissing her.'

'No, no, I wouldn't do that!' Laurent exclaimed.

'No, of course you wouldn't,' Odette agreed immediately, 'it is entirely imaginary, this little scene. But the lady is close and in your arms, you feel her breasts against you, through her ball-gown her thighs are rubbing against yours.'

'This is outrageous,' Laurent sighed, failing to sound at all outraged.

'*C'est la vie,*' said Odette. 'She is incredibly exciting, the beautiful lady in your arms in the moonlight. You put your hand up her gown and feel up her thighs, above her silk stockings.'

'But this is frightful,' said Laurent, 'impossible.' Suddenly he sounded embarrassed, as if her story had stirred a memory he would prefer to be forgotten.

'When you are back in Paris you phone the lady and arrange to meet her,' said Odette, 'she comes to your apartment, you bring her into this bedroom. She puts her arms about you and embraces you. You kiss her and undress her, she lies down naked, on this very bed – you jump on top and do it to her.'

'*Ah, mon Dieu*!' Laurent moaned plaintively.

'That is what I call being unfaithful to your fiancée,' said Odette. She rolled over on the soft cream-coloured blankets and stared down into his eyes accusingly. Her bare breasts lay upon his pullover, by the feel on her skin she knew it was of finest cashmere.

'That is betraying her,' she said, 'there can be no excuse or explanation, none. When she finds out, she will be heartbroken by your perfidy. She will return your diamond ring from Cartier and break off the engagement.'

'But, but . . .' Laurent protested weakly, 'you said before that I *had not* betrayed her. You said there was no question of that. You promised.'

'How slow you are to understand,' said Odette, her pale green eyes boring down into his. 'What I have just described for you was an act of gross and unforgivable betrayal on your part. You made love to a social acquaintance for the pleasure of it.'

'I still don't understand,' he said, and indeed he didn't. He was going to be baffled by female logic, though he didn't know that either. And female logic is not the same as male logic.

'Why can't you see it?' said Odette. 'It is all so simple. I am not an acquaintance, neither of yours nor of your fiancée's. Socially we are strangers to each other. I am your model and I am paid a fee to be sketched.'

'True,' Laurent agreed, 'but what difference does that make? Tell me for the love of God because my brain is rattling round in little circles from your explanations!'

'Everyone knows that artists make love to their models,' said Odette, shrugging her pretty shoulders. 'I read an article about this in a magazine. It is entirely necessary for them.'

'Necessary? But why?'

Now she had turned over, his hand was clasping one bare cheek of her bottom. He lay loose-limbed on the bed, trousers undone, pullover and shirt pulled up above his belly-button. Odette was with a fingertip stroking his limpness almost imperceptibly.

'Because it liberates their genius,' she answered, trying to sound convincing. 'This explains why you were stroking yourself in secret when I posed in the blue knickers – by instinct alone you knew your pictures of me would be improved by exciting your natural emotions. The article I read said all artists did this, especially the Impressionists. They found it necessary to do it several times each session.'

'Manet, Renoir, Degas, Cezanne,' said Laurent thoughtfully.

'All of them,' she assured him, but without the least idea if they made love to their models or not. They were men, and so she assumed they did what men always do whenever they are alone with a naked woman.

'It is true I experience this tremendous urge while I sketch pretty young women in silk underwear,' Laurent admitted. 'It is so overwhelming at times that I an unable to resist it – I have to stroke myself. Did the great painters feel the same?'

'Naturally,' said Odette, 'it is the creative urge expressing itself. But they were not content to stroke themselves – their art demanded more. They laid the model down on a handy couch and did it to her forcefully before they touched brush or paint.'

'I am a magazine artist,' Laurent pointed out, sounding quite modest, 'not a great master.'

'An artist is an artist,' Odette said firmly, 'your creative needs are the same. What you did to me was for the cause of art and culture, it served a higher purpose. It concerns intimately your destiny as artist and therefore it has no bearing on your relations with your fiancée, nothing whatsoever. Now perhaps at last you understand why it is impossible that you could betray her with me.'

'But this is an entirely new way of regarding the situation,' said Laurent importantly. 'I am extraordinarily grateful to you for opening my eyes to the needs of my own artistic nature. For years – ever since I left art school – I have been dismayed and tormented by these urges I feel when I see a model in underwear. You have liberated me! The pictures for *Vogue* tomorrow will be the best I have ever done because my creative nature has now been given full release, openly and frankly.'

'Right,' said Odette, grinning down at him, while he was lost in contemplation of his new artistic freedom to amuse himself in any way his nature suggested with young models wearing exotic knickers. She got her knees under her and grasped his half-hard flesh firmly, threw a leg over him and perched herself over his loins.

The part she had been tickling with a finger to make it swell and grow longer was responding. She rolled it between her palms to hasten the process.

Marie-Claire Villefranche

Before Laurent could absolve himself of his bad conscience in respect of Mademoiselle La Fiancée, Odette intended to involve him even more deeply. She wanted him committed past any hope of retraction – it would make things much easier for her later on, when it was time for him to do favours for her. Financial ones. And to keep him happy while he was paying out, she was going to make him dependent on her for pleasure and emotional support.

'Your artistic talent created this,' she said as her fingers touched the neat *little heart* of curls between her thighs. 'You see to what heights you can aspire when you liberate yourself.'

'It's true, it's true,' Laurent murmured, staring up into her face with a look of surprise. 'I did it – it is a small masterpiece! Before I met you it had never occurred to me to restyle a woman's little fleece.'

'What? Not even Mademoiselle Beaucourt-Villiers'?'

'Never,' he said faintly, and he was blushing.

To keep his mind on what she intended, Odette massaged firmly his stiff throbbing part. With her left hand she opened herself wide to show the wetly pink interior of her *joujou*. Laurent was staring at her, round-eyed, his belly twitching beneath her. She guided the purple head of his stiff shaft between the open lips and sank down slowly to push it into her.

'What savage beasts you artists are,' she said, 'you want to do it all the time!'

Naturally, she was absolutely convinced that Laurent Breville did not do it all the time. Not even a lot of the time. Perhaps only now and then, when the strange fiancée would let him. Poor Laurent, Odette thought, found his amusement

34

BONJOUR AMOUR

sitting on a stool behind his drawing-board, staring at a model in silk knickers.

'Yes, you're right,' he exclaimed, 'all the time – it is our nature! I am a wild beast, I shall ravage you beyond even your imagining!'

Odette slid herself up and down his impaling flesh, watching his gasping reaction to the feel of warm slipperiness about him – he was staring as if mesmerised at her bare breasts jiggling to her rhythm, then down to the *little heart* he was piercing. A powerful image was being imprinted on his mind and his soul in these moments when the thrills of delight rose to their peak of sensation – green-eyed Odette sitting spread-thighed over him.

Marie-Louise Has Serious Doubts

It was early when Marie-Louise woke, only nine o'clock, but the building had been astir for a long time. Sometimes when she got back from a party or a night-club at dawn, ready to sleep until noon, she would meet tenants going out. She in a long dress and her jewellery, they in day clothes. She smiled and said *Bonjour* and they replied politely enough, but they never seemed pleased to see her.

She could hear someone moving about in the apartment, a clink of cup and saucer being set out on a tray. That was Yvette, the maid who came in every day. She was there on the dot of eight-thirty each morning, except Sunday, when she went to Mass and arrived later. One of her duties was to buy fresh croissants on her way in from the baker's shop. For Marie-Louise's breakfast in bed, with *café-au-lait*.

Lying in the half-dark with the shutters still closed and the long curtains drawn across, Marie-Louise could hear the distant whine and creak of the tiny lift – the permanent cause of anger and arguments and tight-lipped confrontations with the tenants. The married couple on the third floor wanted it reserved at all hours of the day for their use because the wife was five months pregnant. The old lady on the top floor who had been there ever since 1932 asserted she had priority, on account of her extreme advanced age and decrepitude.

Almost all were united in a demand to know why Madame Brouage on the fourth floor was permitted to take her savage poodle dog up in the lift. In the interests of public safety and hygiene – not to mention civility and taste – it was blatantly obvious that the animal should be made to walk up, not to have the luxury of a lift to transport it!

Marie-Louise turned on her back and put her hands beneath her head. The movement caused her over-large breasts to roll in her elegant night-dress. It was of silk so fine it was transparent, or very nearly. The neckline was low and with a little ruffle, the waist was high – she preferred the Empire style because she believed it supported her heavy breasts. Perhaps it did, but it made them appear even larger than they were.

She had dreamed that night about Henri Fantour, a dear friend of some years ago. She hadn't thought about him for a long time and she was trying to recall the fragments of her dream before they vanished.

She had been happy with Henri, happier than she had been with any man either before or since, especially the evenings they shared, when she played the grand piano for him in the salon of his house on the Avenue Victor-Hugo. She played very well; usually he wanted to hear Chopin. To please him she played naked.

He would sit on a chair nearby, elbow on the padded arm, head leaning on his hand, listening intently and studying the ripple of her fingers on the keys, the graceful movements of her body, the sway of her breasts. He would have a glass of cognac in his hand, an expression of delight on his face. For Marie-Louise it was oddly exciting to feel the piano-stool underneath her bare cheeks, the touch of the pedals against her unshod feet.

Henri was a man of exquisite sensibilities and understanding. When she reached the end of the Etude or Nocturne and stopped, he went down on his knees by the piano-stool to kiss her hand. At the end of the evening's recital she swivelled round on the stool and turned from the keys, Henri knelt again and took her foot in his hand, her bare foot with pink-varnished nails, and raised it from the floor to kiss it.

He never kissed her anywhere else, or touched any part of her body except her hands or feet. Well, there was once when he had been stirred almost beyond control by a Liszt Rhapsody and he'd stared up into her face with such passionate intensity that she slid her thighs a little apart on the piano stool and wondered breathlessly what he was going to do to her. Lay her down upon her back along the stool? Pull her down to the carpet?

But Henri was Henri, agitated or not. For one brief moment he pressed his lips to her left knee. He thanked her sincerely for playing for him and said his emotions were so deliciously taut that he could bear no more that evening.

Every time she played for him, from the moment she undressed to the moment when she closed the piano lid, she was aware of his huge shining eyes devouring her. He watched so intently, he observed every quiver of her breasts, each twitch of her smooth belly, gloating in perfect silence at each movement of her long thighs when she used the pedals. When he stared at the patch of brunette curls between her legs, it felt almost as if his hand touched her.

Henri's physical adoration of her was intense and obvious,

it seemed to fill the entire salon from side to side just as fully as the music of the piano itself. To Marie-Louise it felt like waves, emanating from Henri and rippling out in slow circles to take up all the available space. It felt like being immersed in warm, scented bath-water. It aroused her in a manner no hand on her breasts or between her thighs had ever aroused her.

It was a long time ago. It had come back to her in a dream – and now she lay in bed in the half-light thinking about the old and happy days with Henri. If he were here now she would get up immediately and strip off her night-dress while he watched her. She would lead him by the hand into her sitting-room where the piano stood, and play two or three short pieces for him.

Or had he changed since those days? Perhaps when she raised her night-dress over her head and he saw her naked he would put his hands on her breasts and push her back down on the bed. And force her legs apart. It was possible – people did change.

The silk night-dress was flimsy, it let the prominent tips of her breasts show darkly. And the dark triangle of curls – that was discernible through the silk. But it was the thought of her breasts showing through that she tried to dismiss from her mind – the truth was that she was embarrassed by their over-generous size. The rest of her body was slender and elegant: her waist was well-defined, her hips stylish, her legs long and rounded – they were devastating in black silk stockings.

But in her opinion her breasts were too big, they were out of proportion. Her discontent with them went back to when she was fifteen and they had grown too bountiful for her liking. She'd spent hours in her bedroom, stripped to the

BONJOUR AMOUR

waist before the mirror, glaring at her swelling breasts and willing them not to get any bigger. She'd used silk scarves to bandage them flat, but they never could be really flattened, not even when she was fifteen.

By the time she was eighteen they had grown to the absurd size they were now. Men found them attractive – almost irresistible, that was something she'd learned early in life. It was no compliment to her – men had deplorable taste. She despised them for it.

Henri in a midnight-blue suit and a striped silk tie, sitting on an armchair with his knees apart, head on his hand, watching her at the piano without blinking. His dark hair tinged silver over the ears, his broad face impassive. The long stiffness in his trousers was decently concealed if she looked round at him. She was happy then because Henri never touched her breasts – or anywhere else.

Women being by nature as they are, eventually this happiness became mingled with a certain mild contempt for Henri – because he was so obviously mesmerised by the sight of her breasts when she played the piano for him. And her long bare thighs. And the curve of her belly. Men were impossible – they were obsessed by flesh, flesh, flesh! Even rich men who loved Chopin.

And to be honest about it, Henri was no saint. Because he had never tried to force himself upon her when she was naked at the piano did not prove that he was above the usual desires of men. Marie-Louise was certain he found his amusements somewhere – it seemed possible to her, probable even, that a man of refinement and delicacy would be the exact opposite when he unleashed his male instincts and gave them free expression.

In a brothel, perhaps, with naked whores – Henri with all his clothes off in an over-perfumed bedroom, his thing sticking out stiffly. Mirrors on walls and ceiling, Henri doing unbelievably sordid things to a paid woman. Or maybe he had two women at the same time! Lying on his back on a bed, with a woman sitting on his face, rubbing her hairiness over his mouth. The other woman lying over him, using her tongue on his stiff part.

Fantasies of Henri giving free play to his desires obsessed Marie-Louise at times. There were days when she could think of little else. The fantasies became ever more incredibly depraved and improbable – if poor Henri could have guessed what bizarre combinations of naked men and women seethed in the brain of the woman who played the piano so beautifully for him!

For the same reason she liked Empire-style high waists Marie-Louise often wore frocks with a wrap-over bodice. She believed this style concealed the weight of her bosom, but she was wrong about that too – a loose wrap-over served to emphasise what she was anxious to hide. Every man she met wanted to get her clothes off and press his face between those sumptuous fleshy mounds.

And where was Yvette with the *café-au-lait*? The little clock of veined green marble and ormolu on the bedside table said the time was after nine. Marie-Louise heard the whining of the lift again as it descended or ascended, then the clonk as it stopped with a heavy jerk at the selected floor. For a moment there was the high-pitched yap of Madame Brouage's poodle Bibi, returning from its first outing of the day. Someone would surely complain the dog had been allowed to bark non-stop for an hour and a half.

There were times when Marie-Louise gave serious consideration to selling the building and ridding herself of these querulous tenants for ever. But it always came back to the same problem – the building was old and run-down and needed money spent on it.

She had taken advice and been told that she would not get the real value of the building in its present state. Even though it stood in one of the most desirable districts of Paris, and from the window of her sitting-room she had a view of the upper half of the Eiffel Tower above the roof-tops.

If Laurent Breville, the fashion artist, had been there in his fiancée's pretty bedroom and seen her lying at ease on her back with the sheet slipping down to her waist and her heavy breasts shown to good advantage by the fine silk of her nightdress – *Ah, le bon Dieu*! Lingerie aroused him furiously, perhaps more than the woman who wore it. For this very reason he had become known as the top illustrator of underwear for fashion magazines. Silk night-dresses drove him to flights of burning fancy, especially with a pair of plump breasts inside.

Had he been there that morning to see Marie-Louise lying with her hands under her head and her breasts protruding through the almost transparent silk, he would have flung himself across her bedroom while he ripped his trousers open! And dived on to her body with his stiff part ready in his hand, to slide it between those generous handfuls of warm flesh!

Apart from this exaggeration of her breasts, Marie-Louise was an elegant woman in her thirties. Her late thirties, that is, almost nine years older than Laurent, but she never admitted that. Her hair was so dark it was nearly black. It was cut short and brushed back in a riot of curls that gave her a provocative no-nonsense look. A woman who said *Non* more often than *Oui*.

For this reason most men saw her as a challenge. There was an extra thrill in getting between the legs of a reluctant woman – a woman who allowed few to get her into bed. Especially one who seemed to embody a contradiction, an aloof manner combined with plump heavy breasts made for pleasure. Many, many men did their very best to get Marie-Louise's elegant clothes off, but only a few succeeded.

She was not beautiful – Odette had been right about that. Nor was she rich – the old apartment building had been her share of her grandfather's will. The old boy had been rich once, and his father before him had been richer. Everything was badly managed and some investments were wiped out by the war. When Grandpapa died six years ago what he left was divided between Marie-Louise's parents, her three brothers, her sister and herself. Her father inherited the neglected chateau southeast of Paris. Grandpapa left Marie-Louise the apartment building.

Yvette tapped at the door and came in with the breakfast tray and Marie-Louise pulled the sheet up to cover her breasts. They said *Bonjour* to each other, Yvette opened curtains and shutters and let the sunlight in. Marie-Louise sat up and arranged her pillows comfortably while the maid poured coffee and hot milk.

Yvette settled the tray across Marie-Louise's lap and left to get on with her work. It was a large apartment, as owner Marie-Louise had taken the best in the building.

An apartment in a good district of Paris, plus the rents from the other apartments. Not as much as they should be, of course, with rent-control in force. Minus the excessive and outrageous taxes imposed on property owners – this was all she had and all she was ever likely to have.

Marie-Louise was not rich, not young, not beautiful. Striking perhaps, and approaching a certain age – Odette was right about that, all of it. Also correct was her assumption that Laurent's fiancée was not much interested in pleasuring him or having him pleasure her. The truth was that Marie-Louise didn't understand what the fuss was about when a man undressed her. Naturally she had tried to find out, over the years, because she could hardly be unaware of the importance others attached to love-making.

She never let the same man do it to her more than a few times because by then she had reluctantly accepted that he was unable to make her experience the sensations others thought so highly of. Male hands all over her naked body – pleasant enough in its way till it came to stroking her breasts, as it invariably did. Usually sooner than later.

That made her uncomfortable and inclined to lose interest in any man who was excited by the fleshy masses that to her were a source of slight shame.

Then came the hand between her legs – the caress which caused her a mild pleasure. Nothing sensational, though she could lie with her legs apart for five or ten minutes while a man teased with a fingertip, or his tongue – some men could hardly wait to lick down there. And it had to be admitted there was a certain pleasantness about it.

If he went on too long she became bored. Usually it was only an interlude before the man rolled his weight on her belly and forced his fifteen centimetres into her. That she found tedious.

Mostly they said things like *Je t'adore, Marie-Louise* as

they bounced up and down on her body. Not once, but again and again, becoming more and more excited. *Je t'adore, cherie, je t'adore.*

For her it was fairly meaningless. She felt the solidity of a man's stiff part deep inside her – a pleasant enough sensation. She felt it slide in and out, becoming harder and faster as the man became more and more aroused. But her own sensations didn't get better and better, they remained on a plateau, so to speak. There was no sudden release for her, however long it continued. She was glad when it was over, when the man gasped *Marie-Louise je t'adore* for the twentieth or the fiftieth time as he spurted into her. On the whole, a massage in a beauty salon was just as good.

Afterwards the man who had pleasured himself on her body just as if she were a passive shop-window dummy would demand if she had shared the ecstatic thrill with him! If she told the truth it would have shattered his fragile male ego. She told him what he expected to hear. And ten or fifteen minutes later he wanted to do it to her again.

There was another reason why Marie-Louise – lying naked in a lover's arms, with a wet patch on the sheet beneath her – would not tell the truth when asked about the supposed supreme moment by the one who believed he'd just provided it. Her motive was simple enough, if she said she found it disappointing it was a confession that she was deficient, that she was excluded from what women friends claimed was the most marvellous experience in the world.

For years she had disbelieved them. She assumed there was an unspoken conspiracy among women to pretend that love-making was very enjoyable, that they could never have enough of it. Women wanted so many things – beautiful clothes, jewels, vacations in exotic places, children, a fine apartment, someone to take care of them – all the things obtainable from a man by pleasing him and flattering his pride. What easier way to keep a man content than by giving an impression of enjoying what everyone knew men wanted? Lie on your back and encourage him to do it – and say you found it thrilling.

This theory of Marie-Louise's crumbled on the day she learned that two of her married friends regularly went to bed together in the afternoons when their husbands were absent. Naively she had asked one of them *Why*? The answer was enlightening, and it led to Marie-Louise experimenting with another woman. It proved even more disappointing than going to bed with a man.

After trying it two or three times Marie-Louise switched back to looking for a man who could make her experience what she was supposed to experience. She decided life had been very unfair to her, to give her plump breasts that men wanted to handle but deny her the pleasure. What stupid irony. She put the breakfast tray on her bedside table, she reached down in the bed to grasp the hem of her night-dress and pull it over her head and off.

She sat cross-legged and naked, hands under her heavy breasts to lift them up while she stared at them in dismay. So full and fleshy, so overstated! What malign fate had made them grow so large – why couldn't she have elegant little pointed breasts? Even though Laurent only used models with small ones, he adored her big ones – typical of a man! If she let him he would drool over them and stroke them and kiss them for hours. Not that she allowed that – it would be too utterly dreary for her.

Laurent was not the first man who had asked her to marry

him. Nor the first to whom she had said yes. To be accurate, he was her third fiancé in thirteen years. She had been able to spin out her two previous engagements for almost a year both times. When the day could no longer be put off, she had decided it was too much to expect of her, to have a man in her bed every night, wanting to drag off her night-dress and lie on her belly.

The engagements were ended, leaving the two fiancés bewildered by her change of heart. This time she meant to go through with it – unless Laurent proved completely unsuitable. At thirty a woman unmarried is talked about by her friends – they think she has a secret lover who is married. If she is still without a husband at thirty-five, friends began to wonder what the problem can be. Single at forty – and all the world knows that a woman's destiny is to be an old maid. Marie-Louise did not want to be that.

With Laurent there were certain advantages and disadvantages. He was easier to manage than his predecessors – less demanding, more pliable. If the marriage went ahead, she would insist that he moved into her apartment and disposed of his own. She would assign him a room, of course – he would not be allowed to sleep in her bed. He would be invited into her room to avail himself of his marital rights – a husband had to be kept contented. And when he'd finished she'd send him back to his own bed.

His profession was not at all to her liking. It was not *comme il faut*, this business of making illustrations of underwear for magazines, even prestige publications. Not an occupation for a person of standing. The best that could be said about it was his abilities were surprisingly well rewarded. Not just magazines, but illustrations for books on fashion and other publications, and not France alone; his work sold well abroad.

Yet to be ruthlessly frank, Laurent's considerable income was made from knickers – it was hard to take him seriously when one knew that. Marie-Louise was sure no member of the de Beaucourt-Villiers family since the time of Louis XIV had had any interest in lingerie except to get it off their girlfriends quickly – to do what men always wanted to do.

No de Beaucourt-Villiers ever made a living, that was beneath them. They owned property, lots of property. Impressive tracts of farmland, *premier cru* vineyards, streets of buildings in big cities with shops below and apartments above. At least they did once upon a time. The present family had lost nearly all of it. They were not exactly as poor as church mice, but they were not wealthy. And no one thought they would be again, there being no talent for accumulation in the family now, only for spending.

From this point of view Laurent Breville was of interest to a woman whose tastes would always outrun her income. Marie-Louise knew that her father and mother were not greatly impressed when she took Laurent to the chateau for a weekend to introduce him. But Papa and Mama knew she was not all that young any more, her choices were becoming limited. So they accepted Laurent with as good a grace as they could manage. But the situation was uneasy.

Laurent had been very impressed by the chateau and the estate – perhaps awed was the word for his reaction. He did not appear to notice how run-down everything was. He saw no awkwardness in his reception by his fiancée's Mama and Papa – he was charming to them. Not that it did him any good, their opinion of him was fixed and unchangeable.

Naturally, after everyone retired for the night he found his way to Marie-Louise's room, frantic to have her in this setting of faded once-upon-a-time wealth. She had expected him, knowing how his mind worked, and was ready. For the occasion she wore a stunning night-dress bought in Paris in the rue Cambon – a wisp of white chiffon, scooped at the neck, coming only halfway down her thighs. It did nothing to conceal her breasts – she frowned when she put it on and stood in front of the long mirror.

Whatever her own feelings in the matter, the revealing night-dress was right for Laurent. He tapped at her bedroom door and sidled in. The lights were on and he stared entranced at her as she lay on her side on her bed, facing the door. He was wearing a pink, lightweight silk dressing-gown over his pyjamas. Marie-Louise actually saw the front bulge out slowly while he stared at her breasts across the room.

No doubt of it in her mind, she could have Laurent as husband – if that was what she wanted. Lying on the pillows she brushed her short dark hair back with one hand, the movement of her arm making her breasts sway in their flimsy chiffon. Laurent was at her bedside in anxious strides, sitting on the edge and leaning over to kiss her mouth while his hands roamed over her breasts. That night she let him do it to her three times, to consolidate her hold, the old wooden bed-frame creaking under them.

He was sleeping heavily at dawn when she shook him awake and told him to go back to his own room before the servants were up and about. He had slept naked, Marie-Louise had put her little chiffon night-dress on. She looked at his slender body when she turned the sheet back to uncover him and so urge him out of bed – and she was surprised to see he was stiff and thick again. He took her in his arms for a parting kiss before he left – so she thought. The kiss became insistent, his tongue probed her lips, his hands were sliding up and down her body.

'No, no, Laurent,' she murmured, 'not now, there is no time – later perhaps. We shall see.'

But her protestations were all in vain, in the chiffon night-dress the question was already settled. Laurent rolled her onto her back and was on top of her, his hands busy with her breasts while he tried with his knees to push her legs apart.

'Laurent!' she said crisply. 'I said not now.'

'*Marie-Louise, je t'adore*,' he moaned, not hearing her words.

'Laurent!' she said again, even more crisply. She had to use all the strength in her legs to keep them together against his onslaught. In the end it made no difference, Laurent abandoned his attempt to force them open, he slid his throbbing stiffness up and down on her belly instead. In a remarkably short time he cried out and jerked frantically – she felt a warm wetness soak through her beautiful night-dress on to her skin.

Now, a month later, Marie-Louise sat in bed in her apartment in Paris and thought about Laurent and her own future. She held her breasts on her palms and joggled them up and down to assess the result. She shook her head and frowned. They were too soft, they were starting to droop a little. A few more years and they would really sag – what man would be interested then? It would be best to marry Laurent Breville, whatever his shortcomings.

She'd always had doubts, of course. His origins were not very impressive, his occupation was best not dwelt on. Against that, he was good-hearted and seemed genuinely to love her.

Marie-Claire Villefranche

But there had been a certain change in the past week or two, Marie-Louise thought. She had noticed something different in his attitude – it was difficult to pin it down exactly. But to be honest about it, she was beginning to suspect Laurent of a love-affair with another woman. The only evidence she had was that he was not so pressing of late about getting her into bed. When he did, once was enough for him.

She would prefer this cooling off of his to mean he respected her feelings, but she didn't think so. Men were quite ruthless about getting their *chose* into a woman. Ruthless and ravenous. It was infuriating, how their absurd length of gristle stood up stiff on every occasion, suitable and unsuitable.

She was meeting Laurent that evening. She planned to find out whether his stood up or not when he touched her. If not, there were certain conclusions to be drawn.

Henri Fantour was different – a gentle, understanding man who loved the music of Chopin and was content to watch her play the piano naked. In retrospect, he was a paragon, a man of delicate sensitivity, who appreciated beauty without wishing to prod his *chose* into it. What a pity they hadn't married. But Henri had never asked her.

That evening Laurent took her to the theatre – an interest of his. She encouraged him in this because he had told her of his lingering ambition to design for the stage. He had drawers full of sketches in his studio, scenery and costumes for plays he'd seen which he was absolutely certain he could do better. It was good to encourage him in this. Marie-Louise considered: if his talents could be switched to the theatre, it would get him away from pretty young models posing in knickers.

On the other hand, when with bursting pride he showed her his theatre designs, it was impossible not to see how significant a role women's underwear played. Whole acts of dramas were moved out of drawing-rooms into bedrooms – in order to have actresses in fabulously chic negligées on stage. Not only modern dramas, he'd even designed Molière's immortal *Tartuffe* to include women in transparent lingerie.

And this was true also for opera – his designs for *Carmen* put the entire second act upstairs in a tavern bedroom instead of the bar. There were sketches of the gipsy-girl heroine in black silk bra and knickers, to entice Don Jose.

'But this is not what Bizet intended when he wrote the music for the scene,' Marie-Louise declared, her eyebrows raised.

'Why not?' said Laurent. '*Carmen* is about sexual attraction between a soldier and a gipsy-girl, everyone knows that. For me it makes good sense to show some of her real charms, as well as her singing.'

As for Victor Hugo's celebrated classic drama *Le Roi S'amuse*, Laurent had transformed it beyond all reason. For the seduction scene he had designed a set which resembled not a royal bedroom but more or less what Marie-Louise once imagined to be the type of brothel Henri Fantour went to for his depraved male pleasure – whatever that was. The costumes were impossible – no innocent young virgin ever wore lacy scarlet knickers like those!

'Well,' said Marie-Louise, trying to be non-committal, 'it is not likely the Comédie-Française will put the play on with your designs, *chéri*.'

But with his continuing interest in women's underwear, there was perhaps only one theatre Laurent could design for, she thought, and that was the Folies-Bergère. But no, that wouldn't get him away from young women in knickers: on the contrary, they would be all round him. She sighed to contemplate the difficulties of redirecting his talents into a more acceptable profession than illustrating underwear.

Artistic Problems For Laurent

That evening Laurent took Marie-Louise to see a new play by Jean Anouilh at the Odeon theatre. He had invited two other friends, who joined them half an hour before the curtain rose – they met on the terrace of the restaurant opposite the Odeon for a drink.

Marie-Louise had met Raymond Carteret before with Laurent. He was an important man at one of the large department stores, concerned with the management of the lingerie department – that explained why he was a friend of Laurent's. He was in his thirties, a round-faced man with a humorous expression, always very well dressed. He had had a different woman with him last time. Today his companion was a slender and well-groomed blonde – near-blonde – he introduced as Pauline Joubert.

The play was amusing, the usual Anouilh confection about love and adultery. It was easy to see why Laurent was so interested, he would have liked to design, if anyone had asked him, bedroom sets and provocative underwear for the actresses. Marie-Louise shook her head as she concluded that Laurent would never get to design for any more acceptable production than a live show for tourists in Pigalle. If the participants – they could hardly be called actors and actresses – did not begin completely nude, they wore some simple type of easily-removable underwear.

Not that Marie-Louise had any experience of live shows – that went without saying. Such entertainments were for foreigners in Paris and elderly men unable to do it themselves. All the same, she wondered if Laurent had ever slipped into one – to see what underwear the women had, if any. Could it be really true – that they actually did it on a tiny stage before a paying audience? A naked woman on her back with her legs in the air, a naked man lying on her and thrusting into her? No, they were miming, the live-show artistes of Pigalle, she felt certain.

After the play the four of them went at Laurent's suggestion to a charming little bistro on the rue Monsieur-le-Prince – and then to a small dark night-club not far away, to drink again and dance. Laurent was a good dancer, even on a floor as cramped as the night-club. He eased Marie-Louise round expertly and he held her very close, murmuring tender idiocies into her ear.

Raymond Carteret was a good dancer too. He held Marie-Louise even closer to him and squashed her breasts against his suit in a manner that was almost breathtaking. The humorous expression on his face was a reliable guide to his temperament, he chatted non-stop and amusingly. He told Marie-Louise how very impressed Laurent had been by the weekend at the chateau, which she knew already from her own observation. But it was good to hear of it from a friend of his.

Marie-Louise was elegance itself that evening, her short dark hair brushed back expertly, her eyebrows black and sleek over a face so beautifully made up it seemed not to be made up at all. Her frock was from a very good hand, mainly black with touches of white to make it dramatic. Her arms and shoulders were bare, narrow straps supported the frock and the over-generous breasts within it. She had a gold chain round her neck with a pendant – a gold circlet set with small diamonds and rubies.

Naturally, Raymond's eye was caught by the cluster of jewels dangling into her bare cleavage. He asked her about it, only as an admirer of precious stones and not because it drew attention to her breasts as it slid about to her dancing. Secretly he was stiff in his trousers, he wanted to plunge his hot face between those beauties and get his hands on them. Everybody wanted to.

The stiffness in his underwear was no secret to Marie-Louise, whatever Raymond might believe. Every man she ever danced with was stiff before the music stopped playing. Even that perfectly saintly man Henri Fantour was no exception to that. Whenever he took her to dinner and they danced afterwards she had felt that unmistakable heavy bulge pressing against her. He always tried to pretend nothing was happening, but she knew.

Pauline was very impressed by Laurent. Raymond had told her he was a celebrated illustrator for the best fashion magazines. She read all of them, she said, she would make a special point of looking for Laurent's work from now on. Was it signed in any way? Yes, he told her, look for a small L in the bottom right-hand corner. This month's *Harper's Bazaar* and *Vogue* next month, he said, and that sent her into eye-flashing delight.

When Laurent danced with her, she pressed herself so close to him her thighs locked with his as they slithered round the tiny dance-floor in the dark. So close that his male part took the hint and stirred. Pauline said it would be marvellous to have a figure good enough to work as a model for a fashion artist as brilliant as Laurent. When Laurent was sure they would not be seen by Marie-Louise he slid his hands down Pauline's back and held the cheeks of her bottom while they danced.

He informed her that in his expert opinion she herself had an admirable figure for fashion work and he found it surprising to hear that she wasn't a professional model.

'You truly think so?' she asked. 'But be candid – have I the right figure for underwear modelling?'

He let go of her bottom long enough to hold her away from him at arm's length and inspect her from her blonde head to her feet – with particular attention to her breasts. Several times.

'Well, what do you think?' she asked.

'Before reaching a final decision it is necessary to see you in your underwear,' he said, 'but yes, it is my impression that your figure is good enough for lingerie modelling.'

So pleasant a time was had by all four of them that a number of bottles of wine were drunk. It was almost one in the morning before goodnights were said and Raymond departed with his near-blonde girlfriend.

At Laurent's apartment, he would have taken Marie-Louise into his bedroom immediately – or so it was once. But he was pleased when she suggested they looked into his studio so he could show her what he was working on. He switched on the lights and waved a hand at the colour illustrations pinned round the walls.

Marie-Louise glanced round with interest; expensively

elegant clothes were very much to her taste. These pictures on display were not all Laurent's original sketches, some were pages torn from magazines that had used them. A set of nightwear pictures for *Vanity Fair* was entrancing – Marie-Louise asked if he knew in which shops the garments could be bought.

There was one set of sketches Laurent said were for *Vogue* and he'd completed them only that morning, he would send them round to the magazine office tomorrow. For some reason she could not explain to herself, Marie-Louise looked with great care at this latest work.

Laurent's style was inimitable – impressionistic watercolour sketches of chic bras and knickers in various pretty tints. And shown on a faceless model with dark hair. It was impossible for anyone to say if the model was the same as for the earlier work on display. Was there a similarity in the stance? A similarity of bust-line and hips? A slight frown wrinkled Marie-Louise's brow.

The closer she looked, the more certain she became it was the same woman – all round the studio. More than that – to her eye there was a *je ne sais quoi* about the sketches, particularly in a jaunty feet-apart pose . . . perhaps just the merest hint that the artist entertained feelings toward his anonymous model that were not wholly professional. A subtle indication of a *sympathy* between model and artist? Nothing obvious or suggestive – not for a fashion magazine of quality. But . . .

'This is your best work,' she said in a neutral tone. 'Who is the model?'

'Oh, I forget her name,' he said with total disregard for the truth, 'a dark brunette.'

'Really?' said Marie-Louise, 'I find it surprising you can't remember her name when she models for you so often. She must be here nearly every day.'

'No, only twice, as far as I recall,' he lied. 'It is not my choice, as you know – I leave it to Madame Drouet at the agency to send me suitable models. It's a question of who is available on her books when I phone her.'

'The brunette whose name escapes you,' said Marie-Louise, 'is she very pretty? You never put a face to your sketches, so one cannot decide. But presumably you make no use of plain women.'

'Pretty?' Laurent repeated, trying to give the impression he was struggling to remember. 'Yes, averagely pretty, I believe.'

'Yes, I thought she was,' said Marie-Louise, still neutral of tone. She put her hands on her hips and stared round the studio slowly, taking in the elaborate screen and the chaise-longue.

'Where did this averagely pretty model undress and put on the black satin underwear?' she asked. 'Behind that ridiculous red leather screen? She stood behind it to strip naked? And where were *you* when she was undressing – behind the screen with her to help her take her stockings off?'

'Marie-Louise!' Laurent exclaimed, sounding slightly annoyed to conceal his perturbation at her suspicions of him – what she suggested had taken place was very nearly the truth.

'I suppose you gave her a hand to take her knickers off,' she continued, not angrily but with a certain determination.

'*Chérie*, we have had this conversation before,' said Laurent awkwardly. 'I have told you over and over again that artists do not look at models from the same point of view as the ordinary man seeing a woman. A model is an object to be drawn, an object to reproduce in paint, nothing more.'

'I find it impossible to believe you,' said Marie-Louise, her tone edgy now. 'I doubt if any normal healthy man can stare for hours on end at a young woman in black satin knickers without becoming aroused.'

Laurent shrugged lightly and smiled with a nonchalance he did not feel, as if dismissing suggestions of his susceptibility.

'No, no,' he murmured, 'you misjudge me.'

'If you were a *pédé* and interested only in young boys,' said his fiancée, 'there would be no supreme difficulty in believing your claim to look at naked women as objects. But I have reason to know you possess all the usual male attitudes. Women's bodies excite you. You were trying most of the evening to see down the front of Pauline's frock – no, don't trouble to deny it, there is no point. It was most embarrassing, especially when you were dancing with her.'

'How can I make you understand that we artists see things in a different way?' he said, ignoring the accusation of trying to see Pauline's breasts.

The decolletage of Pauline's frock was deep and generous, that was undeniable, and she wore no bra that evening. While Laurent was dancing with her, besides feeling her bottom he'd managed to catch glimpses of a fine pair of well-shaped handfuls down her frock. Nothing like as bouncing as Marie-Louise's, naturally – but well worth a look. In his imagination he pictured them in a white lace bra, half-cups with uplift, a glimpse of russet buds through the lace. He would like to sketch her posed like that – if it ever became possible to arrange a visit to his studio.

She had an attractive bottom too, this near-blonde Pauline. Firm round cheeks, not pear-shaped or oval, springy of texture to the hands when squeezed. Smallish white lace knickers to go with the bra he pictured her breasts in. Easy to find a set of that type for Pauline to pose in. Ten sketches of her for his own collection, not as a commission for a magazine. And then!

Yes, then! On her hands and knees on the pink velvet chaise-longue, her pretty cheeks presented to him. Because that's what she really intended to come to his studio for, the posing was a pretence, they both understood that. Kneel close behind her on the pink velvet – trousers gaping open for *petit Jules* to stick out. Slide it into the leg, up under the white lace between the firm cheeks of her bottom.

Pauline would be very surprised not to feel it pushing into her. He'd soothe her with word and touch, his hands holding her hips, while he was thrusting forcefully. In effect, he would be making love to the white lace knickers more than to her – which was what he truly wished to do! There'd been a marvellous moment at the chateau when he'd made love to Marie-Louise's silk night-dress while he was lying on her. She'd kept her thighs together to stop him sliding inside her belly, but he hadn't been trying to do that anyway. She thought she'd won that little struggle – but she hadn't, he'd got what he wanted.

With Pauline on her hands and knees, he'd spurt up into her knickers – and see the wet stain soak through the fine lace.

From this it may be concluded that the direction of Laurent's life had changed. A month ago he had been perfectly pleased to become engaged to be married to Marie-Louise – difficult though she could be when he wanted to take her to bed. He was prepared to tolerate that because he adored her, or so he told himself – he had his own satisfactions which did not depend on her. Girls in pretty underwear posing in the privacy of his studio, it was blissful beyond words.

Then came Odette. She pried into his little secret behind the tilted drawing-board, she was neither offended nor shocked. She offered herself to him for artistic creation. On her young body he had produced a secret masterpiece, the *little heart*. Odette had understood his artistic nature and encouraged his talent in every way she could -- she urged him to do it to her every day. He adored her!. Not in the same way he adored Marie-Louise, of course, that was entirely different and the two would never be confused in his mind.

He was highly satisfied with Odette as a continuing source of artistic inspiration. But now he understood his own nature, why not experiment a little to see if he could find an alternative source of aesthetic vitality? Artists needed to experiment, to try new approaches, to devise new techniques. He felt it to be his duty to himself to find new frontiers. To surpass himself – to explore the limits of his abilities! Pauline in white lace knickers would surely inspire him to new heights of creativity.

'The model in the black satin knickers,' said Marie-Louise, as if half-aware of what was in his mind, 'she was here today, was she? She posed by the chaise-longue, it is in this sketch. She was almost lying on it, as you painted her in this picture.'

Marie-Louise tapped the sketch in question with one vermilion-painted fingernail. It depicted Odette in a very relaxed pose. Laurent shrugged unhappily and said nothing.

'Did you become sexually agitated, staring at her breasts and her thighs?' Marie-Louise demanded. 'Were you hard, Laurent?'

'You misjudge me,' he said again, sadly this time, 'I implore you to have more confidence in me. I am your fiancé – we are to be married.'

'What confidence can be put in any man whose daily occupation is to look at young women in flimsy underwear? What normal man can remain calm in such circumstances? I regret to say that in my opinion you are betraying me, Laurent.'

There! She had said it. Her suspicion was out in the open at last.

An expression of shock passed over Laurent's face. He knew he had *not* been unfaithful to her. What he did with Odette was for the cause of art and culture, it served his creative needs and was necessary to his development as an artist. Odette explained it to him often. When he slipped the black satin knickers down and buried his face between her slender thighs, it was entirely as a preliminary to artistic creation. Naturally it had nothing to do with his tender relationship with Marie-Louise. Nothing.

All the same, women were illogical and it would be impossible to make Marie-Louise understand the purity of his motives. When Odette lay on her back with her legs open for him to pierce the charming *little heart* of brunette curls between them, there was no thought of betrayal in his mind.

Another artist would understand that but a fiancée would leap to the conclusion that he did it to Odette for pleasure. An entirely false conclusion. But perhaps it was better to deny everything than try to explain.

He took Marie-Louise's hand and kissed it and drew her across to the pink velvet chaise-longue, although she let him see that she went with reluctance. She stared at him reproachfully when he drew her down gently to sit beside him.

'You expect me to sit on the very spot on which you betrayed me?' she demanded. 'What brutal insensitivity!'

'I swear to you,' he said, 'I have never betrayed you here on this chaise-longue – or anywhere else. Believe me.'

He said it convincingly because he believed it himself.

True, only that morning Odette had taken off the black satin knickers after he had sketched her, with his trousers wide open and his male part sticking up stiffly. It was Odette's idea for him to work with it out because, she claimed, his pictures were better then. He agreed with her in that. And while she lay with thighs apart he'd dashed across the room and flung himself down on his knees and pressed his lips to her *little heart*.

By no imaginable means was he unfaithful to Marie-Louise when he slid forward on to Odette's smooth belly and pushed into her – there could be no question of faithfulness or unfaithfulness when it was a matter of art and the creation of art. But, naturally, none of that could be said to a fiancée.

Marie-Louise looked at him doubtfully as he put an arm round her waist and held her close. Her knees were properly together, but Laurent was able to slip his hand up under the skirt of her chic black frock. His denial sounded extremely convincing, but she didn't believe him. Men were men and didn't change, she was absolutely certain of that. On the other hand, she didn't want to lose Laurent. Other steps must be taken.

She said nothing and let his hand slide up between her thighs until he was clasping her warmth through her thin knickers. How delicious was the feel of the silk under his hand, the softness of the flesh it covered.

'It is you I adore,' he said devoutly. 'I have no interest in other women. I swear to you this is so.'

To tell the truth, his interest in his fiancée was limited at that moment. For good reason. That morning, after Odette lay on her back for him on the chaise-longue, they went to his bedroom and reversed the process – Laurent lay on his back and she had him, kneeling astride him. He took her to lunch at a brasserie on the Boulevard du Montparnasse, and although he had completed his magazine assignment, Odette suggested she went back to his apartment after they had eaten and shared a bottle of wine.

No sooner was she inside the studio than her clothes were off again. She lay naked and face-down over his drawing-board, her feet widely separated on the floor. What could he do but accept her invitation? In an instant his trousers were undone, he was pressing himself against the bare cheeks of her bottom while he steered his fifteen centimetres up into her.

After his day of artistic creativity with Odette, it was not entirely surprising that he had no great desire to make love to Marie-Louise. Or anyone else, for that matter – though his hand was inside her little silk knickers and his fingertips caressed the warm lips beneath her curls. But he remained limp and small and useless.

'I am not a brute,' he said, 'I am not insensitive, *chérie*, I respect your feelings. Though I am on fire with desire for you, as always, I shall control myself to prove my consideration.'

'Your hand is between my legs,' Marie-Louise said coolly. 'Is that also evidence of your consideration for me?'

'You are unkind to me,' he said.

Marie-Louise said nothing, but she turned her face to him and raised an eyebrow. The gesture was so expressive he could guess what was in her mind – unless he made love to her he was almost admitting he had betrayed her with another woman!

As for Marie-Louise, though she had not the least interest

BONJOUR AMOUR

in making love, she was forcing the issue. Laurent must understand that being engaged to be married to her was a serious business. It did not occur to her, or to Laurent, that the situation was absurd. Neither really wanted to make love and yet both of them were determined to do so, to prove whatever it was each thought necessary to prove to the other.

She freed herself from the arm round her waist and got to her feet to slide her ivory silk knickers down her perfect legs. A sigh escaped Laurent, and then another as she dropped the small garment into his lap and let it lie there. He looked down with wistful eyes at the wisp of silk – if at that moment he had his usual strength he would be stiff as a steel bar. The mere touch of those knickers on his male part and he would be almost ready to spurt all over them. But alas . . .

She sat down again, closer to him, and her legs were a little wider apart now, and his fingers played freely over the soft flesh between. If he could stroke her breasts it would assist him in his search for vigour and determination – usually he went stiff at the mere sight of her over-size bounties.

That first time she had allowed him strip those beauties bare and kiss them – only a few weeks ago – he had become uncontrollably aroused. He had squeezed them in his hands, he had rolled them, lifted them and joggled them, he had licked them, put his mouth on the prominent dark-red tips, he had sucked at them – he'd been in heaven – then he'd gasped loudly and clutched at his trousers, where a wet and warm stickiness was spurting into his underwear.

'Oh, oh, oh,' he had moaned in shame and embarrassment, while Marie-Louise had stared at him curiously and shrugged.

She had never said so, but he came to understand she disliked having her breasts fondled. However desperate he was to squeeze them and lick them, he refrained.

Her hand brushed over the front of his trousers – at last his little friend was roused from his torpor. Laurent was relieved, he'd been desperately afraid he'd disappoint Marie-Louise that evening. But by the time her fingers found their way inside his underwear, there was the usual stiff length of flesh waiting to be grasped. She took hold of it full-handed, she stroked up and down firmly.

'It is not always possible to control one's natural desires,' he said, reversing his previous statement of intent.

'Yes,' she said, 'I understand you perfectly, Laurent.'

Her hand slid easily up and down, he sighed and shivered with pleasure. Marie-Louise had discovered long ago that this was a convenient way to please a man without submitting to the tedium of lying on her back. Naturally, it didn't serve all the time – sooner or later they insisted on her parting her legs for them. Sometimes Laurent could be satisfied by a little stroking until he spurted in her hand.

On this occasion it was insufficient for her own purpose. She was determined to make Laurent demonstrate his devotion to her, in the traditional manner, lying on her belly and thumping away manfully. She stroked him only until what she held was hard and hot and jumping in her hand – he was ready to prove himself.

She parted her legs widely and lay back on the chaise-longue. Her expertly coiffured head lay on a round pink velvet cushion, her dark brown eyes stared at Laurent with expectation and some other emotion he was unable to put a name to – surely it wasn't *doubt*? He slid off the chaise-longue to his knees on the floor and turned her skirt up to her waist. His careful hands pressed her knees further apart and he was staring between her smooth-skinned thighs at her silky brown curls.

Would she ever let him trim her curls into a *little heart*, he wondered. They were darker than Odette's and softer of texture. He could give her a beautiful heart shape to adorn her *joujou* – if she ever let him. He didn't think she would, and the present moment was most certainly the wrong time to ask. But if she did agree one day – how fantastic to have not one *little heart* but two to play with! To stroke, to feel, to transfix. But he knew it would need enormous persuasion before Marie-Louise agreed to allow him to trim her. But perhaps . . .

His hands moved slowly over the curve of her belly. The skin was like satin, so were the insides of her thighs. She reached down with one long-fingered hand, the fingers that had given him intense thrills wrapped round his upright part only minutes ago – the fingers opened the soft lips between her legs and Laurent sighed with pleasure to see the pretty pink interior.

'Make love to me, Laurent,' she said, her eyes closed.

He kissed her thighs, then the tip of his wet tongue flicked over her exposed bud. His experience with other women made him quite sure that Marie-Louise was now ravished by exquisite sensation. But he was wrong, as it happened; she felt only a mild pleasure from what he was doing to her.

Not that she would let him know that! But after only moments she took his head between her hands and pulled firmly to remove his mouth from between her thighs. His lips trailed slowly over her face and her hand reached for his jerking part, to steer it where she intended it to be.

He lay forward over her. They were both still fully dressed

– only her knickers were off and his trousers open, nothing more. The only contact of flesh between them was the feel of his hard part inside her as he penetrated, and the clasp of her softness round his intrusive part. He rode to and fro steadily, watching her face turn pink – with delight, as he thought. Her hands lay on his hips, holding him lightly.

'Yes, yes, yes, Laurent,' she encouraged him, her voice calm, though he was too excited to notice that. He was gasping to the rhythm of his deep and strong strokes into her belly. She heard his ragged breathing and felt his body go rigid – she knew that he was about to spurt.

'Yes, Laurent!' she said briskly – she took his head between her hands and pulled his mouth to hers. He was shaking wildly, his entire body jerking, his hands clutching her bottom. Until now she had been passive under his assault – to finish him off she bucked her belly up at him, meeting his frantic thrusts. It gave her no great sense of pleasure to do this, only a feeling of achievement. His back arched, he gushed his desire into her.

'Yes, yes, yes, yes,' she said – as if counting his throbs to make sure he was not giving her short measure.

He was still panting and twitching when she stared right into his eyes from a distance of five centimetres and demanded if he loved her – truly loved her?

'I love you, dear Marie-Louise,' he gasped, 'I adore you. I am not worthy of you.'

Well, of course you're not, she thought, I am a de Beaucourt-Villiers after all, and you, my dear Laurent, are an illustrator of women's underwear. But I shall make something of you.

She brushed her almost-black hair away from her brow with the back of a hand. Laurent's thrusting had jolted her about on the chaise-longue and ruffled her coiffure against the cushion. She never liked to look untidy after love-making.

Naturally, Laurent hadn't any idea of her private response to his well-intentioned words about not being worthy. To an extent he believed it himself. After all was said, her background and social circle made her such a prize to him.

He was delighted and relieved he'd been able to make love to her so well, after the exertions of the day. It would be useful to restrict Odette's enthusiasm on the days when he was meeting Marie-Louise. If it was possible to restrain her. When they were together he was always keen to do whatever she suggested. But in spite of all that, he had made love very successfully to Marie-Louise and he thought his performance would assure her of his devotion. He was wrong about that.

Marie-Louise was completely convinced now that he was having an *affaire*. With the model in his sketches for *Vogue*. And other magazines. A faceless woman sketched in black satin knickers – a woman with dark brown hair and small feet. And a maddeningly elegant bust-line, not great fleshy things like her own. It was necessary to do something to curb Laurent.

Odette Moves Apartment

The day when Odette moved her clothes and other belongings into Robert Dorville's apartment without an invitation, he was by no means delighted. He'd only known her two days – as a girlfriend she had everything to recommend her, he enjoyed her company and in bed she was inventive and enthusiastic. He adored her madly, but moving in – that was something he hadn't bargained for.

Yet on the day she moved out again, he was seized by feelings of despondency – even though he had begun to suspect that there was another man with the same intimate privileges as he enjoyed himself. Take the matter of the thick brown fleece on Odette's belly and between her legs. Robert found it perversely exciting to look at, to feel, to stroke. And to nuzzle his lips into, searching for the soft fleshy petals the curls covered.

Then one evening, when they had been out to dinner in a small restaurant near Robert's apartment, he kissed her and undressed her in his bedroom – and her fur-coat was gone! He fell on his knees and held her by the hips while he stared unbelieving from a few centimetres away. The wild thicket was gone. And in place of it Odette had a *little heart* of neatly trimmed curls.

She was able to explain her change of style to him. The model agency had sent her to a magazine artist, she told Robert, and the assignment was the most marvellous underwear in the entire world. For *Vogue*, naturally.

Underwear like this was gossamer-thin and almost transparent – as Robert must know from his own past experience. For posing it had been necessary to reduce the size and the thickness of her natural fleece because it showed through.

She was sorry to have to do it, she said with a little shrug, she preferred herself *sauvage*, untamed, in a state of nature!

But what would you do? Posing for Monsieur Breville paid a very good fee. And equally important, she was the type of model that he found agreeable. He said he would ask the agency to send her to his studio again. He was a useful contact, this illustrator. So, as Robert would understand, it had been necessary to make a small sacrifice to get on in her career.

'But why a heart?' Robert asked, sounding disconcerted.

'A whim,' she said, 'while I was shearing my lovely fleece I decided that the usual little triangle was too ordinary. Do you find it chic, my *little heart*?'

His eyes were round and vague as he stared at the heart-shape that fitted neatly between her slender thighs, leaving her skin bare from her dimple of a belly button almost down to the pink lips. There was no doubt that this new style gave her joujou an interesting prominence. It revealed the curve of the full mound and the soft lips that seemed to pout. Robert pressed his mouth to the bared lips in a hot kiss – his tongue slipped between to touch the little bud inside and caress it.

All the same, he was not a complete idiot. Later on, after he had twice had her on her back and his male part lay soft and slack between his legs, he asked an awkward question or two about the celebrated fashion artist who made her take her clothes off and stand about posing in knickers.

Was he young or old, this Breville? Did he stare at Odette's naked body as if he wished to do more than just look? Could he see her while she changed knickers or was there a dressing-room for her use? Did he try to touch her when she was undressing?

'But no, *chou-chou*,' she said, thinking furiously how to invent a story that would allay Robert's natural suspicions, 'he hasn't the least interest in women, me or anyone else – naked or fully dressed. He's left-handed.'

'Are you sure of that?' Robert demanded. He was gripping her breasts so tightly that she began to fear that in his frenzy he might ruin their shape forever. She pried his fingers loose one by one and moved his hand to his own limp part. Let him squeeze that flat if he wished!

'Fashion artists and photographers, dress designers and hair-dressers, they are always left-handed, you know that,' she said sweepingly. 'In those professions it is almost obligatory.'

'Some are,' Robert agreed, 'but how do you know this one is? What does he look like?'

'Oh, he's reasonably good-looking, in a weak sort of way,' she said, 'but believe me, *chéri*, women know at once where a man's interests lie. It is an instinct. Monsieur Breville could stare at me stark naked all day long and never go stiff. You need not be concerned for me. But if I were a pretty sixteen-year-old boy, I would be very doubtful about posing in underwear for him.'

Robert thought it over for a while and let it go at that. But as days passed and she went out each morning at ten to take the Metro to Breville's studio Robert began to ask himself if there might be more than she said. She went to work so cheerfully, it seemed unnatural.

Perhaps, as she claimed, she was the right type for Breville's work. But why was it she modelled only for him and never anyone else? Did he demand her exclusive services? How important was a particular model to a fashion artist – surely she was only a clothes-horse? Any woman with a good figure would do.

And to be absolutely truthful – the neat *little heart* between Odette's legs troubled Robert. It was exciting, yes, he admired it and he loved having her strip naked for him and stroll about his apartment while he looked at it. But the truth was that it seemed so contrived, so blatant. It was the sort of fancy a man might have, rather than a woman. Perhaps it was Breville's idea and not Odette's.

And if Breville was interested in Odette to that extent, then he was certainly not left-handed. And if she let him design her little fur coat, then she let him make the obvious use of what it covered. Or used to cover – in its present state everything was displayed!

Not that Robert's growing suspicion prevented him from making love to Odette every night when they went to bed. Even without her thick brown fleece she was very exciting to hold and touch and do things to. But Robert couldn't help thinking, even while he kissed between her spread thighs, before he lay on her belly and pushed into her, he might be tracing another man's route.

Suppose Breville had kissed her *belle chose* that morning

and penetrated it? Or that afternoon. Or morning and afternoon.

For Robert it was a time of confusion, not knowing whether he was sharing her with Breville. Not for absolute certain, though his suspicions hardened to near certain. He said nothing to her and asked no more questions about Breville. Probably because he didn't want to know the truth. Then one morning Odette told him she was moving out. She had found a little place of her own, on the Left Bank. Robert didn't know whether to feel sorry or glad at the unexpected news.

'When?' he asked.

'As soon as the taxi arrives,' she said.

That was it. She packed her belongings into two suitcases, a large and a small, and had Robert carry them down to the street entrance of the building. She was very amiable to him, she said how grateful she was to him for putting her up while she got on her feet. She let him stroke her breasts through her silk shirt and slip his hand up her pencil-slim skirt and touch her *belle-chose* while they said *Au revoir*. And Robert being Robert, if he had half a chance she'd be on the sofa with her skirt round her waist.

'There is no time,' she murmured, her hand on the stiff bulge in his trousers for a friendly farewell squeeze, 'another time, Robert, we shall meet often, I promise you.'

She wanted to remain on good terms with him, in case she ever needed to move back in. She saw no necessity to advise him the rent of the small apartment she was moving to had been paid for six months in advance by Laurent Breville.

She had been Breville's model for three weeks. His only model — and at top rates, of course. She rewarded him with fantasies of delight, she made him open his trousers to expose his length of stiff flesh while he was sketching. He'd been doing that for ages, of course, long before he met Odette – but in the past he had done it furtively, behind his tilted drawing-board, hiding what he was doing from the model posing for him.

Now it was out in the open, so to speak, his model was urging him to do it – she stood there almost naked and smiled to watch him handle his fifteen centimetres while he eyed her *nichons* in an almost transparent white satin bra and her slender loins in matching lace-edged knickers. She flashed her trim *little heart* at him as he hunched over his drawing-board open-mouthed and in a trance of delight – paint-brush trembling in his hand. In two minutes, no more, he completed the sketch before he let himself succumb to her wiles.

She kept his feeling of guilt simmering by asking often about his fiancée. Did Mademoiselle Beaucourt-Villiers do *this* to him when she visited his studio? Did she sometimes stand just here in her underwear and make him spoil a sheet of drawing-paper so he had to do the sketch again? Perhaps she had no interest in his work in the studio and preferred elsewhere in the apartment for her amusements?

In the bedroom, that went without saying. But it demonstrated a certain lack of imagination – and an artist like Laurent must bring his imagination to life. Did his fiancée stand naked with him in the shower, to be lathered all over? And stand with her legs wide open and her back against the tiles for him? Surely she must want to be swept along by his spirit of adventure? Did she bend over the kitchen table while he did it to her from behind? Or sit on his face while he lay on the sofa? Did she scream loudly when she reached her climax?

Laurent never answered her questions – or any other questions about Mademoiselle la Fiancée. His face would turn a deep pink with embarrassment and he needed to be reassured very regularly that he was not in any way betraying Marie-Louise.

With his stiff part in her hand, Odette could persuade him of almost anything. The strange thing was, after all that nonsense about liberating the creative urge by making love to the model, his work did seem to be actually improving. It had always been first rate, or top magazines would never have commissioned his illustrations. There was a touch of something new about them in the last couple of weeks, a certain wittiness, a vivacity and a stylishness that brought favourable comments from editors.

Things were going well for Laurent and only when he was alone at night did he remember that he was balancing on a knife-edge. Odette in silk knickers sitting on his lap every day and Marie-Louise in his arms by night. Some nights, that is. It needed a logical mind, courage and determination to cope with situations of this complexity.

Cope he must, there was no question of it – in less than a month Odette had become very important to him. He blessed the day she had first arrived at his studio when he was working on the bras and knickers for *Vogue* magazine. After that momentous day he phoned Madame Drouet at the model agency to thank her and arrange that in future she sent only Mademoiselle Charron, no one else. And Madame Drouet, who had been long in the business, realised from the tone of his phone call that certain personal interests were involved here.

She explained to Monsieur Breville that she would do anything in her power to accommodate so valued a client as himself, but it was very difficult to guarantee a particular model on short notice. Especially one so much in demand as Mademoiselle Odette Charron. Her services were requested by commercial artists and photographers all over Paris. Laurent believed her because his power of reason was suspended in regard to Odette. What was in his trousers had taken control of what was in his head. In fact Odette's services were not in demand by anyone except him.

She hadn't worked for weeks before the morning Madame Drouet had sent her to Laurent's studio – she'd been hard-up and without much hope, which was why she'd moved uninvited into Robert Dorville's apartment. But only till she was on her feet again – and it seemed that Laurent was the opportunity she needed. Meeting him was an astonishing stroke of luck – she had been given the assignment because the model booked for him had disappeared with a married man the previous day, and only Odette was available.

Naturally, in business matters these little considerations of fact and truthfulness are often changed around to the advantage of who is in the stronger position. By misrepresenting Odette's lack of professional success and so deceiving Laurent, Madame Drouet was able to secure a bonus payment for herself from him. And top rate fees for Odette – as if she were a model established in the top fashion houses and constantly in demand. Everyone concerned was satisfied, Madame Drouet, Laurent, and Odette.

At last things were going well for Odette. In less than four weeks Laurent had become besotted by her, he paid the model fee for her to come to his studio almost every day, whether he had a commission for a magazine or not. He took her to lunch, once or twice he took her to dinner, to discreet restaurants where he'd be reasonably sure of not being seen

BONJOUR AMOUR

by anyone acquainted with his fiancée. And Odette provided all the sexual pleasure he was able to cope with – sometimes more.

After she had hinted carefully about the problems of finding an affordable apartment, Laurent had an idea he thought was his own – he found one for her. And paid the rent in advance to let her see how interested he was in her career. It was closer, he said, it eliminated the inconvenience of a journey on the Metro to reach his studio. Odette looked at him with an expression of interest, but not giving in too quickly.

The apartment he had found was small but comfortable, he told her, it was much better to have a place of her own than sharing with two other girls. That was what she had said when he asked about her living arrangements, a harmless little lie to protect him from the anguish of knowing she was living with a man.

Laurent pointed out it would be possible for him to visit her in her own apartment. He made this sound like a great advantage – perhaps he had visions of rolling her on her own sitting-room floor and pulling her knickers down with his teeth. Odette saw no advantage at all in an arrangement where he could drop in on her at any time – presumably he would have a key. She was doing all that needed doing to make sure he stayed besotted – either in his studio or in his own bedroom.

Nevertheless, this offer of a place of her own was important, it was necessary to establish guilt in his mind. Paying rent on an apartment for a woman was something no fiancée in the entire world could misunderstand or ignore or forgive, Mademoiselle de Beaucourt-Villiers included, if she ever found out. Laurent was really putting himself at Odette's mercy! Once installed, she could really get him to promote her modelling career.

But she knew that even sure-fire plans went wrong as often as they went right. If her career under Laurent's patronage struck serious problems, it would be useful to have the option to move back into Robert's apartment instead of using her own money for rent and food. This presented no great difficulty – Robert had never been able to say *No* to her.

What she had to do was simple enough, phone him once or twice a week and visit him and let him undress her and play with her *little heart*. With this in mind, she left him on terms of close friendship, if short notice. She kissed him warmly on the lips, holding his face between her hands, when he carried her luggage out to the waiting taxi.

Robert stood on the pavement with hands in his jacket pockets looking forlorn. He had a very prominent bulge in his trousers. How absurd men were, Odette thought as she gave him a fond wave through the window. How easily persuaded they were when in that state – how little it took to make them stiff! The taxi-driver grated his gears noisily and accelerated away from the kerb and Robert and along the Boulevard de la Madeleine, as if competing at Le Mans. But everyone knows taxi drivers are demented.

The tiny apartment Laurent had taken for Odette was situated conveniently near his own. It was in the Quartier Latin, about twenty minutes' walk away, up on the second floor of an old building in the narrowest possible of streets, somewhere between the rue d'Ulm and the rue Mouffetard. Odette was not impressed the first time she saw the apartment and the area. Picturesque, no doubt tourists came in coaches to see it every day. Laurent was enthusiastic about the steep little streets of sagging ancient buildings and the market-stalls along the rue Mouffetard.

It was colourful, Odette agreed, shrugging. The open-fronted shops extended out on to the pavements – the shoppers walked in the road. There were stacks of every possible type of fruit and vegetable, there were cranberries and melons, almonds, carrots, onions, apples and bananas. There were bakeries producing fresh bread, baguettes and croissants, wine shops and cheese stalls with every variety of cheese ever devised of cow milk and sheep milk and goat milk.

On the corner there was a busker in an old and badly-fitting jacket, patched trousers and cracked shoes. An old young man – no more than thirty but with a lined face. He was playing a tune on an accordion, his sweat-stained cap lay on the pavement by his feet for passers-by to drop cash in.

He was playing *La Vie en Rose*, not very well, and by the look of him his life was lived in shades of dark grey, not pink. But he grinned at Odette and she could guess what was in his mind – he'd like to have her up against a handy wall with her knickers round her knees. She returned his glance in a very offhand way. *You can keep your insolent thoughts to yourself, accordion-man,* her look said. *What's between my legs is valuable.*

The rue Mouffetard was all very well if food and cooking were your main interests. Meat, poultry, fish – it was all there on offer. What was far more interesting to Odette was that she counted ten cafés along the street. She sat with Laurent at a table outside one of them and pretended to listen to his fervent descriptions of the attractions of the rue Mouffetard, its long history, its colour and vivacity.

What she wanted was a modern apartment in a modern

building, with no concessions to history or tradition. Instead of that he was putting her in two tiny rooms in a building two hundred years old! Artists were idiots, she decided! Laurent was the biggest idiot of them all.

Naturally, it would have to be changed for something far more appropriate. For the present she would have to accept it, there was nowhere else to go now she'd left Robert's very comfortable apartment. It was necessary to teach Laurent her preferences in accommodation. If he found the rue Mouffetard so picturesque he could live there himself and paint melons and cucumbers all day long, instead of lingerie for *Vogue* magazine.

But no – with the inconsistency for which men were notorious, he talked about a rich cultural heritage but he made sure that he lived in a spacious building with tall windows, wrought-iron balconies and an air of anonymous distinction, with every modern convenience – and a stroll from the Boulevard du Montparnasse. That's where the famous restaurants and cafés were to be found – the places where people of intelligence and eminence in arts and letters congregated. Where a woman with a good face and figure could meet charming and useful people.

And who was she likely to meet around the rue Mouffetard but pregnant wives with heavy shopping-bags filled with cabbage and bottles of cheap red wine for their husbands' dinners? To say nothing of penniless university students who needed a haircut! What use were people like that to her new career?

Laurent was going to have to do better. It was necessary to apply a little discreet pressure. The next time he lay panting on her bare belly, he would have to be reminded how disastrous

BONJOUR AMOUR

it would be if by some unfortunate mistake his fiancée ever got to know about the source of his marvellous artistic creativity. Not blackmail, of course, that was crude and criminal. It made enemies, and she wanted to stay friends with Laurent. That way she'd get much more from him.

No threats. Just a hint, no more than that. Guilt was the way to influence Laurent and persuade him to open his bank account. Odette meant to make him feel very guilty indeed.

Life is full of little ironies – in spite of Odette's opinion she would never see anyone of the least interest in the area of her new apartment, she did, only a few days after she moved in. She had a morning off from posing in knickers for Laurent – and other things she did for him after she slipped them off. He had a business meeting in an editor's office, he said. Odette lazed in bed till after ten, then made coffee and dressed to go out – it was a bright sunny day.

She cut through the narrow streets to the Boulevard St-Michel and was sauntering along with her dark-haired head full of plans and possibilities, when she heard a man's voice call her name. She stopped and turned, and saw Jacques Brolin. A friend, one might say, from the past. Friend was not really the correct word – he was a boyfriend once, a different thing altogether. One of many men who expected her to get into bed with them after they paid for dinner and a bottle of wine in a cheap restaurant.

It was two years since she'd seen him last. He kissed her on both cheeks – he smelled pleasantly of hair lotion. He told her she was looking more beautiful than ever. Privately she agreed with him, she'd been to the hairdresser only the day before and her hair was skilfully cut. She was wearing a summer frock in a *café-au-lait* colour, with a matching little square jacket and a necklace of jade green beads – not jade, of course, but pretty. The effect was to draw attention to her pale green eyes.

Jacques took her arm and led her to the nearest café and a table outside under the awning, saying she must spare five minutes to talk to an old friend. He was looking moderately prosperous, in a light-grey trilby hat – the brim turned dashingly down at the front – and a fairly new blue suit. The waiter came and Jacques ordered beer for himself and *kir* for Odette – he remembered she liked that.

He was a salesman when she first knew him; he still was, she learned, though not for the same company. He was selling shoes for a well-known manufacturer now. And he was married and had a new-born daughter. He lived in the suburbs, miles out of Paris, a boring train-ride morning and evening. To Odette that was as much as to say Jacques had resigned from the human race. People lived in Paris, anywhere else didn't count.

Naturally, when he got round to asking her what she was doing these days she didn't tell him too much, boyfriend once or not. She was a firm believer in keeping her secrets to herself. She told him she was modelling for fashion artists and let it go at that.

They talked for half an hour, the café was filling up fast as the hour for lunch approached. Jacques suggested she had lunch with him, he knew a very good little restaurant not ten minutes walk away. Odette was a little surprised by the invitation, but she accepted and off they went. She had a feeling he was taking her to one of the cheap Latin Quarter places where students ate basic food for their few francs, but it proved to be a pleasant little bistro with good cooking.

Over the meal and a drinkable red wine Jacques talked mostly about the days when he and she were close friends – in love, he seemed to mean – though Odette was certain she'd never been in love with him. While they talked and laughed together she tried to recall what it was about Jacques Brolin that appealed to her back in those days. He'd liked to dance and often took her to a *café-dansant*. He liked the cinema, especially gangster movies – they'd seen plenty of those together.

Perhaps it was the wine – perhaps it was because Jacques was of no significance to her now and no effort was called for, but by two-thirty and after two small glasses of cognac Odette felt quite friendly towards him. Affectionate? No, that was overstating it. *Sympathetic* might be closer. She understood him, they were from the same background, the dreary wasteland of streets round the Place Hebert, between a railway shunting yard and the noisy goods depot. A depressing area, young men like Jacques leaning on street corners with their hands in their pockets. Women like Odette getting pregnant at eighteen to make sure the boyfriend would marry them.

Jacques was not happy, that was evident. He had escaped from the all-night clatter of the railway shunting yard, or had he? He hadn't really escaped. Wife, baby and home in the suburbs – that wasn't his style, never had been. He was a creature of the boulevards and bright lights, dance-halls and bars. Girlfriends and late nights, steaks and *frites* on the Place Blanche at one in the morning, rumpled beds in cheap little hotels when he had the money, standing up in dark doorways if not. No promises, no commitments, that was Jacques' way. If he'd been born rich he'd have been a natural playboy.

This or something like it was in Odette's mind when they

left the restaurant. She felt she understood Jacques very well
– and to understand was, they say, to forgive. Her goodwill to
him was very sincere. When he suggested they went to her
apartment she agreed without giving it much consideration.
They went on foot, chatting vivaciously, until Jacques whistled
in surprise to see the area where she lived, the narrow streets
and old buildings.

'Not what I expected of you,' he said. 'When we were
talking over lunch I pictured you in a modern luxury block,
with a rich boyfriend paying the bills. Uniformed porter on
the door and a marble bath big enough for two – that's your
line, not the back streets.'

'You've a lot to learn, Jacques,' she said, 'haven't you any
feel for tradition and cultural heritage? Surely even you can
see how picturesque the area is. And further on there's the rue
Mouffetard and the market, fruit and wine and cheese.'

'If you say so,' said Jacques, though doubtfully.

In her heart she agreed with him, of course; a marble bath
in a modern apartment was her own dream too. But she was
not going to let Jacques Brolin feel superior. After all, he
lived out in the suburbs somewhere!

When he saw the inside of her tiny apartment he was
impressed by the decor and furnishings. Laurent had done that
part well – at least his artistic talent was good for something
beside bras and knickers. Odette took off her little summer
jacket and went to the tiny kitchen to make coffee and find a
bottle of cognac. Jacques flung his hat into a corner and
slumped down on a chair. The room was too small for a sofa,
it held two armchairs, an elegant coffee table and a tall
electric floor-lamp with a milk white globe on a swan-neck
chrome shaft.

BONJOUR AMOUR

Odette set the bottle and glasses on the table, and before she could return to the kitchen Jacques reached up to seize her wrist.

'We had coffee at the restaurant,' he said with a grin and he pulled her down to sit on his lap. In a moment he held the back of her neck in one hand while he kissed her – his other hand up her frock and between her thighs.

Odette remembered clearly now why she had liked him once – it was not his thinly handsome looks, nor his dubious charm. Cheap was the word for him. But at one thing he was superbly good and he knew it.

'Jacques – you are impossible,' she said as his fingers found their way into her little white knickers and stroked the fleshy lips between her thighs.

'What's this?' he demanded, his whole hand between her legs, his palm rubbing slowly. 'What's happened – you used to have a pelt like a she-bear! What have you done to it?'

Odette didn't answer, it was more amusing to let him find out for himself. He was still holding her tight by the nape of her neck, as if to prevent her from running away, but with his free hand he pulled her frock up and her knickers down her thighs to examine her. '*Alors*!' he gasped, when he saw her *little heart*.

'It's sad, but when I started to work for celebrated magazine artists I had to trim my fleece,' she told him. She was already becoming aroused, it was that hand of his gripping her neck, he always had that effect on her when he held her like a rabbit.

Jacques' fingers were probing inside her, making her slippery wet. She stared at him, her green eyes half-closed, and he gave her a wicked grin.

'I like it,' he said, 'it's classy.'

'Yes,' she murmured, hardly able to speak for the surging of her emotions, as his skilful fingers manipulated her rapidly to the brink of ecstasy, 'yes, Jacques!'

'Take them off,' he said quickly, pulling his hand out of her knickers and squeezing a breast through her frock. But he kept a firm grip on her neck so she couldn't get up off his lap. She wriggled them over her knees and down her legs – she kicked off her shoes. And while she was doing this Jacques ripped open his trousers, jerked his loins, and she saw the stiff length poking out at her.

She knew that fifteen centimetre part well – when she was nineteen she'd had it up her twenty times a week. It was an old friend, strong and thick, purple-headed, tireless. She ran her fingers lightly up the shaft and over the swollen head.

'Ah yes, feel it – I can see you've missed it,' said Jacques with his usual ill-placed and annoying confidence. That was one of the things Odette disliked about him, his assumption that he was always right. But he was doing marvellous things to her and sending exquisite thrills through her belly – at least this was something he always got right!

He turned her on his lap to face him, forcing her legs apart with hands busy above her stocking-tops. She was open and wet – a strong push took him into her, right up in her shaking belly.

'Jacques . . .' she moaned, '*chéri* . . .'

'We've a lot of time to make up for,' he gasped thickly. 'I'm going to have you till you can't stand on your feet.'

Her pretty summer frock was bunched up and creased round her waist, it would need pressing before she wore it again, but she was too far gone in sensation to notice or care.

Jacques' right hand gripped the nape of her neck to press her lips on his in a hard kiss.

His other hand was behind her, holding her bare bottom – his middle finger between the cheeks. Odette was driven helplessly on by his jabbing inside her, she was ricocheting from orgasm to orgasm, shaking violently as she hung from the hand gripping her neck.

The Problems Of Being A Man

When Jacques finished with Odette on the armchair and sank back shaking, she collapsed against his chest, chin on his shoulder. She could feel his heart thumping under his shirt, she felt the heat of his body against her. She hadn't the energy to lift her head, not after all he'd done to her – but she was sure that if she could see his face there'd be a sly smile on it.

He was still in blue suit and shiny grey tie, he had conceded the very minimum necessary to do it to her – just the front of his trousers gaped open for his stiff part to stick out and ram up into her. His hands were at rest now and lay on her bare and widely parted thighs, his thumbs in her groins.

But not to stroke her, for her pleasure or his own – it was a gesture of possession, and Odette understood it: his statement that he was in her, he'd ravaged her, he'd had her and used her for his satisfaction. Which, said the placing of his thumbs, was how it should be – he was a man, rampant and dominant! He took what he wanted from women. That's what men did, that was how it had always been. She was a woman, man had a slit to be made use of – *et voilà tout*!

'Just like the old days,' he said, very pleased with himself, 'I bet your boyfriend can't make you squeal like that.'

I must be out of my mind to bring him here, Odette thought

to herself. Now he knows where I live he'll come round whenever he feels like it and try to jump on me. Suppose Laurent was here – as soon as he saw Jacques I'd lose my hold over him. I've been a fool!

Jacques represented everything she didn't want. And not only because of the threat to her dealings with Laurent. Jacques was a part of her past she wanted to leave behind; he brought back all her memories of growing up in a poor and drab district. The struggle to get out, the unreliability of everything to do with men, the ever-present uncertainty.

When she knew Jacques before, he too was full of plans to escape, but he hadn't managed to – he'd settled for dreary married life in the suburbs. That was her own worst fear. She knew how close to failure and giving up she'd been only a month ago when she ran into Robert. Without knowing it, he'd given her breathing-space till she met Laurent. She didn't want Jacques sliding back into her life to distract her from her career as a model.

And yet she had to admit to herself with a feeling of shame and anger that it was going to be very difficult to resist him, almost impossible. Jacques always had this effect on her – from the first day she met him in a dingy *café-tabac* years ago. When Jacques put his hand up her skirt, her mind switched completely off. Her belly started to shake and her legs slid apart without any conscious decision by her. When Jacques stroked her between the thighs she was overcome by an almost irresistible desire to lie on her back and let him do what he wanted.

It was impossible to explain rationally, but nobody else ever did it to her like Jacques. She was nineteen when she first met him – not a virgin, of course, she'd had several boyfriends.

She knew all about love-making, or so she believed. When Jacques had her that night on a market porter's barrow parked in a baker's yard her climax was tremendous. She'd experienced nothing so intense before. She passed out underneath him, on the dirty old barrow. After he'd finished he slapped her face, forehand and backhand, to bring her round. And she begged for more.

They suited each other – if he'd asked her to marry him she'd have thought herself the luckiest woman alive and jumped at the chance. It was her idea of heaven come true – a small apartment with a big bed and Jacques flinging her on her back three times a day. Well, almost her idea of heaven.

Except that in those days he had no interest in marrying. And hadn't now. A wilier woman than Odette had managed to catch him by letting her belly swell. Some determined woman had been able to persuade no-promises-no-commitments Jacques into a permanent sort of commitment. Not all that permanent, though, when he was slumped here in Odette's armchair – less than a year after he'd married someone else. She felt his softening part beginning to slip slowly out of her.

To be truthful, even at nineteen, Odette's sights had been set on a more elegant and prosperous way of life than Jacques would provide. If she had married him, they would not have been together long, only until being flung on her back throughout the day became so familiar a routine that it ceased to be enthralling. She would have left him to strike out on her own – she was sure of that – left him for a career that took her into different circles and very different possibilities.

But having said all that, she felt it was a pity she had never had the ten or eleven months of ecstasy with Jacques – it would have been the most memorable part of her life. But that was all in the past. The problem now was to save herself from becoming his twice a week drop-in when he was in this part of Paris.

She was turning over these thoughts in her mind when Jacques slid his arms round her waist and stood up quickly, lifting her with him. She clamped her legs round his thin body and her arms round his neck and clung tight. In this way he carried her into the bedroom. She'd known all along, from the moment she sat on his lap and he slipped his hand up her frock, that he'd want to have her on the bed sooner or later. Jacques was a glutton – he took everything. There was a greed in him that was insatiable – he'd rather die than leave anything untasted or untouched.

The bedroom was small, but thanks to Laurent it was pleasing. The walls were painted a pale pastel pink, the window curtains were pale lemon velvet. And the bed! Laurent had provided her with a broad modern bed, very impressive. Obviously he planned to share it with her when the mood took him. So far he'd had no opportunity to make use of it, she'd satisfied him well in his own apartment and kept him away from hers. She grinned to think that Jacques was going to be the first to have her on Laurent's new bed.

The room was tiny and the bed was large, it almost filled it. Jacques set her down on the near edge, took half a step back and was almost touching the door.

'Get your clothes off, girl,' he said, licking his lips, 'and let's have a look at you – you're as skinny as you always were. Don't you eat enough?'

'I'm a model,' said Odette proudly, 'I have to stay slim. No one wants a fat model in the fashion business.'

'You'd be better with more meat on your bones,' said

Jacques. His trousers were still undone from having her on the armchair, his limp part dangled outside. His hand was under it and he was playing unconsciously with it while he spoke. 'I like something to get hold of. A nice broad belly to lie on and solid thighs.'

'I suppose you mean like that fat blonde girl you were having when you met me,' Odette said caustically, 'Marianne Loiseau – same age as me, we were in the same class at school. A backside like a wine-barrel and great flabby *nichons* hanging down to her belly-button. That's your type, Jacques.'

He grinned at her wolfishly and took his jacket off. He undid the knot of his tie, pulling it down impatiently with a finger. Odette stood up to undress and saw how her frock was creased. She threw it over the straight-backed wooden chair in a corner. Her knickers were in the sitting-room, stuffed down the side of the armchair. Off came her stockings and garter-belt, her white satin bra. Jacques leaned against the wall watching her strip. He eyed her well-shaped pointed breasts with interest.

'Nice pair of *nichons*,' he said, almost leering. He was still playing idly with his limp part. 'They're not all that big, but I like them.'

'I'm sorry I can't compete with Marianne,' said Odette with a sneer, 'with the handling you gave her they must have been long enough to wrap round your neck before you'd finished with her.'

But Jacques was more interested in the small neat heart shape fitting neatly between Odette's slim thighs, to leave her belly bare above the pouting pink lips. He was so interested, in fact, that he got down on his knees on the maroon carpet and held her with his hands on the bare cheeks of her bottom while he stared at her neatly-clipped *joujou*.

'Used to be like a she-bear in the circus,' he said, shaking his head in a doubtful way, 'I liked that. I could push my hand down your knickers and get hold of a handful of curly hair. And when you opened your legs for me I used two fingers to find the way in. What a muff you had! Why did you cut it off?'

'Because it's pretty like this,' said Odette.

Laurent had given her *little heart* its twice-a-week trim with scissors and safety-razor only the day before. This he tackled with unfailing enthusiasm, it was never just a quick trim, he'd developed it into a sort of love-ritual. He'd take half an hour fussing over her as she lay on a bath-towel on the side of his bed, with her feet on the floor and her legs wide apart.

When he'd finished shaping her brunette curls to his complete satisfaction, he devotedly kissed the long pink lips he'd bared and parted them with gentle fingers. Then the tip of his tongue slipped in to lap at her little bud. When he heard her sighing, and that never took long, he slid forward over her and put his belly on her belly. He was tremendously aroused by fussing over her curls – he impaled her *little heart* with a single push.

That was Laurent's way, not Jacques's way. By nature Laurent was sensitive and artistic, Jacques was by nature uncouth. His blunt fingers played over the lips that split the *little heart*, but he didn't kiss them.

'So it's pretty,' he said with a dismissive shrug of his thin shoulders, 'though who cares what it looks like? It's what you can do with it that matters. Plump or thin, hairy or bare, some are nicer to be up than others, and it's nothing to do with how they look.'

'You're the big expert,' said Odette, sounding unimpressed.

'You're right about that,' he said with a grin, taking it as a compliment to his prowess. 'In case you'd forgotten after all this time, I gave you a reminder while you were sitting on my lap just now. The way you were squealing!'

The annoying truth was she wanted to feel his hardness inside her again. His attentions to his dangling male part were having a visible effect, it was getting longer and thicker. But Odette wasn't going to let him think he could do what he liked to her.

'It wasn't bad on the armchair,' she said, trying to sound as casual as possible, 'I've had better. You're not really much of an expert, Jacques, you get a woman's knickers down and all you think of is getting inside her quick. I don't believe you even notice whether she's blonde, black or ginger down there, you're so anxious to get up it. Mine's the first one you've looked at in years. You never had any finesse and you never will.'

'That so?' he asked. He turned his hand palm upward and ran his middle finger up the lips of her *belle-chose* to open them, exposed her little pink button and tickled it slyly.

Odette wanted to sit down on the bed, she wanted to lie on it and feel Jacques on top of her. But his free hand held the back of her thigh and kept her standing while his fingertip caressed around and over her wet bud.

'Jacques – lie on me and do it,' she murmured, surrendering to the delicious sensations, 'I want you.'

'When I'm ready,' he said, finger busy in the slipperiness of her *joujou*, making her belly squirm with sensation.

She put her hands on his shoulders to support herself as her legs trembled and lost their strength. She sighed and shook all over, her green eyes were cloudy with overwhelming emotion. And Jacques, coarse and brutal monster, was staring up at her face, revelling in his power over her. He could throw her down on her back whenever he felt like it – climb on her belly and ride her senseless. And he could make her wait for it – make her beg him to give it to her.

Which was the way it should be, he was a man with a big thick thing to stick into girls, women, wives, widows, all of them – they all wanted him to slip it up them, it was born in them to understand what they were there for: to lie down and get their legs open for him. Including Odette, she'd been his years ago; she'd learned some independent ways since then but that made no difference at all – she was his for the having. He gloated as he watched her face, his fingers tantalising her. She was his for as long as he wanted, she couldn't help herself.

But it happened sooner than Jacques expected. She gave a long shriek and her legs folded under her. She fell back on the bed, writhing in ecstatic convulsions, bouncing on the mattress. Her legs were flailing the air – he trapped them in his armpits and held them while his fingers flicked at her bud to intensify her spasms. Then she was still, except for an occasional tremor of her belly and thighs.

She opened her eyes to see Jacques between her legs, grinning at her and very pleased with himself once more.

'That got you going,' he said.

Odette saw he was stiff, *Jacques-le-Grand* was jutted fiercely and proudly up out of his open trousers.

'What's the matter,?' she asked, to taunt him and get her own back, 'can't you do it a second time, *chéri*? You used to go on for hours, but I suppose being married has tamed you.

BONJOUR AMOUR

Does your wife roll over and turn her back to you after you've done it to her once? They say married women behave like that after a year or so, they open their legs twice a week and no more.'

That took the grin off his face. He raised a hand in a threat that made her think she'd gone too far. With a scowl he slapped the inside of her thighs hard, leaving a pink handprint.

'Mind what you say!' he growled. 'I'm master in my own house – what I say goes. And don't you forget it! If I want my wife on her back seven nights a week, there's no argument about it – I have her.'

To show her he was a man to be reckoned with, he stood up and pushed his undone trousers down to his knees. In another second he was on top of her – his hand jerking at his stiffness while he guided it to the wet lips between her legs and pushed hard. Odette grinned cynically and parted her legs wider. She let him penetrate her to the very limit, her grin growing wider.

His hands gripped her breasts almost painfully tight while he slid backwards and forwards in a very determined manner – as if to ravish her and subdue her and destroy her. Odette sighed in delight, jerking her hot belly up at him. Her head was tilted backward on the bed to thrust her chin towards the ceiling, her mouth was open to show her white little teeth.

Her legs were round Jacques' waist, her heels drumming on his back as he plunged and plunged into her belly. He was sweating and panting, hard at work, when in a crescendo of shrill cries Odette's back arched off the bed, lifting his weight on her. He realised her orgasm had taken her and he cursed and pumped away at her, making her squirm under him.

'Oh yes, Jacques, yes,' she was moaning, 'show me how

strong you are . . . just like you always were . . .'

He let go of her breasts and slipped his hands beneath her to grasp the bare cheeks of her rump. She squealed shrilly to his powerful in-and-out, her hands on his back, fingernails scoring down his shirt.

'Yes!' he groaned, ramming faster and deeper into Odette's slippery warmth, his belly smacking against hers brutally, until he spurted in spasms that shook his body from head to foot.

Later on, while they were half-dozing, his head pillowed upon Odette's warm belly, he tried to recall the last time he'd had her. She'd been his girl for longer than most, he liked her and he liked doing it to her – but he also liked to play the field. It was inevitable she found out sooner or later. There'd been a row, he remembered that well enough, she screamed at him in the way women do when they realise they don't own a man after he's slipped it to them a few times.

But when was the last time he'd had her on her back before the break-up, that he couldn't remember at all. And why should he? He'd had her so many times in those days. The first time – that was up an alley, he was fairly sure of it. He'd still lived with his parents at twenty and the job he'd had then didn't pay very much, which meant he had to take girls up dark alleys and stand them against the wall after the cinema or the dance-hall.

There was an occasion in an apartment, he remembered, whose he was not sure. Perhaps his family were all out, or perhaps hers had gone out, though she had two or three brothers and sisters. Well, wherever it was, what stuck in his mind was standing with his jacket off and his trousers gaping open in a small bedroom. He had his sticker out in his hand,

BONJOUR AMOUR

stiff as a broom-handle, he was flashing it at her, he always did that, to let women see it was big and strong and he was a man who stood for no nonsense.

They loved it, they wanted to feel it up them and they wanted to be ridden. She'd fallen down on her knees at the sight of it – that's how much she wanted it – and she'd had it in her mouth.

He grinned as he stared down to where his thick strong thing stuck out of his open trousers and Odette's head was bobbing up and down on it. Her eyes were closed, her face was rapturous in the intensity of its expression. Her tongue was lapping quickly over the unhooded head of his jerking part – she heard him moan and pulled him out of her lipstick-scarlet mouth and looked up at him. Her green eyes stared boldly at his face while she held his solid fifteen centimetres tightly in her fingers and massaged.

'I love it,' she said, 'I want to feel it all night long.'

'You've never had one like it up you,' he boasted, laying his hands on her head to urge her to lick him again. She opened her mouth wide and seemed to swallow his long length of wet flesh – her nose was pressing against his belly and his thicket of black curls was touching her chin.

He held her tightly by the nape of her neck and slithered in and out of her mouth. Her hands went into his trousers and into his underwear to reach round and grasp the cheeks of his bottom fiercely. He groaned when she sank her nails into him. He heard the gurgling noises she made as he slid in and out of her mouth with mounting excitement – two more seconds and he'd do it!

The thought stopped him instantly. He stopped his in-and-out, he gripped her tighter by the back of the neck to hold her head still. She was trying to make him do it in her mouth, trying to make him do what she wanted – sucking his strength right out of his body instead of waiting for him to shoot it up her when he was ready. That wasn't the way of it, women did what he wanted, they didn't get ideas of their own. He scowled down at her with eyebrows drawn together while he pulled out of her wet mouth.

'What are you doing?' she gasped.

He wasted no words on answering her, he reached down and slid his hands into her armpits. With one quick heave he had her up off her knees and threw her sideways on to the iron-framed bed. She fell across the edge, landing on her side, and instantly he had her under the knees and twisted her on to her back. She was wearing a plain white blouse tucked into a dark skirt as far as he could recall; she worked in a draper's shop then.

The sudden fall on the bed had knocked the breath out of her, her face had turned pale and she was wheezing. He didn't intend waiting for her to recover – he dragged her skirt up around her waist. He stood leering for a moment at her bare thighs between her stocking-tops and her knickers, that stretch of smooth flesh he often stroked in the darkness of a cinema. Plain white knickers – he remembered that clearly.

He gripped her thighs and made his fingers sink into the warm flesh, putting his mark on them. Her body jerked and she gave a muffled groan – and tried to kick up between his legs and force him to stop. He laughed and dragged her knickers right down to her knees – here was her thick, dark-brown bush, wild, natural, not the miserable little heart-shape design she had between her legs now.

'On your back, girl, that's more like it,' he said, grinning down at her with approval. He plunged two joined fingers deep in her curly thicket and opened her up – she gave a stifled shriek at his rough handling. He threw himself forward on her body and the shock of his weight made her gasp for breath again. He held his throbbing part in his hand, clasping it and manipulating it smoothly while he steered the purple head between her thighs.

But he couldn't get her legs properly apart to penetrate her, the knickers round her knees held them together. He pushed and huffed and cursed and got nowhere at all – the best he could do was get between her thighs and carry on until he spurted there, not inside her. To Jacques that was like admitting defeat by a woman. In exasperation he levered himself off her and stood up while he grabbed her ankles and hoisted her legs up in the air. She tried to heel him in the face, but he held her without much trouble one-handed while he ripped her knickers up and over her feet.

He prised her legs apart and pushed his belly forward, aiming for the long pink lips now visible in her curly thicket. With a long grunt of triumph he slid into her – she was wet and ready, warm and soft, although the awkward position made it impossible to get more than half of *Jacques-le-Grand* in.

'Jacques, Jacques, yes,!' she cried as he held her ankles and stabbed forcefully into her. The brief struggle had aroused him so intensely that it took only seven or eight strokes before he spurted into her trembling belly.

'Don't stop!' she screamed as his spasms faded away, but he was balancing on bent knees and legs that were shaking with the strain of his position. He let himself fall forward against the backs of her upraised thighs, his weight pressed her legs down on to her body, her knees touching her breasts.

The change of position had pulled him out of her, he was fast going slack. On her face was a pleading expression as she stared up into his face, suspended just above her. She expected him to take her the rest of the way to her climax, not to leave her in this condition of desperate frustration. But Jacques had no intention of letting a girl dictate his actions – she'd have to wait twenty minutes till he went stiff again. Or use her own fingers, if she couldn't wait.

Long time ago, that – two years at least, maybe three. But it had stuck in his memory because that was the day he understood Odette was more independent-minded than the other girls he had. He wasn't all that sorry when they had a row over another woman and she flounced off in a huff. Soon after that she'd left home and found a different job. And he hadn't seen her since – until he ran into her this morning on the Boulevard St Michel by pure chance. And he'd seen straight away how much better groomed she was nowadays, better dressed, sexier than ever before – he knew he had to have her. To prove that he could.

She couldn't resist him – just as he guessed. Jacques grinned and turned over. His head still rested on her warm belly but he was facing up towards her *nichons* now, not down at her muff. He decided to suck them, though they weren't as big and soft as he preferred for that, but it would be good to touch her up again and let her see who was boss. She gave a long sigh as his mouth closed over the russet tip of an elegant pointed little breast and moved her legs apart on the bed.

It was starting to get dark outside the windows when finally Jacques yawned and sat up

'Have to go,' he said, 'I'm expected home.' Without a kiss

or an embrace, without even a touch, he slid off the bed.

Odette rolled on to her side and watched him dress. He sat on the side of the bed to pull on his socks. He'd told Odette that she was skinny and made fun of her, but like her he was slender and long of thigh. Not much flesh on his bones either. But very well equipped for the pleasuring of women – when he stood up to put his trousers on, Odette stared at his useful part. She knew from personal experience that it was impressive, even slack. It hung down long and thick – not much smaller in repose than when it was at full-stretch. The hair round it was thick and dark.

He noted what she was looking at and grinned at her. He put a hand under his dangler and joggled it at her.

'Pity I've got to go,' he said, 'I've a train to catch or I'd stay and have you all night.'

He sat on the bed to put his shoes on, trousers undone so his limp part remained on show, as if to remind her what marvellous sensations it had given her. And would again when he found time for her.

'You always did have a very good opinion of yourself,' Odette told him, 'that hasn't changed.'

He winked and grinned at her in the dressing-table mirror as he knotted his shiny grey tie.

'Why not?' he said.

He slicked his hair back with Odette's comb. He shrugged his shoulders into the jacket of his blue suit and turned from the mirror to face her, announcing he was ready.

Odette slid on her bare bottom to the foot of the bed and sat with her legs on either side of him while she took his dangling part in her hand and looked at it curiously.

'You're an idiot, Jacques,' she said with mocking affection, 'you think you only need wave this at women and the whole world is yours.'

'It gets me everything I want,' he boasted, hands on his hips and head on one side to look down at her as she pulled his soft part to see if it would grow stiff again.

'All it gets you is a roll on the bed,' said Odette, 'is that all you want, Jacques? And you're not even fussy about who you lie down with – any available slit will do for you, you said so yourself. Plump, thin, hairy or bare, it doesn't matter, that's what you said.'

'What of it?' he asked, a crease appearing between his thick eyebrows as he puzzled over what she meant. 'I love them, every one of them – not for what they look like but for what I can do to them. I've done plenty to yours this afternoon!'

'Poor Jacques,' she said, 'you'll never get anywhere in life, you understand nothing. So go home to your wife and baby – this is no good now it won't stand up.'

She tucked his limp part inside his trousers and did them up for him. He was still wondering what to reply when she slid off the bed and led him by the hand out of the room. She went to the apartment door with him just as she was, naked. She felt he deserved a last look at her in return for all the pleasure he'd given her that day – coarse and impossible though he was in his attitudes. And it was his last look, her mind was made up.

There was a certain turmoil in Jacques' mind at that moment – he was uneasy because Odette had spoken to him in a pitying and mocking way, and he didn't know why. Women never talked to him like that after he'd had them, they lay with their eyes glowing and skin perspiring and they displayed proper gratitude for his attentions. Some of them crawled on their knees to him when he said he was leaving and kissed *petit-Jules* to make him go stiff again. Their mouths smeared him with their lipstick, while they begged him not to go. Odette had just flipped his pride and joy into his underwear and said it was no good to her any more!

Naturally, she'd said that because he was going, now he came to think about it, that was obvious. She wanted him to stay but wouldn't give him the pleasure of hearing her beg! Now it made sense. Well, he could have taken a later train if he'd wanted, but he had a reason for getting out of her apartment. It stood to reason she had a boyfriend who paid the rent, not that she'd said a word on the subject. But she was a pretty girl and had a *little heart* between her legs – she hadn't gone to that trouble because she was a model, whatever she said. Jacques was no fool, she'd done it for a man's pleasure, no other reason.

In Jacques' experience, men often went to see their girls at this time of day, feeling a need to have their knickers off for a lie-down on the bed before the evening's entertainment.

Not that it would bother Jacques if Odette's boyfriend turned up and found him stark naked on top of her. It was her problem, not his. For him it would be comic, putting one over Odette and her boyfriend at the same time – it would show the pair of them who was the better man. And for identical reasons Jacques found particular pleasure in getting astride a married woman; when he pushed up into her belly it made him feel he was scoring a win over somebody, asserting his right to have anything he wanted.

His job as salesman left him time and opportunity to look for married women. He never seemed to have much trouble persuading them to let him put a hand up their skirt. And everything else he wanted to do. There were five or six he knew scattered round Paris and its environs who made him welcome any time of day their husbands were out at work. Now he could add Odette Charron to the list. Every time he did it to her he'd be thinking about how he was putting one over on the man who paid her rent.

But for now it was better to leave. There was the possibility the boyfriend might be big and violent – Jacques had no desire to be involved in a brawl. Not over a woman.

At the same time, he meant to reassert himself before he went and show Odette who was the idiot, him or her. Before she could open the apartment door for him to leave he pressed her against the wall with his body. He held the back of her neck tight with one hand, the other slipped between their bodies to wrench his trousers open. He pulled out his growing part and flicked it up and down vigorously in his hand.

'Feel that!' he said, grinning wolfishly at her.

Odette smiled slyly as she took hold – strength and stiffness had returned, the warm length of flesh twitched in her fingers. Jacques slid his own free hand between her bare thighs to touch her *little heart* and she sighed, liking the cruel grip on the back of her neck. With impatient fingers Jacques prised the wet lips of her *joujou* open and pushed a fingertip inside to stroke her. She was slippery and hot to his touch, she was trembling. He grinned to know she wanted him inside her – that's how women were supposed to act when he got his pride and joy out.

She wouldn't wait – she moved her knees apart and steered him into her. She pushed her belly against him to force him in.

'Who said it wouldn't stand up stiff again?' he mocked.

'What do you think of it now? Too much for you? Too bad – I haven't finished with you yet.'

He let go of her neck and reached behind her with both hands, grasping the bare cheeks of her bottom to hold her fast while he pushed further into her, until his belly pressed on hers. He rolled the warm cheeks and pinched them and squeezed them hard, digging his fingernails into the soft flesh.

'Ah, ah!' Odette gasped, to feel herself stimulated fore and aft at the same time.

He was rocking back and forth in a quick, rhythmic motion that made her gasp in pleasure. She gripped him around the waist and held on very tight.

'Not every girl has it done to her up against the wall in her own apartment,' he gloated. He had the ridiculous idea that he was showing her who was master – demonstrating his superiority. It would be comical if the boyfriend turned up now – suppose he knocked on the door at this very moment, while Odette was being ravaged against a wall just inside it! Imagine pumping away at her like this while the boyfriend on the other side of the door heard the moaning and sighing and knew what was going on! What a joke – boyfriend banging on the door in a frenzy and kicking at it and shouting *Stop that* while Jacques spurted up her!

The thought tickled him so much it made him laugh, though the time was absurdly unsuitable. Odette's bare belly was thumping at him in double-quick rhythm – Jacques thought she was frantic to reach her climax, but he was mistaken, she was determined to milk him of his remaining strength. He was the one learning who was master, but he didn't know it yet. He gasped for breath and shook as he struggled to control his laughter.

The involuntary jerking of his body pushed Odette to the edge of ecstatic sensation and over. Her head went back against the wall, her green eyes were wide and staring, seeing nothing. Her wailing cry of release drowned out Jacques' laughing. The rapid little spasms of her *joujou* milked him of his passion in spurts that shook him so furiously his legs buckled and he almost fell down on the floor at Odette's feet. He was kept upright by her arms round his waist.

Long after he was finished and stood trembling on shaky legs, she continued to hold him tight against her and jerk her belly at him. Only when she was quiet again did she release her grip and let him slide out of her warmth and take a step back away from her. He felt for the door-handle, grinning at her in a way that was more nervous than jubilant.

'Let your bush grow again, Odette,' he told her, sidling out of the half-open door, 'it's better the old way, not this fancy little moustache you've got now. Next time I see you I want you like a she-bear again. *Au revoir.*'

'*Adieu*, Jacques,' she replied, but by then he was halfway down the stairs and didn't hear her, which was just as well.

Odette At A Rehearsal

Part of Odette's plan for her new career as a fashion model was to be introduced by Laurent to all the useful people he knew so she could take full advantage of their influence. Naturally, as a well established fashion artist he had a wide acquaintance of magazine editors and other illustrators, buyers, manufacturers, designers, fashion writers on newspapers, publicists, everyone. At Odette's urging he took her to cafés and bistros and bars to introduce her. He made it clear to everyone that Odette was not his girlfriend, which made them certain she was, especially the ones who knew he was engaged to be married to someone else.

Among the many Odette met as Laurent's protégée was a charming and interesting man named Daniel Rocart. He was a publicist and among the important clients of his highly specialised company was a major fashion house. It was at a table on the terrace of Fouquets on the Champs-Elysees that Odette became aware of this useful information about Daniel. Without a word she set out to let him understand she found him absolutely fascinating. But with particular care not to let Laurent see her sudden interest in his friend.

It goes without saying that women are very skilful in letting men who seriously interest them become aware of it.

Before five minutes had passed Daniel was trying not to look at her breasts while he was chatting to Laurent about the forthcoming fashion shows. She was looking very desirable that day, in a green and grey wool costume she had bought half-price at the Chanel sale, no blouse under the jacket, a lot of delicious cleavage on show to halfway down her elegant pointed breasts. While Laurent was distracted for a moment ordering more drinks from a waiter, she stared frankly into Daniel's eyes and pouted at him briefly.

He understood – what man wouldn't? He crossed his legs under the little table and Odette smiled for a moment to realise she had made him stiff inside his underwear. That was good, she was sure he would want to get in touch with her as soon as a chance occurred. She casually mentioned the picturesque and historical traditions of the rue Mouffetard, to make sure he knew where to find her, there being no telephone in her apartment.

He was wearing a pale grey suit Odette found imposing in its cut and material – it looked like mohair but she dare not touch a sleeve to be certain, not with Laurent present. But it was by a good hand and was expensive, that much was obvious. It fitted him so perfectly that it almost disguised a certain plumpness. He was full-faced and thick-necked, this Daniel, there would be a round little pink potbelly under the suit, Odette knew. She put his age at forty or just over. His curly hair had receded in front to give the appearance of an intellectual forehead – and why not? He was a man who knew his way around, a man who could be very useful when his interest was caught.

Half an hour later they all rose to leave. Daniel pressed her hand quickly but intimately, and walked off in the direction of

BONJOUR AMOUR

the Avenue Montaigne. As all the world knows, it is here and in the adjacent Avenue George-Cinq that the grand couturiers have their establishments. Now that the twice-yearly celebrations of chic and good taste were about to be presented to the world in the fashion shows, Daniel was very occupied with his client.

Laurent said he wanted to walk for half a hour in the Bois de Boulogne while the fine weather lasted. Odette shrugged and got into a taxi with him. He instructed the driver to take them to the lake in the Bois, then leaned back and looked curiously at Odette.

'If I didn't know better, I'd have said you were making up to Daniel back there,' he said slowly and deliberately.

'What?' she exclaimed in outrage. 'How can you think such a thing? What do you mean?'

'It was written all over his face,' Laurent insisted, 'it was obvious what he was thinking. You must have encouraged him.'

'It's not my fault if a man finds me attractive!' said Odette in high dudgeon. 'You'd prefer it if I were plain and dowdy, I suppose. Shall I sit with you in the most important café in the whole of Paris wearing an old frock and laddered stockings? What was he thinking, then, if you are a mind-reader now?'

'He was thinking he'd like to put his hand up your skirt and feel between your legs, ' said Laurent, his face pale.

Odette laughed at that and snuggled closer to him on the taxi seat. She slipped her hand into his trouser pocket – right down into it, over his thigh.

'And if he had,' she said, her mouth so close to his ear that he could feel her warm breath on his skin, 'he'd have found the charming little token I have of my affection for you, *chéri* – a neat and pretty *little heart* you created specially for me – and which I adore.'

Through the pocket-lining and his underwear, she just managed to touch with a fingertip Laurent's limp part.

'Do you really adore it?' he asked doubtfully, his intellect going into hibernation the instant his male part stirred.

'It is the nicest compliment anyone has ever paid me,' Odette assured him, 'at night in my apartment, when I am alone, I take off all my clothes and stand before the long mirror – I look at my pretty *little heart* and I think of you, Laurent.'

'Odette . . .' he sighed, 'is this true?'

She withdrew her hand from his pocket and slipped it down the front of his trousers, between his shirt and his belt, to grasp his stiffening flesh with her bare hand.

'It is beautiful, your design,' she murmured in his ear, 'if a photograph could be taken, it would be so thrilling! Perhaps there will be a day when you arrange it for me, *chéri*. I adore the little sketches you made of me naked in your studio – and I shall treasure them for ever. If you adored my *little heart* as much as I do, you would buy a camera and make pictures of me.'

'But I do adore it,' Laurent murmured, 'it is my inspiration. No one believed my work could ever be any better than it was – yet everyone now acknowledges that it has improved. And this is because of you and what I have learned from you about myself as an artist.'

Odette held the swollen head of his jerking male part between her fingertips and stroked lightly up and down.

'But how can I believe you, after so monstrous an

accusation against me?' she enquired doubtfully. 'I exchanged a few polite words of conversation with Monsieur Rocart, no more than that, but you become jealous and enraged – you behave as if I'd pulled my skirt up and showed him my bare thighs!'

'Forgive me, Odette,' he said, 'the truth is that my feelings for you are so formidable I cannot help assuming that every man who looks at you feels the same way as I do.'

'I hope they do,' she murmured as her fingertips eased slowly up and down the hot-flushed head they held inside his trousers, 'after all, I am very attractive. I know it as well as you do, but it doesn't mean I want every handsome man I see to put his hand up my skirt – only you, my poor Laurent.'

'*Chérie*,' he moaned, '*je t'adore . . .*'

He sat upright for a moment to tell the taxi-driver there had been a change of plan and he was to drive them to the Boulevard Edgar-Quinet – and fast!

'Are you sure you want to do this, Laurent?' Odette murmured in his ear. 'You told me you're meeting Mademoiselle Beaucourt-Villiers this evening to have dinner with friends. Consider, my dear friend, if you take me to your apartment now, we know what will happen. You will fling me down on my back on your bed and rip off my knickers – it will be absolutely delightful, but you won't be much use to your fiancée this evening.'

'That doesn't matter,' he said faintly, 'I have to touch your *little heart*, Odette – I want to kiss it and caress it and . . .'

'So you shall,' she assured him, her hand motionless now – it would be a pity if a mishap occurred in Laurent's trousers, before they reached his apartment.

In the event it took Daniel Rocart three days to find Odette.

She returned to her apartment one afternoon to discover a card slipped under her door – his business card with the address and phone number of his company. On the rue de la Paix, she noted – an address of importance for an office. On the back of the card he had written a few words in an elegant hand, a suggestion she might call him before noon the next day.

She phoned, and a secretary demanded to know her name and why she wished to speak to Monsieur Rocart. Perhaps Mademoiselle would prefer to leave a message? Odette put on a disdainful tone and informed the secretary her name was Charron and Monsieur Rocart was expecting her call. There was a pause of perhaps twenty seconds while her statement was verified, then she was given an apology for being kept waiting and put through.

Daniel sounded very busy, but he was pleased she had called – he suggested dinner that evening. When she hesitated purely for effect, he said he had no wish to upset his good friend Laurent Breville, that went without saying, of course ... Odette replied that she thought Laurent had made it clear that she was not his girlfriend.

Naturally, said Daniel, it was well understood – her life was her own to do as she pleased. He had wanted to meet her to talk about many things of importance – when they had been introduced at Fouquet's there had been no time. But it had occurred to him then, and later, that so elegant and beautiful a model ought to be known to his publicity company, who often put forward names of models to clients for photo sessions and other engagements.

In short, it would be extremely worthwhile if they could meet for a discussion of these and other matters of mutual interest. What better time or place than over a meal and a bottle of fine wine? Meetings in offices were so impersonal – didn't she find it so?

Odette agreed with him. As well she might: her intention was to become very personal with Daniel Rocart, though it was quite unnecessary to tell him so – he'd guessed that already. But she put a warmth and a promise into her voice when she accepted his invitation to dinner, a hint that she would have no objection if he wished to become personal with her when they met – just as personal as he liked.

So it was agreed. They met at eight in a fashionable bar and he took her to an expensive restaurant. By half past ten they'd got to know each other a little, though Daniel said not a word about her career as a model – past, present or future. Nor did Odette, that was for discussion later, when he truly understood how very satisfactory she could be as a girlfriend. They took a taxi from the restaurant, over the Seine by the Pont Alexandre, to the Left Bank.

In the taxi Daniel put his arm round her waist and kissed her – she would have been astonished if he hadn't. He put his hand on her knee and slid it under the skirt of her taffeta evening frock till he could stroke her bare thighs above the top of her sheer silk stockings. That too was as it should be, she said to herself – there was something odd about a man who didn't try to get his hand between a pretty girl's legs in the back of a taxi by night.

Before eleven o'clock they were climbing up the stairs to her tiny apartment, his arm round her waist. There was no necessity for polite preliminaries – chat, more drinks, music – they both understood the position. She led him straight into the bedroom. He glanced once about the tiny room, then with approval at the bed, before he slipped his jacket off and

Marie-Claire Villefranche

casually let it drop to the floor. He undressed Odette very neatly and expertly – he felt behind her to unzip the close-fitting bodice of her frock and raised it up and over her head without disturbing her hair.

He took off her little satin bra and then stooped to take off her knickers – and caught sight of her little heart.

'*Ah, très chic!*' he said, pausing to feel it. But only for a moment before he had her suspender-belt undone and was rolling her stockings down her legs. When she was naked – not a process which took long with Odette – he sat her on the bed and went on his knees to stroke her pointed little breasts and kiss her.

She put her toes against the bulge in his trousers and rubbed it slowly. She unbuckled his belt and unzipped his trousers and let them slide down his thighs to his knees. She slipped a hand under his shirt and stroked his warm plump belly. She felt down lower and grasped the stiff and throbbing part aimed up at her.

His fingers were doing the most exquisite things inside her – she pulled at his stiffness, murmuring to him to put it in her. She sighed into his mouth and parted her legs widely for him to slide it in. But he eased away from her with a little smile on his face and took both her hands. He stood up and pulled her to her feet.

'Say your prayers for me, Odette,' he said, his hands were on her hips to turn her round until her back was to him. And then they were on her shoulders and pressing her downwards. She sank to her knees, not in the least surprised by the absurdities of men's desires. Her knees on the floor and elbows on the bed, she assumed the right attitude for prayer, though that was far from her mind just then. She heard the

BONJOUR AMOUR

rustle of clothes behind her and felt Daniel press his warm naked body against her back while he held her breasts in the palms of his hands.

Poor Laurent, she thought, he bought this big handsome modern bed for me, but he's had no benefit from it, none at all. First Jacques ravaged me on it and now Daniel is about to – it is like being married and deceiving a husband, I suppose.

'What shall I pray for?' she asked Daniel, twisting her neck to see him over her shoulder.

'For what you want most,' he said, hands stroking her breasts in delight.

'And you – what do you pray for?' she asked while she rubbed her smooth bare bottom against him.

'For unending pleasure, of course,' he murmured.

He put a hand between her legs and opened her with so precise a touch that Odette was impressed by this evident experience of women's bodies. She felt something that was thicker and harder than a finger touch between her legs and push up into her. She spread her knees wider on the floor and sighed in pleasure as a firm length of flesh slid up her wet *joujou*. Daniel's hands on her hips held her fast – she closed her eyes and surrendered to the sensations brought by the rhythmic slide of his hardness.

She was greatly aroused, but Daniel was even more so, it soon became apparent. His fingers dug into the flesh of her waist so hard she winced and murmured in discomfort – he rammed into her strongly, his belly made smacking noises against the cheeks of her bottom. Three more seconds and she heard him cry out like a girl – he spurted into her, his body shaking against her back.

When he was finished she pulled away slowly and got up

on the bed, taking his hand to urge him to follow and lie full-length beside her. She was aroused and unsatisfied – it was too quick, much too quick. She was sure Daniel regretted it as much as she did, and she was right. He started to apologise, he said he was overwhelmed when he saw her naked and totally unable to control himself.

'I suppose I should be flattered,' she said lightly, her hand on his chest. Now he was naked she saw she was right about the little dome of a belly from good-living. He had no hair on his chest, his skin was remarkably smooth and pink all over, like a well-fed healthy baby. She stroked his plump belly, guessing it would arouse him quicker than playing with his limp wet part.

'A compliment, yes,' Daniel said, 'though an unfortunate one. You have a perfect body for a fashion model, *chérie* – beautiful little breasts and long slender legs. I could lie here and look at you for hours. If you come to my office I will lock the door and you shall parade naked round the room while I admire you. I find you adorable, Odette.'

'But you haven't mentioned my best feature,' she objected.

He rested his hand lightly between her thighs, it covered her *little heart* completely.

'I can't think of words adequate to describe it,' he told her breathlessly, 'it is superb, magnificent, sumptuous – what more can I say?'

'You could say sexy,' she reminded him.

'Ah that, yes!' he murmured, 'undoubtedly that, *chérie* – you saw what happened when I got into it.'

'I didn't actually see,' she said, 'but I felt what happened. I am pleased you enjoyed me, Daniel, but we must slow you down, if you and I are to remain friends.'

That wasn't strictly true, of course, she was prepared to let him do what he liked to her without taking any pleasure herself – if he would use his position and influence to further her own career in the fashion business. No point in telling him that – men had to be made to feel slightly uneasy or they would tread all over a girl.

She continued to stroke Daniel's pink round belly, and before long his hands were roaming over her body. He was exploring her, touching every part of her, the hollows under her arms, between her small pert breasts, the insides of her long slender thighs, the crease between the taut cheeks of her bottom. She thought the time was right and slid her hand downward on his belly. His sticky male part was half-hard again. She rolled it in her hand and tugged at it.

'Yes, *chérie!*' he sighed, 'very soon . . .'

Odette said nothing – she slid her hand up and down his moist length of flesh to stimulate its enlargement. And the moment it felt stiff enough, she rolled over on top of him and opened her legs wide outside his. Her fingers gripped him and directed him into her, she pushed down with her belly and impaled herself on his stiffness. A gentle thrusting of her loins slid him in and out very agreeably.

'Odette, *chérie* . . .' he sighed, his body flopping loosely on the bed to the rhythm of her movements on him. Her orgasm came very easily – Daniel chuckled to hear her long gasp and sudden heavy bounce on his belly. When she was quiet again he took her face between his hands to kiss her lips and eyelids, and the tip of her nose.

'So you got what you prayed for,' he said.

'Not yet, Daniel,' she said, 'but I will, I promise you!'

She locked her arms round his neck, her legs round his

legs, and rolled sideways, dragging him with her. He resisted her for a moment before he understood what she intended, then went with her. Clutching tight together, they rolled until their position was reversed and he was on top. His stiff flesh was inside her still, jerking a little – her orgasm had merely aroused him and made him ready again.

Odette spread her legs widely apart and sighed in pleasure to his thrusting. *Yes, yes, Daniel* she moaned, instantly aroused by the feel of him inside her. She panted and writhed to the rapid in-and-out penetration, faster and faster – her body arched off the bed and she cried out in spasms of ecstasy. Daniel had his timing right – he spurted into her shaking belly at the peak of her pleasure.

Her prayer was answered next day. Daniel took her with him to the Avenue Montaigne to see the final rehearsal of his client's autumn show. The designer had not the international reputation of Chanel or Dior, not yet at least, but he was a *grand couturie*r, this Jean-Luc Marigny, highly respected by Parisians who could afford his clothes. Odette wore her little Chanel suit for the occasion, it would never do to look drab in this setting.

The high-ceilinged, long room, with a narrow raised platform running down the middle between rows of gilt chairs, was almost empty when she and Daniel arrived. Eight or nine women sat together on one side of the room and talked incessantly. Daniel explained that they were heads of departments, assembled today to see the results of their endeavours. One was responsible for buying materials, for example, another for furs, one for hats – a fashion house was a complex organisation.

Odette regarded all this thoughtfully and pictured herself

as part of it. Through the open white double doors came a crowd of women, modestly dressed, chattering and cheerful; they were the seamstresses, Daniel said – the women whose nimble fingers made a reality of Jean-Luc Marigny's designs, a reality great ladies with very rich husbands or lovers paid huge sums of money for.

They settled themselves on the opposite side of the platform to the heads of departments and their conversation continued in half-whispers. There was a pause; in came a woman alone and all conversation ceased. She was dark-haired, slender and graceful. She wore an elegant suit of midnight-blue with a grey chalk-stripe, very businesslike and *très chic*.

Daniel was on his feet, striding towards the newcomer, on his face a respectful smile. He kissed her hand, he radiated charm, it was as if he had been granted audience with a visiting Queen – Odette realised that the woman in the beautiful suit, whoever she was, held a position of considerable power here at Jean-Luc Marigny. Daniel half-turned and beckoned to her to join him and be presented.

'Mademoiselle Odette Charron,' Daniel introduced her, 'she is a model who has appeared mostly in the magazines rather than at the shows. My colleagues and I believe that she has interesting potential. Odette, I have the honour to present you to Madame Barras, the driving force here, the great organiser – she alone makes it possible for Jean-Luc's creations to be made up in satin and silk and displayed to the world in an appropriate manner.'

The woman held out her hand briefly to Odette. Seen close up, she was halfway through her forties, but her face and neck were unlined and smooth. She had dark-brown eyes that saw everything and missed nothing of importance, her mouth was wide but tight. Her only jewellery was a gold chain round her neck with a small diamond pendant. Odette felt herself being scrutinised closely; her hair, her make-up, her clothes, her shoes, her posture. She tried to keep a tranquil smile on her face – but it was hard.

'You are charming,' said Madame Barras – her face without any expression at all.

Before there was time for any more of this, a bustling at the door announced the arrival of Jean-Luc Marigny and his retinue. Everyone stood up for him, he smiled briefly and gestured with elegant hands they were to be seated. He made a little speech – he thanked them for their diligence and loyalty. He praised all their work, he told them how essential their abilities were to the flourishing of the great house of Jean-Luc Marigny.

He reminded them that the underlying philosophy of his autumn collection was the inverse triangle – this signified a unity of design that was generous of shoulder, tapering downward through understated bosom and hips to slenderness of ankle. There was a nervous little hush following this statement, perhaps all those present were praying he'd got it right and their employment was safe for another six months.

'Sit here with me,' said Madame Barras, putting her hand upon Odette's arm to draw her down to a chair in the front row.

Daniel sat on the other side of Madame Barras, very attentive to everything she said. Jean-Luc Marigny seated himself, easing up the knees of his perfectly creased trousers. He flicked away an imaginary speck of fluff from his lapel, took a handkerchief of fine linen from his sleeve and dabbed elegantly at his lips. When this performance was over and he was ready, whoever was in charge backstage gave the word and the first model came out on the raised catwalk.

She was a dark-haired girl in a blue suit, which had padded shoulders, was close-fitting at waist and hip, with a pencil-slim skirt – all in accordance with the great man's inverse triangle theory for the season. Odette watched with great care, less interested in the clothes than the staging of the show itself. Model after model swung along the catwalk and back in the disdainful manner that rich overweight women customers envied desperately and men became so aroused to see they let their wives spend fortunes on clothes that were only suitable for young models.

There were nine models; Odette counted them, and guessed that behind the scenes there must be high drama and frantic activity bordering on frenzy in the dressing-room to get the girls in and out of clothes so that each sauntered out on cue – looking tranquil and perfect and beautifully dressed.

An elegant blonde strolled along the catwalk in a winter coat with huge lapels and a leather belt tight round her waist – yet another illustration of Jean-Luc's upside-down triangle.

'She is beautiful,' said Odette, studying the girl's face and expression of hauteur, not the coat.

'She is a fool,' said Madame Barras, raising one elegant eyebrow. 'Kiki, she calls herself – she lives in one room near the Santé prison with a drunken writer. He takes all her money and deceives her behind her back with sluts while she is working.'

'But why?' Odette asked, knowing quite well the reason why.

'She believes she is in love with him,' said Madame Barras, a tiny shrug of her shoulders indicated the idiocy of it.

'When I consider the opportunities that were offered her, which she threw away, it drives me to despair. What can one say? It seems there are women who are born to be slaves.'

'Not all of us,' Odette said quickly.

The fashion show lasted for an hour and a half, and ended to enthusiastic applause from the audience of employees. They rose to their feet again when Jean-Luc Marigny stood up and bowed in acknowledgement. Off he went, smiling to left and right, Madame Barras just behind him.

'That was fascinating,' Odette said to Daniel, 'thank you for bringing me. Can you leave now or will they want you again?'

'No, all my part is finished,' he said, 'the magazine writers are invited, the advertisements were approved weeks ago. I must go back to my office for a meeting with another client.'

'I hope to meet Madame Barras again,' said Odette, 'when she has time to listen to me and advise how to become a model for a *grand couturier* like Jean-Luc Marigny. What will be best to do, Daniel – phone her next week to see if she will give me half an hour?'

'Why no,' he said, 'she told me to ask you to wait for her in her office. The conference with Jean-Luc will only take twenty minutes or so. I think she means to take you for a drink – come with me and I will show you where her office is.'

It was a delight of an office – the desk a Louis XVI writing-table, the walls lined with green-brocade silk, the honey-brown parquet floor adorned with red-and-gold Aubusson carpets. This room with fresh flowers in crystal gave a clear indication that Madame held an authority second only to Marigny himself.

'I've come to the right place,' Odette said aloud when

BONJOUR AMOUR

Daniel had gone and she was left alone to wait. On the desk she found the latest issue of *Vogue*, she sat on a small gilt armchair and leafed through it, too excited by the opportunity that had been presented to see the illustrations – not even those of herself in underwear. It was twenty minutes before the door swung open and Madame Barras made an entrance like an actress on stage.

Odette stood up, the older woman smiled and put a hand on her shoulder to press her down again on the chair.

'I hope you enjoyed our rehearsal, Odette,' she said.

'It was fascinating, Madame – I am impressed by all you do.'

'Ah yes, so much work,' Madame Barras murmured. 'Few realise that – they see the girls and the clothes and think it happens almost by itself. Tomorrow will be an incredibly busy day. The collection will be shown to the most critical audience in Paris – everything must be perfect. I can never sleep before a show – I lie awake all night and worry myself insane.'

She hadn't sat down, she was standing by Odette's chair, with an expression of rueful anguish on her beautifully made-up face, and it occurred to Odette that Madame Barras had been a model herself once . She retained the slim figure, the elegant stance, the gait. She put a hand on Odette's shoulder and half-smiled.

'Daniel told me you have ambition to find a position as model with a *grande couture* house like this,' she said, 'but I wonder if you realise how many pretty girls with good figures apply to us. Perhaps one in a thousand is taken on. But I don't want to discourage you, I think you may have potential.'

'Thank you, Madame,' said Odette, smiling most charmingly.

'I've had enough of this place for one day, I must get right away from it and try to relax a little before tomorrow,' Madame said. 'Come with me and I will tell you about this fascinating and infuriating world of mine over a drink. If you have time.'

If she had time! Odette suppressed a smile. If the President of the Republic had been waiting at the Elysée Palace to dangle the Grand-Croix of the Legion d'Honneur round her neck and kiss her on both cheeks, she would have left him waiting in order to find time for the woman in the beautiful midnight-blue suit. Of course, by this time she had formed an opinion about the interests of Madame Barras – but what of it?

A taxi was waiting for them outside on the Avenue Montaigne. It drew away from the kerb without the need for any directions to be given – Odette assumed it was there every evening for her companion. Yes, she had very certainly come to the right place.

Madame put an arm round Odette's waist and laid a gloved hand on her silk-stockinged knee.

'I am wearier than I thought,' she said softly, 'do you mind if we go to my apartment first? I really must get out of these clothes and take a shower to wash away the problems of the day. Is that all right?'

'But of course,' said Odette. It was too dark in the taxi for a little smile to be seen and appreciated, so she put the smile into her voice. Madame Barras half-turned on the seat to press her lips to Odette's in a brief and delicate kiss.

'Take my glove off, Odette,' she murmured, and raised the hand that had been on her knee.

'Oh Madame!' said Odette, a little breathless now the moment was fast approaching. The glove was of exceptionally fine white leather, she eased the fingers up one by one, giving the simple act an intense erotic significance.

'My name is Giselle,' Madame Barras said, 'call me Giselle.'

Her long-fingered hand was bare, it returned to Odette's knee without delay. But only for a moment — it slipped up her skirt and along her thigh. *Oh Giselle* . . . murmured Odette, closing her eyes. She tried to imagine it was a man beside her in the taxi, a man's hand under her skirt and above her stocking-top. But it was impossible to pretend, the costly perfume Giselle wore made it evident her would-be lover was a woman.

Knowing fingers slid between her thighs, touched her lightly, sought a way into her underwear, found it and caressed the lips between her parted legs. She turned her head to look at Giselle in the light of a street-lamp, she was aware her own breathing was becoming uneven as familiar thrills of pleasure ran through her body. Giselle was smiling a shadowy smile and the hand that played with Odette was very expert.

'Giselle, I must tell you,' Odette said, 'I have a boyfriend. I've never done this with another woman.'

In spite of her arousal, it almost made her smile to think of Laurent Breville as a boyfriend — he was too submissive, he was a pigeon to be plucked. But the way things were going, Giselle might soon see a living example of his design work. And as for Daniel, he could not be considered a boyfriend either, he was a sympathetic man who took what he wanted and gave back something in return. Jacques Brolin was neither friend nor boyfriend — he was just a forgotten figure from her past, who had the knack of reducing her to whimpering ecstasy.

To be truthful, her last boyfriend, properly so described, was Robert and she hadn't seen him for weeks. Not since the day she left him standing on the pavement outside his apartment – with a sad look on his face and a hard bulge in his trousers. But it was important to tell Giselle she had a boyfriend as a reminder that she was not just there for the taking.

'But naturally,' Giselle murmured. 'What of it, *chérie*? This evening no such creature as a boyfriend exists.'

Her middle finger caressed inside Odette's *joujou*, a soft and gentle touch that was driving her insane with desire, her mouth whispered against Odette's cheek, her perfume brought a sensual rapture of mind and body and soul – and Odette was held gasping on the brink of shuddering ecstasy by an expert, for as long as the taxi ride lasted.

Giselle At Home

When the taxi arrived at the rue Monceau and drew into the kerb Odette's legs were trembling from the thrills she had been made to experience. She had been held breathless and shaking on the very brink of ecstasy throughout the journey, but never allowed to achieve the release of orgasm. Giselle got out of the taxi, a smug little smile on her face as she took Odette's arm under the elbow to support her while she reached the pavement.

The buildings were old and imposing in this part of the city, great mansions built for the prestige of bankers, stockbrokers, property speculators and other swindlers of the Second Empire – now redeveloped as apartments of distinction for those with the means to afford them. And as Odette's breathing became tranquil again and she assessed her surroundings it occurred to her that from the Parc Monceau to Robert Dorville's apartment was only a ten- or twelve-minute walk down the Boulevard Malesherbes.

Giselle led her into the building, talking softly to her, but it was in Odette's mind that she had neglected Robert since the day she moved out of his apartment and waved *Au revoir* and left him standing in the street with a bulging trouser-front. And he didn't know it, but he was her refuge if her career as fashion model should go wrong and leave her without an income.

She knew she ought to visit Robert, as soon as she had time, and let him take her to bed, just to be sure he remained on her list of reliable friends: a very short list of names. Not that she'd get as far as the bedroom, he was much too impatient for that – he would be too excited to wait while he undressed her.

If Odette understood his character – and she did – the instant she set foot over his threshold he'd have her on the sofa, with her clothes up round her neck and her knickers round her knees. Later on, when he paused for breath, then he'd take her to bed.

To be truthful, Odette admitted to herself, Robert was always good at it. He did exciting things to her. A night with him was an experience to remember for days afterwards. And besides that he had a comfortable income from his father. What a pity he was not the type to be interested in marriage or in other long-term arrangements.

But Robert was fickle, she understood that clearly. He adored women – young and pretty women – but he soon became bored with the woman of the moment. Odette believed he might perhaps stay interested in her longer if he only had her occasionally, when she arranged it herself. On the other hand, it was weeks since she'd moved out – and he had surely found someone else.

Yes, it was important to see Robert soon. She would phone him tomorrow and arrange to meet. Or perhaps not tomorrow – it was impossible to know how energetic she would feel in the morning, after being taken home by Giselle for advice on her career. And Giselle's arm was round her waist, her hand was on her bottom, stroking through her skirt. Robert must wait his turn – tonight it was imperative to capture Giselle's heart.

If Giselle had a heart to capture! If not, then another part of her pampered body must be captured. Daniel would also expect to be told of her success with Giselle, and to be rewarded for the introduction. On her knees beside the bed, no doubt, giving thanks for the blessing bestowed on her – Daniel gripping tight from behind and pleasuring himself on her naked body. She hoped she had the strength for it tomorrow.

The apartment was exactly what Odette wanted for herself – it was spacious, expertly designed and furnished, all done with an eye trained to appreciate perfection. It was impressive and yet comfortable. As soon as they were inside Giselle pulled off her hat, a flower-pot shape of black velvet with a large brooch of diamanté pinned on it jauntily. She put her arms around Odette and held her close, standing there in the entrance hall.

'Welcome to my home,' she whispered into Odette's ear. 'I hope this will be the first of many, many times you come here.'

Her hand rested on Odette's thigh to trace the smooth outline through her fine woollen skirt. Her mouth was gently insistent on Odette's, her kiss so commanding it dissolved reservations. A sigh escaped Odette when Giselle's hand slipped up inside her skirt. It paused between her thighs, to stroke her with little controlled movements.

'Those green eyes – you are adorable,' Giselle murmured while she gazed into them. 'I wonder if they go darker at the moment of ecstasy? Well, I shall find out before we part.'

She took Odette into her bedroom, a large and beautiful

room, and asked her to help her undress to take the shower that would restore her good humour and verve, after the many exertions and annoyances of the day. Odette stood close while she unbuttoned the jacket of Giselle's elegant midnight-blue suit.

'It is chic,' she said in admiration, 'it must be by Jean-Luc Marigny.'

'Of course,' said Giselle, 'all my clothes are – it would be unthinkable to wear anything else. Perhaps one day you too may be fortunate enough . . .'

She let the thought trail away unfinished. But Odette did not miss the point, she took it as a half-promise. If. There was an *if* in everything desirable in life, she understood that.

She took Giselle's jacket off, sliding it down her arms, then folded it and put it on a chair. Under it Giselle wore a white silk blouse with a turn-down collar. Odette undid the buttons and eased it out of the skirt, to reveal Giselle's breasts in a bra of white lace. Very chic.

Giselle did nothing to assist her. She stood gracefully poised with her arms hanging at her sides, a sly little smile on her perfectly made-up face. Odette stepped closer and her cheek lay against Giselle's cheek while she reached round her to undo the bra and let it fall loose.

Giselle's perfume was so sensuous – so insistent – she must have sprayed it on just before leaving her place of work. For a moment Odette stood breathing in that heady fragrance, cheek on Giselle's cheek, arms lightly round her waist. Then she stirred herself to continue the undressing – she removed Giselle's lace bra completely and took a short step back to look at her.

Her breasts were small and pear-shaped, the tips pink and

BONJOUR AMOUR

not at all prominent. She had a model's figure, an ex-model's to be more precise – although she was twenty years older than Odette, her breasts drooped only a little now they were unsupported by the white lace bra. Her smile had a trace of triumph in it now that she was allowing herself to be displayed.

Odette unfastened the stylish midnight-blue skirt and it slid down long and slender legs to the floor. Giselle stepped out of it and kicked it to the side as if it were a mere rag bought in a street-market. Her knickers matched her bra – white lace that permitted glimpses of pale flesh. Odette knew what was expected of her – she slipped the knickers down and knelt to kiss the dark-brown curls she had exposed.

So dark the hair was, and neatly clipped to a small triangle above the long thin lips that had been bared by the trimming. A pretty thing to touch and play with – kept purposely so for the pleasure of Giselle herself, and whoever she chose to pay devoted attentions to her.

But only for a moment did Odette kiss those long lips under the triangle of curls – and only the most fleeting kiss, before she rolled Giselle's silk stockings down her legs. She took off the white satin suspender-belt that supported them, and Giselle was naked – except for her diamond pendant. Odette stooped down to kiss the tips of her breasts and stood upright again to kiss her mouth, her hands roaming sensually over Giselle's warm body from collar-bones to groins.

If the truth were told, Odette was surprised to think she was doing all this to a woman. She was allowing herself to be used, that went without saying, but what of it? The cause was good – therefore the means to it were perfectly acceptable. Women were flat on their backs with their legs open every day and night for the pleasure of men who could promote their careers. Why not for a woman who could do so?

And it had to be said that Giselle was not old and plain – on the contrary, her body was excellently well cared-for – and her face was still beautiful, even if her habitual expression was disdainful.

'Good,' said Giselle, freeing herself from Odette's hands and mouth, 'take your clothes off and join me in the shower.'

She turned and walked gracefully out of the bedroom into the adjoining bathroom, leaving the door open. Odette stared at her retreating back, envying that haughty posture, the slow rhythm of taut bare cheeks rising and falling to her steps, the gentle and almost imperceptible sway of her breasts seen in profile.

In seconds Odette had her own clothes off and thrown across a brocade-backed chair. She made for the bathroom, trying to copy Giselle's walk, catching a glimpse of herself from the side in a tall mirror as she passed. What she saw pleased her, her body was lithe and smooth. She had youth and beauty to offer Giselle – she knew she was as attractive as any model she'd seen on the catwalk at Jean-Luc Marigny that day. And casting aside modesty where it was pointless, Odette was sure she was much better looking than any of them.

That included blonde Mademoiselle Kiki in the winter coat of blue with the wide leather belt. Odette's guess was Giselle had once entertained a warm desire for Kiki – a desire thwarted by the blonde model falling in love with a drunken writer who took all her money. Odette was no such fool as to bestow herself on layabouts. She had much to offer and would naturally expect to receive gratitude in return, gratitude expressed not in words alone – or sentiments – but in very real favours.

BONJOUR AMOUR

She remembered what Giselle said to her about Kiki – *it makes me despair when I consider the opportunities offered to her and which she threw away*. One thing was very certain, whatever opportunities were offered Odette would be grasped firmly with both hands.

The bathroom floor was tiled in black and white. The bath was big enough for two to share without crowding each other unless they chose to. The shower was separate, a square basin let into the floor in one corner. Giselle was under the spray, head back and eyes closed, her arms hanging loosely, enjoying the cascade on her long lean body.

Odette went close and stood silent, looking at her. Her hair was longer than had appeared when she was dressed – it had been pinned up behind. There was not a line or a wrinkle, a fold or a crease to be seen anywhere on her face, neck, her flat narrow belly, her rounded bottom or her thighs. Odette was impressed – she hoped she too remained as perfect when she was twenty years older herself.

Giselle opened her dark-brown eyes and stared at Odette – she observed every centimetre of her, slowly and minutely, from the top of her head down to her pink-painted toe nails. Centimetre by centimetre, missing nothing, appraising everything. Then she came back to the *little heart* of curls between her thighs – the charming design of rich brown curls that Laurent had created.

'*Oh la la!*' she said with a wry smile, 'how very unexpected, *chérie*.'

She stretched out her arm to offer her hand to Odette and tug her gently under the shower with her. The water temperature was very carefully adjusted, not hot, not cold, pleasantly warm and soothing.

'I'd like you to wash me,' she murmured and leaned her back on the pink-tiled wall while Odette soaped her body all over with a scented *crême-de-bain*. She did it slowly and carefully, her hands gliding very sensually over Giselle's pale skin. When she touched her small pear-shaped breasts that sagged just a little now they were free, the buds became slightly more prominent and firmer to the fingers, though not much.

'You think my breasts are drooping and ugly?' Giselle asked.

'The shape is extremely elegant,' said Odette, 'I adore pear-shaped breasts – my own are too round.'

To prevent any further questions that might lead into awkward discussions, she wiped the scented lather off Giselle's breasts with a handful of water caught under the spray and bent down to flick the small pink buds with the tip of her tongue.

'Ah,' said Giselle softly – a tiny exclamation of pleasure as Odette's hand caressed her belly in a circular motion. Her feet moved apart for scented lather to be smoothed between her legs.

'How long has Daniel Rocart been your boyfriend?' she asked, surprising Odette with the inappropriate question.

'Ah no,' she answered, her fingers stroking between Giselle's thighs, 'you are mistaken – Daniel is not my boyfriend. We know each other a little because we are in the fashion business. We are friends. But nothing more than that.'

'Really?' said Giselle, her perfectly drawn eyebrows rising in disbelief. 'But he can do nothing for you, *chérie*, he is not important in the world of *haute couture*, he is only a publicist.

He would be as happy to promote saucepans as the creations of Jean-Luc Marigny, if he were paid as much.'

There was a change of mood, Odette discerned, from passive to active and from minor key to major key. Giselle stood away from the pink wall-tiling and straightened her back. She resumed her normal hauteur of manner and facial expression – even naked and wet, with blobs of creamy lather sliding down her belly and her thighs. She put her hands on Odette's waist and placed her with her back to the streaming wall. She took a palmful of *crême-de-bain* and smeared it over Odette's breasts.

'We are very different, you and I, Odette,' she said. 'But it is possible you could be a very good model, perhaps, if you had the proper training and guidance. As you admitted, your breasts are too round for elegance, but at least they are not too big – that spoils many a girl's chances of success.'

But not with men, Odette thought, they are besotted by girls with big breasts. Think of the showgirls and film stars who have made their fortune by owning a pair of melons. She said nothing of this aloud, of course, knowing that Giselle would despise so blatant an appeal.

'Raise your arms above your head,' said Giselle, 'right up!'

Odette was a little surprised by the request – if it was that and not a command – but she reached up as high as she could. It lifted her small round breasts, the posture, and it exposed her armpits. This was what Giselle wanted, she filled those tender, smooth-shaven hollows with thick white creamy lather, washed it off and turned her head to press kisses to the warm skin.

'Turn round,' she said, and Odette did so, her arms above

her head still and her palms against the tiles. She felt Giselle's hands washing – or caressing – down the length of her back. And over the neat round cheeks of her bottom.

'As round as your breasts are,' said Giselle, appreciation in her voice – mild appreciation, naturally, nothing ever received fulsome approval from her, 'a perfect shape in this part of the body, *très chic*.' Odette almost giggled when Giselle bent down and kissed each wet cheek in turn. Her suppressed giggle became a sigh as Giselle stroked those cheeks and pulled them apart to tickle between with a fingertip.

She turned round again when Giselle asked her to. She put her hands on Giselle's narrow hips and let herself be kissed on the mouth. She felt Giselle's palm sliding down to the *little heart* between her legs, where the curls were plastered wetly against her flesh.

'A charming little conceit,' Giselle said, 'I have never seen one trimmed like it before. Some might think it a little vulgar – a little too *circus-artiste*? But at least it shows you have a certain imagination. What gave you the idea?'

Her fingertips were teasing the soft lips within the design – a caress that was half affectionate and half disdainful. Odette sighed at the sensation, wondering what to answer. It had never been her own design, of course – it was Laurent who had created it with scissors and safety-razor. It had been Laurent alone of all the men she knew who disliked her thick natural fur-coat of walnut-brown, thought it too *sauvage*. He had persuaded her to allow him to remove her thatch – for his own pleasure, of course. But for Giselle a different explanation was necessary.

'Like you, I like to be well-trimmed,' Odette said, 'it isn't chic to be hairy. It occurred to me one day that a little heart design was more interesting than the usual triangle.'

'I suppose that means more interesting to a boyfriend?' said Giselle with a little sneer.

Odette opened her thighs a little wider for Giselle's hand to slide between and denied any thought of pleasing boyfriends was in her mind at the time. It is necessary to sound convincing if convenient untruths are to be believe – Odette hoped she could give the impression of complete sincerity.

'This Daniel Rocart,' said Giselle, apparently not convinced, 'I have heard things about him, rumours, gossip. But there must be some element of truth in them. Unpleasant things to do with his attitude to women. And what he does to them. Or tries to do to them. I would be desolated to think you permitted a man like that to do anything at all to your pretty body.'

Her finger opened the lips between Odette's thighs and gently inserted itself.

'I swear to you – he is not my boyfriend,' Odette insisted in a sincere tone. She dare not claim Daniel had never touched her – if he had a reputation for getting his way with women Giselle would never believe her. 'He would like to be, of course, but I am not interested in him.'

'Not another word – I don't want to hear about him!' Giselle exclaimed, her finger sending little spasms of pleasure through Odette's belly.

The hot water splashed down between her body and Giselle's in a constant cascade of pleasurable sensation. It ran over their breasts, the pretty round ones and the elegant pear-shaped ones – and down between their bellies. And all that time Giselle was stroking Odette's *joujou*, with a look of disdain upon her face as if she had not the least interest in what she was doing. But for all her apparent indifference, she was careful not to allow Odette to reach her climax – she judged her caresses carefully and kept pausing whenever she saw Odette was getting too close.

As for Odette, subjected to this teasing love-making, she was on the brink of hysteria after fifteen or twenty minutes of it. Her breasts were heaving and falling as she laboured to breathe – she moaned and panted. Her fingernails sank sharply into the flesh of Giselle's hips, and though it must have been painful, Giselle never winced and the expression of hauteur on her face did not change.

'Please . . . please . . .' Odette moaned, pleading abjectly for the *coup de grâce* to release her from the overwhelming sensations. She seized Giselle's hand and pressed it harder against herself – she tried to rub the teasing fingers fiercely against her bud and bring on her orgasm. She stared imploringly into Giselle's face and all she saw was a thin smile. An instant later Giselle had freed herself from the clawing grasp and stepped out of the shower.

'Come, *chérie*,' she said, 'too long under the water will make you look like a prune – and that would be far from attractive. Come and dry yourself and we will go into my bedroom.'

Odette stared aghast as her friend wrapped herself in a large white towel. Two more strokes and she would have dissolved into ecstasy – Giselle knew it and deliberately stopped it happening – this was a game of cat and mouse she was playing! Odette took a deep breath and willed her legs not to tremble while she stepped out of the shower.

Giselle was ready with a pair of bath towels in her hands and a scheming look on her face. Evidently she was enjoying her sly little game – she paid particular attention to the little heart between Odette's thighs. She made her stand with her legs apart while she patted the trim little curls dry. And when Odette had in turn dried her body, they went back to the bedroom naked.

'*Chérie*,' said Giselle, with a little smile as they stood by the bed, holding hands, 'you look to me as if you will have an orgasm in two more seconds – what a state you have let yourself get into. I think that one little touch will drive you over the edge . . .'

She kissed Odette's face three or four times and made her sit on the side of the bed, her feet on the floor.

'I cannot bear to see you suffer any longer,' she said, as if she herself had had nothing whatsoever to do with Odette's arousal. She knelt in front of her and put one hand on her thigh and the other between them, on the *little heart*. She stroked it gently, murmuring *not elegant, I know, but pretty in its way* . . .

Odette's eyes were half-closed, she was on the very brink of orgasm. Because her legs were spread her *joujou* was open like a pink rose – Giselle spread the lips wider to see how moist she was. She touched Odette's secret bud with a fingertip, she bent her neck and touched it with the tip of her tongue.

Odette moaned and fell backward on the bed, the sensations of pleasure were so intense she felt she would go insane if there was no resolution of them very soon now. Giselle leaned forward and pressed her tongue in again – the little bud stiffened like a kissed nipple.

'Giselle . . .' Odette moaned, her long slender thighs shaking.

Giselle slid her hands under Odette's bottom and took hold

of the cheeks firmly. She squeezed them hard as her tongue played with determination – she knew she had taken Odette to the limit and must let her reach her climax before her nervous system was overloaded and burnt-out and incapable of responding again for many hours. Her mouth took possession of Odette's *joujou*, as if she was asserting her ownership of it.

'*Mon dieu, mon dieu . . .*' Odette was moaning, past all coherent thought or speech. Giselle's tongue moved strongly and conveyed the message clearly that she was wholly in command, that Odette was her plaything. Even in her advanced state of sexual arousal Odette understood that message – but only for an instant before she convulsed under the attentions of that skilful tongue. Her back arched off the bed and she sobbed and shrieked in orgasm.

Afterwards they lay naked and close together, Odette at ease on her back, her hands under her head, Giselle propped up on an elbow beside her, her hand roaming lightly over Odette's body. She was soothing her now, not arousing her, she caressed every part of her and her touch was like a whispering summer breeze. She touched the hollows under Odette's raised arms, her throat, under her chin, between her small round breasts, over her belly – but she did not put her hand between Odette's thighs. And she spoke without the habitual disdain in her voice.

'Do you find me at all attractive, green-eyes?' she asked in an uncertain tone. 'Tell me the truth, what do you really think of me?'

'I have never met anyone as elegant as you,' Odette told her, 'or half as intelligent – I think you're absolutely marvellous, Giselle.'

While Giselle basked in these words of praise, Odette

turned on her side and put her lips to the small pink bud of her right breast. Giselle sighed and put her arms round Odette's neck and held her close while she licked her bud firm.

'Are you telling me the truth?' Giselle said, almost humble, but never truly so.

'But of course,' said Odette, her lips relinquishing the soft pear-shaped breast, 'I want you to love me.'

'Ah that,' said Giselle, 'I do not think so.'

'Not yet, perhaps,' Odette told her, keeping her tone mocking and light, 'but you will.'

She spread Giselle flat on her back on the bed and pushed her legs well apart. Her fingers brushed over the clipped triangle of dark curls above Giselle's bare *joujou*. The time had come to pay close attention – devoted attention – to the soft hairless lips that lay with seeming modesty between Giselle's thighs. It was a deceit, this modesty, this fastidiousness, this disdain: it was a pose, perhaps to conceal an inner lack of confidence. The truth was Giselle had played at cat and mouse with her ever since they got into the taxi together in the Avenue Montaigne.

In the taxi and under the shower she had put Odette through a seemingly endless experience of sexual arousal – only to let it conclude naturally when she chose, here on the bed. She had let Odette wash her in the shower, soap her breasts and between her legs – but she had avoided being stimulated to orgasm. Perhaps for Giselle loving was only what she did to others – but didn't let them do to her. *We shall see*, said Odette to herself.

She changed position on the bed to lie between Giselle's open legs. She put her fingers to the long lips between them and for a long time she caressed gently up and down, teasing them until they parted a little of their own accord. Giselle was breathing hard and rolling her bottom a little on the bed, as if to break free from the touch between her legs – yet never doing so. She gasped when Odette's tongue touched her wetly.

'What are you doing?' she moaned. 'No, no, *chérie!*'

Naturally, Odette had experience of taking a man's long stiff part into her mouth – beginning with Jacques Brolin's when they were friends years ago. But this was the first time she had set her mouth to a woman's *joujou* and it seemed very strange to her – but what of that? The first time a boy had pushed his length of hard flesh into her – she was sixteen at the time – that seemed strange too. Yet how quickly she had come to love it.

At least she had an advantage here – she knew exactly what it was that pleased a woman. Some men seemed not to know or not to care – all they wanted was to get inside and ram away for three minutes. But there was Giselle's little bud, now she had opened her, and there was nothing in the least difficult about putting the tip of her tongue against it.

Giselle moaned a little and trembled. She wanted this done to her, but only while she herself was in control of the situation – she was afraid of being at the mercy of another. When she was becoming highly aroused she gasped out *no more, no more* and her hands reached down for Odette's head to push her away. But this was no longer in her power. Odette was determined to continue – to force this superior person to surrender to the sweet torment at her hands – or rather, her tongue.

She put her hands firmly on Giselle's thighs and pressed them down against the bed to immobilise her, while her tongue worked to good effect. *No more, no more*! Giselle cried again, and she sounded a little desperate now. She tried to sit up to get away from the relentless tongue that was ravishing her, but halfway up she was seized by spasms of pleasure that weakened her will. She flopped back, legs jerking and arms pounding up and down.

Odette felt a thrill of triumph, she gripped Giselle's thighs harder still and took her all the way, ignoring her breathless little cries and pleas. You like to play cat and mouse, Giselle *chérie*, she said silently, now the mouse is playing with you – the cat is lying on her back with her legs up to have her belly tickled, and I shall tickle it well for you, your furry little belly, believe me.

At the final moment Giselle's body went into rapid shudders, she strained upwards and she shrieked three or four times. Then she was still, the sheen of perspiration on her skin.

'Odette, what have you done?' she moaned when the ability to speak returned. 'Ah, *chérie, chérie* – do it again!'

'Ah yes,' said Odette, raising her head to stare up along the length of Giselle's naked body, past her little tuft of curls, over her smooth belly and between the mounds of her breasts, to her pink-flushed face, 'yes, Giselle.'

All night long if you want me to, she said to herself – after I have done it to you five or six times, Giselle, you will find that you adore me. You will want me to be with you every night. It will not be long before you decide to help my career.

Marie-Louise Makes A Discovery

It was not very difficult for Marie-Louise to trace the address of the model in Laurent's sketches for the fashion magazines. A faceless woman in black satin knickers, a slender brunette with small feet – and an elegant bust-line. Marie-Louise was certain her fiancé was having an *affaire* with this unknown woman.

Laurent had denied it, naturally, and insisted when asked about her that he *never* chose models for his work – all of them were complete strangers. He required a good figure and the face was of no importance because he didn't give his drawings faces. His job was to illustrate stylish underwear, the body inside it was of no significance to him.

He left the question of choice completely to Madame Drouet at the agency. She sent whoever had an appropriately slim figure and was available. It was surely obvious to Marie-Louise that a professional artist like himself regarded studio models as mere clothes-horses. No, he really couldn't remember the name of the dark brunette who posed for him twice. He thought it was twice, but so many models passed through his studio it was impossible to recall them as individuals.

A likely story, Marie-Louise thought, *he is not a convincing liar, my Laurent.* But when she challenged him again about the model in black satin knickers and demanded to be told if he had been sexually agitated when he looked at her breasts and thighs in the flimsy underwear, Laurent admitted nothing. He only said that his fiancée ought to have more confidence in him.

It was a pointless discussion and the outcome was necessarily unsatisfactory. Marie-Louise said no more at the time, but she was determined to find out the truth. She knew the name of the model agency run by Madame Drouet, the phone directory gave her the address. She went to the office, a not very impressive pair of rooms three flights up on a noisy commercial street. A thin receptionist in a roll-top grey pullover stared at her above a new typewriter and asked her to take a seat.

Around the walls of this outer office were large photographs of young women. Head and shoulders, full-length, profile, full-face. Some were in long evening dresses, some in chic day-wear, some in country clothes, riding jackets and narrow trousers, as if departing for a weekend of shooting wild boar at an aristo's chateau, these glamorous young women who had never been further from the Arc de Triomphe than the end of the Metro line!

Some were photographed in elegant beach wear, swimsuits that clung to their bodies and revealed a lot of smooth young skin, and a few were in underwear – naturally, the revealing type men find so interesting, lacy bras and sleek-fitting knickers.

While she was waiting for Madame Drouet to become free to see her, Marie-Louise examined the photos of models posing in their bra and knickers. All of them were pretty, of course, and some were more than pretty. All had good figures – slender, shapely, with small elegant breasts – and this was infuriating to Marie-Louise when she compared them with her own fleshy bounties.

But the model she was looking for was not among the photos on the wall – at least, not recognisably so. Granted, Marie-Louise didn't know what face she was looking for, but she was clear in her mind about the figure and breasts and hips of the woman she was after. And none of these in the photos quite fitted.

Madame Drouet was a middle-aged talkative person, her hair a silvery tint that required her hairdresser's regular attention to maintain. She wore a plain black frock and had several rings on her hands, only diamonds, suggesting that business was going well. She eyed with approval Marie-Louise's clothes, frowned at her over-large bosom, and asked her to sit down. She opened the conversation by asking, "How old are you? I never take on anyone over twenty-five."

Marie-Louise explained curtly that she hadn't the least wish to become a model. Her reason for calling was of great delicacy and she trusted that Madame Drouet would respect her confidence in this matter.

'If you are hoping for information about any particular model it is the firm policy of the agency never in any circumstances to divulge names and addresses,' said Madame Drouet. 'You would be appalled to know how many perverts telephone or write to ask for the phone number or address of a model they have seen in an advertisement – need I tell you what these degenerates would do to my girls if they had the chance?'

Marie-Louise remained undaunted. The curious ways of

men held no surprises for her. Men were absurd, there was no mystery in that. She explained she was there in connection with a certain client of the agency – Laurent Breville – a fashion artist who always hired underwear models for his work. At the mention of Laurent's name the frown on the face of Madame Drouet deepened to a scowl. She glared in fury at Marie-Louise and asked her to leave at once.

The truth was that Laurent had offended Madame Drouet. He had lied to her. And worse, he had deprived her of regular fees he used to pay for the models. This was unprofessional and foolish of him. When he first became besotted by Odette he had arranged with Madame Drouet that she was to be his exclusive model – and he paid top rate. All concerned were pleased. But after a while – when his attentions to Odette's *little heart* were daily – she felt she was so well established in his life that it was a pity to let the agency take its percentage of her fees.

Madame Drouet had been in this business enough years to know what was going on when Laurent phoned one day with instructions to send no more models. It was that *petite salope* Odette he was so hot for – they'd done a deal together to cut the agency out of its due! She said so to Odette, who denied it to her face – and had the brazen impudence to claim she was available for any photographic work or for fashion shows. Naturally Madame Drouet didn't believe a word of it.

She was very suspicious at first of Marie-Louise, thinking it was a question of some sort of trick to her disadvantage. But a frank admission by Marie-Louise of her situation apropos of the underwear artist finally convinced Madame Drouet her caller was in truth Laurent Breville's fiancée – and so had every right in the world to concern herself with his interest in other women. Especially those who posed for him in the privacy of his studio wearing skimpy silk knickers. Everyone knew what men were like, let them only catch a glimpse of bare thigh or bosom – and they turned into raging beasts!

There were tales Madame Drouet could tell of the infidelities of her husband – now long since kicked out and vanished – which would shock and amaze Marie-Louise! Open infidelities with the models of the agency itself, some of them were no better than little whores, and Drouet went after anything in skirts.

An understanding grew between Marie-Louise and Madame Drouet. The name of the brown-haired model who had posed so very often for Monsieur Breville – would you believe she had been with him every day for three weeks before he said send no more models! Her name was Odette Charron. She was twenty-two years old and her vital measurements were . . . never mind that, it was not important now. Her address – yes, one moment, here it was – a superior address for a girl like that: Boulevard de la Madeleine.

'Well!' said Marie-Louise, raising one eyebrow, 'Your models evidently earn more than I imagined.'

'I only know what they earn as models,' said Madame Drouet, a noncommittal look on her face. 'This address – it is sure to be the apartment of a man she lives with. It is not the address of Monsieur Breville, we both know that. But she could have other friends, of course.'

'Of course,' said Marie-Louise, tight-lipped, 'I feel that it is my responsibility to find out. I must protect my fiancé from this scheming woman. He is very susceptible – men are such idiots in these matters.'

Madame Drouet nodded her heart-felt agreement. And as

she had her knife into Laurent Breville for cheating her over fees, she had no compunction about revealing something else about him.

'It is not for me to tell tales, Mademoiselle,' she said, her expression stony, 'but as his fiancée it is only right that you know the worst. Before Odette Charron went to work for Monsieur Breville I used to send him a girl named Annette Delorme, twice or three times a week. One day Annette vanished without a word. She ran away with a married man – this was why I sent Odette to him, there was no choice at such short notice.'

'Are you suggesting,' said Marie-Louise, her face pale with shock or anger, or both, 'that you think something was going on between Monsieur Breville and this Annette?'

'As to that,' said Madame Drouet with a shrug, 'I cannot say for certain. There were hints from Annette, half-suggestions of something improper. It is difficult, you understand, when it is a question of underwear models. Annette never complained to me about Monsieur Breville, but I received the distinct impression that his behaviour was not strictly professional towards her.'

'What are you saying?' Marie-Louise demanded.

'Nothing,' said Madame Drouet, rolling her eyes upward, 'but when I asked Annette she would never give me a straight answer. What was I to think? Monsieur Breville is a *voyeur* – an artist must be, if his work is drawing underwear. Beyond that, does he molest his models, I ask myself? Does he expose himself to them? Who can say what goes on in privacy between a young woman in fancy underwear and a successful artist?'

'You have given me much to think about, Madame,'

Marie-Louise said, shaking her head in dismay. 'Can it be arranged for me to speak to this Annette? Perhaps she would be willing to tell me more than she admitted to you.'

'Alas no,' said Madame Drouet. 'First she went to Corsica with the married man I mentioned. Then I heard she was back in Paris some weeks later, but she never got in touch with me and when I phoned her there were different people in the apartment.'

Marie-Louise took a taxi straight to the address she had been given for Odette – determined to lose no time in her search for the truth. Or whatever she was searching for. The apartment was one floor up. She ignored the lift and climbed the well-tended stairs and rang the doorbell. It was a little after ten in the morning – she had called at the agency not long after it opened for the day's business. When the bell stopped ringing there was a long pause. She rang again and waited. She had decided no one was in when she heard steps. The door opened – a man in a silk dressing-gown peered out at her enquiringly.

It was Robert Dorville, of course. This was his apartment and Odette had given the address to the agency when she was staying with him. In view of the subsequent disagreement over fees, she had not bothered to advise the agency of her change of address when she moved into the tiny apartment Laurent had rented for her. Marie-Louise stared back at the man in the doorway. She liked the dressing-gown, it had the expensive and stylish look of the rue St-Honore about it. The man wearing it was good-looking and had dark curly hair. He was about thirty, she concluded. Evidently she had woken him up and dragged him out of bed by ringing – he belonged to the same privileged class of people as herself, who stayed out late and slept late and had no interest in working.

'*Bonjour*, Monsieur,' she said, 'I would like a few words with Mademoiselle Charron.'

It was in Marie-Louise's mind that the brown-haired model was in this man's bed, still asleep.

'Ah,' said the man in the silk dressing-gown, stifling a yawn behind a well-manicured hand, 'Mademoiselle Charron. I see. Are you a friend of hers, Madame?'

'We have mutual acquaintances,' said Marie-Louise cautiously, 'I am Mademoiselle Marie-Louise de Beaucourt-Villiers. And you, Monsieur, are . . . ?'

'Robert Dorville,' he answered, his brain starting at last to function. Here was a most elegant woman of a certain age on his doorstep asking for little Odette, who deserted him weeks ago! He wished he knew where she was – he'd slept alone for the past two nights and he was in dire need of the consolations that she knew so well how to provide. What could the connection possibly be between darling green-eyed Odette and this big-bosomed woman in a leopard-skin jacket with a Courrèges handbag swinging from her shoulder on a long leather strap?

'I regret Mademoiselle Charron is not here at the moment,' he said, which was only the truth, he really did regret she wasn't there. If only she were he'd keep her in bed and do delicious things to her till midday.

'When will she return?' Marie-Louise asked.

Robert glanced along the landing and smiled. He meant to find out more about his caller before he volunteered any information that could be to Odette's disadvantage.

'It is ridiculous to stand here talking,' he said, giving her his most charming smile. 'As you see, I am not dressed. In fact

I have just woken up and I am in urgent need of coffee. Please come in and have a cup with me while you are asking questions.'

Marie-Louise accepted the invitation, there was no reason not to. She liked the apartment when she saw the interior – not her own taste, of course – but pleasantly furnished in a well-to-do bachelor manner. Robert proposed she should wait in the sitting-room while he made the coffee, but she suggested she went with him to the kitchen to assist, having put him to so much trouble and waking him up, etc. They were both extremely polite to each other, intent on gaining the information they wanted.

The kitchen was large and well-equipped but little-used. All Robert did was make coffee in the mornings and wash up the champagne and brandy glasses from the previous day. All this Marie-Louise took in with one glance. Robert Dorville very obviously ate his meals in restaurants. And equally obviously, his girlfriend did nothing by way of cooking. Women like that never did, their scene of action was the bedroom. For at this point Marie-Louise still believed that Odette lived with Robert and was having an *affaire* with Laurent on the side.

Robert busied himself boiling water and Marie-Louise prepared the filter and spooned in ground coffee. She began to think she was wrong about Odette being in the bedroom and naked, sleeping soundly after the exertion of the night. One had to ask oneself if this Dorville would invite her in so readily if she were.

'You were telling me when Mademoiselle Charron will be back,' she said to prompt him.

'Yes,' he said, again treating her to his charming smile. 'It is not easy to be precise about her movements, from day to day. Her hours of work are necessarily irregular, you understand.'

Robert was determined to give nothing away until he knew what his visitor's interest in Odette was.

'Are you also in the fashion business?' he asked.

'No, I have nothing to do with business,' said Marie-Louise. Her tone indicated that she was above all that, she was a woman of independent means.

'Yet you have friends in common with Mademoiselle Charron?' Robert said thoughtfully. Without waiting for a reply he picked up the tray on which Marie-Louise had set breakfast-cups and he steered her back to the sitting-room.

It was pleasantly warm in the apartment, Robert suggested she took off her leopard jacket. He poured *café-au-lait* for both of them. When she was sitting in one of his leather armchairs and he handed her the cup he saw that her breasts were as bountiful as he had thought. He sat down facing her and took care when he arranged his dressing-gown over his knees – a little flicker of interest down between his legs advised him that there was going to be something to conceal from his visitor soon.

Marie-Louise was speaking quickly – she evidently felt it was necessary to answer the question he had asked in the kitchen: what friends had she and Odette in common? Robert had forgotten the question and paid no attention to the confusing answer – he was much too interested in the jiggle of Marie-Louise's big breasts in her frock. It was a stylish autumn frock, made of fine wool in a peach shade and fitted close to her body. It had a scooped neck-line, sleeves to the elbow and the hemline two centimetres below her knees. The close fit showed Robert that her body was slender and elegant, her waist well-defined – and her legs, now the skirt had ridden up a little, long and rounded.

An attractive woman, he thought – for her age. Women over twenty-five had as little interest for him as for Madame Drouet, though for different reasons, of course. But this woman was fascinating to him because her breasts were so out of proportion with the rest of her body. It was Robert's guess she was extremely proud of them – a man's point of view that happened in this case to be totally wrong. Robert wanted to see them bare; down between his thighs there was a stiff and jerking length of flesh that would not leave him in peace.

'I see,' he said when Marie-Louise stopped talking. The words were inaccurate – he'd understood nothing much of what she'd said about knowing Monsieur Laurent Breville, the celebrated fashion artist. And the reason for his incomprehension was not only his interest in Marie-Louise's superb breasts, it was partly due to her deliberately ambiguous approach – very naturally she had no intention of telling a stranger his girlfriend was lying on her back for her fiancé – that was too mortifying!

But the name Breville was one Robert remembered very well. It was after Odette first posed for a magazine illustrator by that name that she trimmed away the impressively *sauvage* brunette thicket between her legs. Sheared it and tamed it to a *little heart* of neatly clipped curls. For sketches for *Vogue*, she claimed when Robert asked why she had done this to herself. He never wholly believed her story, not even when he was pressing kisses to her newly-prominent *joujou*. Odette insisted that Breville was left-handed, but Robert could never dismiss a suspicion that it was for Breville that she had created the heart-design.

If he had known that it was Breville himself who had created it, then Robert's suspicions would be certainties. But then she had moved to an apartment of her own and speculation about whether or not the fashion illustrator was doing more to her than draw her in silk knickers became pointless. Now here was a woman of style and substance come to ask about Odette and mentioning the name of Breville. It made Robert very determined to explore the mystery fully.

He didn't yet know it, but the matter was not entirely in his hands. He was confronted by a woman equally determined to probe the situation fully. And Marie-Louise knew what all intelligent women know – which is how to get their own way. She listened to Robert's vague chatter disclaiming any direct acquaintance with Monsieur Breville while she studied him closely. Naturally, she knew precisely what was in his mind, the way he kept looking at her breasts made it obvious – it was the way men always stared at her. Usually she ignored it, sometimes it irritated her, now she thought of a way to make use of it by putting Robert in the wrong and on the defensive.

'Really, Monsieur Dorville!' she exclaimed, her tone replete with outraged modesty. 'I will not be insulted. I shall leave instantly!'

'But what do you mean?' Robert asked, amazed by this sudden outburst.

Marie-Louise was up on her feet – reaching for leopard jacket and expensive handbag before sweeping out of the apartment.

'You understand very well what I mean,' she said coldly, 'you are exactly like one of those pitifully imbecilic creatures of tramps who lurk in dark corners and expose themselves to little girls. This is disgraceful!'

'But . . .' said Robert, glancing down into his lap, 'I have not exposed myself to you, Mademoiselle.'

'Do not quibble with me,' she said angrily, making no move to go, 'it is perfectly obvious that you have deliberately aroused yourself – the evidence is plainly to be seen. From the instant I entered your apartment you have been staring at my body in an ill-mannered and insulting way.'

It was impossible for Robert to deny that he was stiff in his pyjamas. He thought his dressing-gown concealed this condition, but not so, his visitor had discerned movement under the silk. But she had mistaken her man – Robert was not Laurent Breville, he was not intimidated by a woman professing outrage and anger. He decided to play her at her own game.

'Ah, you have noticed,' he said, smiling pleasantly up at her as she stood over him, fiddling with her handbag, 'the truth is that I am so strongly attracted to you that I have lost control of my physical reactions. But to take this as an insult is very strange – it is a great compliment to you.'

Before she had time for any more outraged comment, he untied the belt round his waist and pulled open his scarlet and yellow dressing-gown to show her his hard fifteen centimetres standing upright through the slit of his pyjama trousers. She stared in amazement, her cheeks turning bright red.

'But this is atrocious!' she said, her voice shaking. 'Cover yourself at once, Monsieur!'

'There is no point in doing so,' said Robert very reasonably, 'now that we both know the state of arousal I am in, this will dominate our discussion, though we never again refer to it.

You understand what I am saying? We were two talking, now there is a silent third present at the conversation.'

'Then there is no more to be said,' Marie-Louise told him.

'On the contrary, we have much to say to each other,' Robert said, feeling his upright part throb under her stare, 'you have questions to ask about a certain young lady, there are things I wish to ask you. Why not continue, we have the time and this is as private a place as you will find anywhere.'

'Well . . .' said Marie-Louise, hesitating, 'perhaps . . . but what you said about a third being present makes it embarrassing for me to continue.'

'Yes, but the problem would resolve itself easily if two more joined the conversation,' Robert pointed out.

'Two more? What do you mean?'

Robert smiled his charming smile and gestured briefly in the direction of her breasts.

'Those two, of course,' he said.

'Well really!' she said. 'I've never in my life been treated with such bare-faced effrontery.'

'It is not only my face that is bare,' said Robert amiably.

'Of that I am aware,' she said, sounding thoughtful – an idea had flashed into her mind that almost took her breath away. She had come to this man's apartment to face the brown-haired model and tell her to stay away from Laurent Breville. Not that she'd thought it out clearly – or what to do next if the girl laughed at her. But now an alternative suggested itself.

Suppose Marie-Louise allowed this man to make love to her; he very obviously wanted to, this man who kept Odette. Get her own back by doing with him what the slut did with Laurent. And then inform the man his girlfriend was betraying him with Laurent? That would infuriate him. When Odette returned he would scream at her and call her names and kick her out into the street. And Marie-Louise would tackle Laurent and tell him his model friend was also opening her legs regularly for a man named Dorville.

The more Marie-Louise thought about it, the better her scheme sounded. Permitting Robert Dorville to touch her and make love to her was of no significance at all – she knew from experience the act was brief and physical and did not engage her emotions. Nor her intellect. And with some men it never even engaged her interest – she lay there while they did what men want to do.

'I cannot entirely disagree with what you say,' she told him, her mind now made up, 'two more could with advantage join us in conversation.'

She dropped her handbag and fur jacket on the chair to reach behind her back and slide down the zipper of her frock. Robert stared entranced as she slipped the bodice off her shoulders – it fell to her waist and the oversized beauties he was panting to see were held in an stylish bra of white and black satin. In another moment she was sitting on his lap.

Events followed their natural course. With the skill of long practice Robert unfastened her bra and felt her breasts to his heart's content. *But how magnificent* he murmured – Marie-Louise took this as proof he was as idiotic as other men. They admired flesh in quantity, they gave no consideration to the person who had these much-too-large breasts hanging under her chin. But it had to be admitted that she felt a mild pleasure when they were handled with finesse. And without question, Robert Dorville was extremely skilful in his handling of women.

Down in his lap Robert's unruly part was twitching wildly and Marie-Louise smiled as she took hold of it – she was well aware that a certain amount of judicious stroking here had the effect of speeding up a man's performance when he threw himself on her and pushed it in. And since there was little by way of pleasure for her in being entered, the shorter the duration, the better.

'It's so hard,' she murmured, knowing that praise of a man's pride excited him and made him anxious to proceed to the usual, 'and so big!'

She was absolutely correct about Robert – the words delighted him and the part in question throbbed in her hand. He moaned in his throat and struggled to his feet, lifting her in his arms. She held on tightly as he carried her to the bedroom. The broad bed was rumpled but empty – no sign of the slut of a model. She must be at work, Marie-Louise thought – perhaps with Laurent at this very moment! On her back on that garish chaise-longue in his studio, laughing at me while he sprawls on top of her. Well it's my turn to laugh now – I'm going to have your boyfriend!

'Put me down,' she said softly, 'let me take my clothes off.'

He set her on her feet and helped her wiggle the peach frock over her hips and down her legs. She sat on a chair and crossed her legs modestly while she undid her suspenders and started to roll her silk stockings down. Instantly Robert was kneeling in front of her to assist in this delicate and exciting operation. For it is almost a law of the universe that if a woman allows a man to take her stockings off, she will also let him take other garments off – in particular her knickers. And when a woman has permitted a man to remove her knickers, she will most certainly have no objection to his continuing by putting his hand between her thighs. And in due course she will be naked on her back and her legs will be apart waiting for him to slide his belly on to hers ... and all this from the innocent act of letting him help her take off her stockings!

This is how things went, till Robert with his fifteen centimetres sticking fiercely out of his pyjamas was staring in fascination at Marie-Louise spread out naked on his bed. He leaned over and flicked the dark russet tips of her breasts with his wet tongue until she sighed. His fingertips moved like butterfly wings on her belly. Marie-Louise found these early stages very pleasant, the touch of male hands on her naked body. As for her breasts – it was too much to hope that a man would leave them alone – she preferred it when they were licked rather than handled. But not too much of that, either – whatever was done to them was always a reminder of the permanent massiveness that displeased her.

'Robert, take your pyjamas off,' she said, encouraging him to get on with it. The victory she intended over that brown-haired slut of a model depended on having this man – there was nothing to be gained by stretching it out. Get it over with quickly and then tell him his girlfriend was deceiving him with Laurent.

Her hand gripped his thigh and her fingernails bit into soft flesh. Robert flung off his exotic silk dressing-gown and his pyjamas as if they were old rags, he gazed in rapture at Marie-Louise's superbly formidable breasts. At the long dimple of her belly. At the neat triangle of dark hair between her open legs. So dark the curls, as dark as the expertly cut hair of her head on the pillow, as dark as her curving eyebrows.

Robert leaped naked on the bed, to lie between her open legs and kiss that neat little triangle and the pinkish lips below. Marie-Louise spread her thighs wider apart – in her experience to kiss a pretty *joujou* had a marked aphrodisiac effect on men. Apart from that, if she were truthful about it, the rapid touch of a tongue between her legs evoked mild sensations of pleasure: she felt herself becoming moist and open – not that it led to anything of interest. The orgasm women talked about and claimed to adore never manifested itself in Marie-Louise's body.

'Robert,' she said, using his first name, 'come to me.' Naturally, he believed she was highly aroused and not able to wait another second to feel him inside her. But in fact she was becoming bored by what he was doing to her and wanted to get it over with. Happily ignorant of the truth, Robert spread himself on her warm belly and guided his distended part to the pouting lips he had been playing with. In a long push he sank deep into her. Her arms went round his neck, not in passionate embrace as he believed, but to hold his head down, his cheek against hers – so he would not observe the look of indifference on her face.

Poor Robert – all unknowingly he was taking part in an act of love that was one-sided. He might just as well have been on top of a shop-window dummy with its legs twisted apart. But men in a state of arousal are totally beyond taking note of matters of that sort – their only concern is to stab away into the warm wet *joujou* offered for their delight. And Robert had been alone in bed for two nights – he sighed and thrust away joyfully.

Marie-Louise felt the solidity of his stiffness deep inside. It filled her, it stretched her pleasantly. She tried, as many, many times she had tried, to let the in-and-out slide carry her up to a higher plane of excitement – where the impossible might happen. The hard flesh ravaging her was becoming bigger and was thrusting faster – Robert was approaching the peak of arousal – but the sensations were not becoming more exciting for her. She accepted that, as in the past, nothing was going to happen for her. She held Robert's cheek close to hers, arms round his neck tight, and forced herself to suppress a sigh of disappointment.

Then Robert spurted – so powerfully after two nights and days without a friendly *joujou* that he was sure she could taste his outpouring in her mouth. Or so in his climactic throbs he told himself. Whereas in truth she only knew when he did it because he cried out and she felt the spasms of his belly on hers. *Good,* she said to herself, *that's over and done with now and I've had something that slut of a so-called model thinks belongs to her.*

Meanwhile, she was bumping her belly up at Robert and moaning in an imitation of orgasm. This she had learned to do years ago because men were apt to become dismayed and upset it they found that they'd made no impression. Sometimes they became enraged. It was easier to pretend they'd thrilled her.

Robert rolled off her and lay with his head close to hers on the pillow, his hand on an over-bounteous breast – evidently he was fascinated by them.

'*Je t'adore*, Marie-Louise,' he murmured, 'I am so pleased you came here this morning.'

From the slow and sensual manner in which he was fondling her fleshy breast Marie-Louise could guess what was in his thoughts – she had experienced this before with certain men. When he was ready again – a matter of ten or twelve minutes – he would want to make love to her breasts, she was certain of it. As soon as he was stiff again he'd want to slide it up between her breasts and squeeze them close round it and spurt there! But she had no intention of letting him do so. Not unless it was absolutely necessary to find out what she wanted to know.

'I wonder if you realise how exciting your breasts are,' said Robert, toying with them, 'they are insanely exciting, *chérie*.'

Jacques Does It His Own Way

To conduct a serious and important discussion naked in bed with a perfect stranger is not easy. There are obvious distractions, when one of those concerned is a suave and charming man and the other is a woman with a pair of magnificent breasts. But Marie-Louise ignored all distractions. She had a sense of achievement from scoring over Odette – she had got Robert to betray his so-called model friend not once but twice in twenty minutes!

'I'm sure you've forgotten, in all the activity,' she said to him in an encouraging tone of voice, 'but what I am really here for is to speak to Odette Charron. About a personal matter.'

'Ah, darling Odette,' Robert said, stretching himself lazily at full length on the rumpled bed. He was very relaxed now the intolerable pressure of two nights and the day between had been released. All that time – forty-eight hours or more – without the solace of a woman's company, it was atrocious!

'To be truthful, *chérie*,' he said, his charmer's smile much in evidence, 'I'd forgotten about her completely. Can you tell me why you are so anxious to see her?'

'She is your girlfriend,' said Marie-Louise, sitting up on the bed, her knees up and her thighs together, 'but that didn't stop you for even a moment, did it? The moment you met me you insisted on exposing yourself disgracefully. She'll be furious when she finds out about you and me. But on the other hand, you will be equally furious with her when I inform you she is deceiving you with a man named Laurent Breville.'

'The underwear man!' Robert exclaimed. 'I guessed as much.'

'You suspected her?' Marie-Louise asked, her eyebrows rising, 'and yet you did nothing about it? Why is that?'

'Odette is not my girlfriend,' said Robert with a shrug. 'She stayed here for a while after she'd been kicked out of her room for not paying the rent. I felt sorry for her, and to be frank, she is amusing and attractive. But it's weeks since I saw her. She phoned me the other day, for a chat, but we didn't make any arrangement to meet.'

'What!' Marie-Louise shrieked, turning pale as she realised she'd let this total stranger take his pleasure on her body for no reason at all.

Before there was time to explore the dilemma any further, she heard quick footsteps approach the bedroom. A moment later the door opened wide and in walked the subject of their discussion, Odette herself. She had a different hair-style and was wearing a new coat and dress in the rich tints of autumn leaves.

She stared at the couple on the bed and grinned. Robert stark naked, lying on his side, his main asset dangling limply on his thigh. A woman of forty with massive breasts sitting on the bed at his side, a shocked expression on her face. It was obvious what they had just finished doing – Robert's look of content and the wet smear between the woman's melons explained everything.

If Odette had arrived at the bedside a few minutes earlier, a comic scene would have unfolded before her – the woman propped in sitting position with pillows and Robert straddling her legs on his knees to grip her *nichons* with trembling hands – sliding his fifteen centimetres between them. *But what are you doing* Marie-Louise exclaimed in a doubtful tone, again and again. *You know what I am doing, chérie* was Robert's breathless reply.

He had squeezed her breasts together round his stiff part and thrust fiercely into the fleshy purse they made. This she never intended to happen, but she let him do it because she saw it as a step in the process of turning him against his girlfriend. To speed things up and get it over she put her hands under him and grasped the lean cheeks of his bottom. She dug her fingernails in and heard his gasp.

He thrust hard and fast, she glanced down at the shiny purple head that emerged and withdrew with great rapidity in the cleft of her heavy breasts. His body jerked to his sudden spurting on her skin. *Ah, chérie, chérie*, he moaned, *they are marvellous*! After that, when he lay at ease beside her, she felt the moment was right to start her questions about Odette. Now that Robert was satisfied he would surely tell her everything. But what she heard was not what she wanted to hear.

Standing at the bedside, where so much had taken place in so short a time, Odette was surprised to find Robert had taken a woman of Marie-Louise's age for his pleasure. Usually he had no interest in anyone over twenty-five or twenty-six. Could it be he was desperate, she asked herself – handsome and charming Robert Dorville? Or was it her enormous *nichons* that attracted him so greatly that he ignored questions of age for once?

The reason Odette could walk straight into Robert's apartment was that she still had the key he gave her when she lived there. Very conveniently she had forgotten to give it back when she moved out. Well, she expected to look in from time to time. As now. Before midday was a good time to find him at home.

'Oh Robert,' said Odette with a grin, 'a thousand pardons for interrupting. I dropped in to say hello – I had no idea . . .'

'*Bonjour chérie*,' he said, not at all perturbed to be seen by her naked with another woman. After all, Odette had left him.

'*Au revoir, chéri*,' she said, 'I'll visit you some other time when you are not so preoccupied.'

With a little wave of her hand she was gone. Robert rolled on his back and laughed – Marie-Louise turned to glare at him, her face scarlet. She had never seen Odette before – only faceless sketches of her in black silk knickers and little bras. But she had a dreadful feeling in her stomach that the woman who'd just seen her naked in bed with a man was Odette Charron.

'Who was that?' she demanded.

'I thought you knew,' said Robert, 'that was Odette – the one you came to meet – the one you said is Breville's girlfriend. I find myself confused, perhaps you will explain what is going on in simple words I can understand?'

'*Ah, mon Dieu!*' Marie-Louise gasped in deep dismay. 'She saw us naked together. She will tell Laurent. I shall be disgraced in his eyes. He will break off our engagement!'

In fact, Odette had no idea that the woman in bed with Robert was Marie-Louise de Beaucourt-Villiers. There were no photos of her on show in Laurent's apartment, and she'd never bothered to ask what his fiancée looked like – whether she was dark, blonde or a redhead. Laurent never talked about his fiancée. His face would turn pink with embarrassment if Odette referred to her in any way at all.

The woman in Robert's bed was just a dark-haired woman with a telltale smear down between her fat *nichons* – Odette giggled at the memory as she went down the staircase and into the street. Poor Marie-Louise assumed she had been recognised.

'Engagement?' said Robert, astonished by her words. 'What on earth are you talking about? You said nothing about this when you arrived – you told me you and Odette had friends in common. Am I now to understand I am in bed with Breville's fiancée? It is absurd!'

'It is a catastrophe!' Marie-Louise contradicted him as she slid off the bed and began to dress in haste. 'I must stop her before she talks to Laurent. Do you know where she lives?'

There was only one bright little streak in an otherwise black and gloomy prospect, as far as Marie-Louise was concerned – the model was not on her back on Laurent's gaudy chaise-longue that morning. If Marie-Louise could get to her in time and speak to her reasonably, perhaps all would not be lost. An offer of money – women like that were always ready to take money.

And a little pressure on the question of Odette strolling so casually into Robert Dorville's bedroom... if Laurent knew that he would be bound to assume Odette had gone there for the usual reason. He would be very angry to think he was sharing her with another man. It would be the end of their *affaire*. So a promise of silence on that in return for a promise of silence on Marie-Louise's presence in Robert's bed. It might work.

Less than half an hour after being caught naked, Marie-

Louise was paying off a taxi in the Quartier Latin outside the ancient building where Odette lived. Robert had given her the address – he was well enough disposed to her for the morning pleasure she had given him to divulge it, an address he hadn't known himself until Odette's phone call of a few days ago. And he owed nothing now to Odette, he felt, not after the revelations about Breville.

Marie-Louise stared up and down the narrow street, unsure of what sort of people lived in these decrepit old buildings. She shrugged and climbed the stairs – and there on the second-floor landing was a man in a blue suit and a grey trilby hat knocking at the door of Odette's apartment. He heard Marie-Louise behind him and turned to stare at her. Early twenties, thin faced and with a self-assured expression. Not the sort of person Marie-Louise knew socially, not in that cheap-looking suit.

'Is anyone in?' she asked.

'No, I've been ringing and banging for ten minutes,' he said, 'I thought she might be asleep, but she's out.'

'What a pity,' said Marie-Louise, 'I've just come half across Paris to see her.'

'And I've come even further,' said the man. He added the name of the distant suburb he'd travelled from that morning by Metro but it meant little to Marie-Louise. She'd never been there, it was just a name on the underground rail network guides stuck on the wall at stations.

'You're an old friend of hers, Monsieur?' she asked him in a thoughtful tone.

'None better,' he said with a leer, suggesting a very intimate acquaintance with Odette. That gave Marie-Louise pause – she asked herself if she could persuade the man in the

BONJOUR AMOUR

blue suit to reveal enough scandalous and damaging information about the so-called model to discredit her in Laurent's eyes. It appeared to be a useful line of enquiry, she was certain that Laurent would recoil in distaste from the prospect of sharing his girlfriend with a flashy cheapjack from the dingier suburbs.

'I saw her quite recently,' said Marie-Louise, which was true enough, she'd seen Odette only thirty minutes ago – and Odette had seen her, in highly embarrassing circumstances. 'I thought we'd arranged to meet here this morning. But I must be mistaken.'

Needless to say Jacques Brolin had been staring all this time at Marie-Louise's bosom – men always did. He licked his lips.

'Is there a café near here?' Marie-Louise asked. 'I've had a very busy morning so far and it would be good to rest a while.'

It was no more than the truth – she'd had a very busy morning – first at Madame Drouet's agency and then in Robert's bed. And the morning was not over – here was this man to be questioned tactfully to see what could be learned.

What was in Jacques' mind was exactly the same as what Robert had thought earlier – he'd like to get his hands on those plump *nichons*. And he'd like to get Jacques-le-Grand between them. It never for a moment occurred to him that someone had pre-empted him. With an ingratiating smile on his face, he offered to take her to a café he knew round the corner in the rue Mouffetard.

When she accepted, Jacques naturally took it to mean that she was interested in him. Women were always interested in him – it was a simple fact of life. They wanted him to feel them between the legs and lie on their back for him to slip it in. Including this middle-aged woman in the expensive-looking leopard jacket. In fact, middle-aged women were even hotter for him than young ones, in his experience. He knew more than one who was so keen on him she practically raped him when he dropped by.

The café he took Marie-Louise to was small – it had two tables on the narrow pavement. The weather was cool and the sky overcast but it was possible to sit outside. She ordered coffee and Jacques had a glass of cognac. By then they had introduced themselves.

'How long have you known Odette Charron?' Marie-Louise asked as casually as she could.

'We're from the same neighbourhood,' Jacques told her, and in his role of backstreet Don Juan he added with a bold grin, 'I was the first to have her.'

He said it for effect and to show what a devil of a fellow he was. It wasn't true, but Marie-Louise took him at his word. She asked delicately how old they'd both been at the time and where this interesting event took place. Jacques concocted a suitable story – he'd had so many girls in the old days round the shunting yards that they had become confused in his mind, and one was as good as another. Marie-Louise took it all in and congratulated herself on her adroitness in extracting such useful information from her boastful companion.

'You're still very good friends, of course,' she suggested.

'She's crazy about me,' said Jacques with a fearful leer. It hinted strongly that he had called on Odette to oblige her, for old times' sake. This was what Marie-Louise wanted to hear him say. Being shrewd, Jacques saw where her interest lay and used it to his own advantage.

'Where do you live?' he asked. 'Far, is it?'

'Not really, why do you ask?'

'There's a lot I could tell you about Odette,' he said with a knowing wink, 'but not here in public. I thought we could go to your place for a bread and cheese lunch with a glass of wine.'

And seeing Marie-Louise hesitate to take him to her apartment he said quickly: 'She trims the hair down between her legs into the shape of a heart. And I know why.'

'No!' Marie-Louise breathed. 'I don't believe it. For a man, is it?'

Jacques tapped the side of his nose in the gesture that means *ah, the secrets I could tell you if I wanted to*! Marie-Louise hesitated no longer, she told Jacques to pay the bill and in no time they were in a taxi and on their way to her apartment. She said nothing to him about owning the building, it was imprudent to let anyone know too much about private matters. And Jacques Brolin was not the sort of person who would normally be invited into her home. In the taxi he was reasonably well-behaved – he didn't try to put his hand on her knee, but she was very aware that he was staring at her breasts for most of the journey. His chatter was heavy with sexual innuendo, not amusing at all.

They rode up in the creaking little lift. Confined though the space was, she felt he stood closer to her than was necessary – his hand brushed against her thigh. When the lift stopped with its usual abrupt clatter at her floor, he stumbled for a moment and his hand was on her bottom, steadying himself. Marie-Louise blushed slightly and tried to glare at him, but all she got was an insolent grin in return.

It was Yvette the maid's half-day, she finished at midday,

or Marie-Louise would never have taken Jacques there. She regarded him as a type of upper workman – not the one who came to repair the lift but the type who came round to measure windows for new curtains.

'We'll eat in the kitchen,' she told him, 'there's some very good Camembert, I think. And you can tell me about this curious personal decoration you said your friend Odette has.'

Jacques knew it was all a smoke-screen, this talk of Odette – the reason the classy lady had brought him here was to open her legs for him. That was fine, he expected no less from women of her age and he was rarely disappointed – but he wasn't going to be treated like a servant.

Well-off or broke, it made no difference, women did what they were told. They didn't order him about, they waited for him to tell them to take their knickers off. He glanced round the big kitchen and decided the table in the middle would do for lesson number one. He waited while she removed her leopard skin jacket and hung it on a chair-back.

'Right, Loulou,' he said with a grin, hanging his trilby hat on the same chair, 'let's see what you can do.'

The abbreviation of her name startled Marie-Louise as much as his coarsely ambiguous suggestion. Well, almost as much. He was a vulgar lout, this friend of Odette Charron in the cheap blue suit – what else could one expect of these people? A graceless oaf, an offensive nobody . . . yet he had a certain fascination. It was completely inexplicable, it was against logic and reason but a powerful sexual attraction radiated from him, commonplace though he was.

And while these thoughts churned about in Marie-Louise's head Jacques stepped close and she smelled the cheap scent he put on himself in a misguided attempt to increase his allure to women. He didn't try to kiss her, he grinned again and put his hands on her hips. Marie-Louise stared at him speechless – she could feel the stiffening part in his trouser leg press against her thigh. At close quarters his sexual magnetism was overpowering.

Without another word he gripped the back of her neck hard – a startled gasp escaped her to feel the strength in his fingers. He pushed her head down and bent her over – in a moment she was face-down over the table, unable to free herself or even kick him. He'd flicked up the skirt of her peach-coloured frock and was standing between her legs.

'This is absurd,' she said, perplexed by her own reaction and why she wasn't furiously angry to be handled so very boorishly. 'Let me up!'

'Not bad for a woman who'll never see thirty again,' said Jacques in a tone so condescending as to be insulting. He'd dragged her knickers halfway down her legs and was feeling her bare bottom. His hand pushed between her thighs, fingertips probing the soft lips there.

'You really must stop this now,' said Marie-Louise, unable to understand why she was not violently enraged. To tell the truth she would be sorry if he did stop – but she felt she owed it to herself to protest at this impossible lack of respect. And that was something else she couldn't explain – why did she want this common young man to go on touching her? He could no doubt tell her stories about Odette's disreputable past, but to allow him to go this far in return was out of the question!

She tried to push herself upright with her hands flat on the table-top, but his fierce grip on the nape of her neck held her pinned down. Her face was crimson as she looked at him over her shoulder and told him to let her go. But Jacques never paid any attention to what women said or wanted – they said such idiotic things. All that mattered was his pleasure.

'Hold on, Loulou,' he said, 'don't be impatient – I'm going to give it to you now.'

The fingers between her legs pinching the soft fleshiness of her *joujou* moved away to flip his trousers open and release his stiff male part. Marie-Louise gave a little shriek as she felt it touch her.

'No, you're going too far!' she said, as a strangely unfamiliar and exciting sensation throbbed through her belly.

'I'm not even in yet,' Jacques retorted as his fingers opened her wide for his entrance. He pushed hard, she squealed to feel him penetrate her. He slid in deep, she squirmed, his belly was hard against her bare bottom and he was thrusting in-and-out in a fast rhythm.

Whether Marie-Louise was angry or outraged was a question with no answer – sensation swamped her and she was incapable of thinking anything. Jacques gripped the back of her neck firmly to hold her in subjection – as much psychological as physical. His other hand was free to slide underneath her and squeeze her soft oversize breasts through her frock.

'You've got a lovely pair of *nichons*, Loulou,' he gasped, his engorged fifteen centimetres stabbing her fiercely, 'I'm going to strip you naked after this and have a real look at them . . .'

Marie-Louise lay bewildered, her body shaking to his thrusts, an unfamiliar sensation of triumphant near-ecstasy growing to an incredible intensity within her. Nothing like the usual mild thrill of pleasure most men could give her, this was savage and ferocious, intimidating . . . unendurable!

'*Ah bon Dieu*!' she moaned as the powerful throbbing increased beyond anything she imagined possible – then with a shriek she achieved orgasm for the first time in her life.

'No – wait for me!' Jacques cried out hoarsely.

He was indignant that a woman dare anticipate him – mortified and incensed! It wasn't supposed to happen that way. *He* did it first and that set the woman off – that was the right way. What did this rich bitch think she was doing – doing it before him? There was a lot she had to be taught and he was the man for it. His belly pounded hard against her, until with a vicious cry of triumph he spurted into her convulsing body.

He lay trembling on her back while his breathing returned to normal, then he stood up and smacked her bare bottom. She gave a sighing gasp but made no move. Jacques saw that her eyes were closed and her face pale – it made him grin to realise he'd had so profound an effect on her, it restored his normal feeling of superiority. He hauled her off the table-top and made her stand on shaky legs, his arm round her to keep her upright.

'Where's the bedroom?' he demanded, shaking her roughly.

She pointed vaguely, he dragged her in that direction, out of the kitchen into a passage, opening doors with his free hand as he went, until he found the room with the broad comfortable bed with an ivory satin coverlet. He dumped Marie-Louise face-down on it and stood back to take off his jacket and tie and shoes. While he was doing this she rolled on her back and stared up at him curiously. She was stunned by what had happened – it was so fast and unexpected – so uncontrolled, so violent.

She understood now what her women friends were talking

about when they discussed love affairs and lovers. But as to whether she ever wanted to undergo that annihilating experience again – that was a major question in her mind.

Jacques had his knee on the bed and turned her on her side to get at the zip down the back of her frock. While Marie-Louise was murmuring in surprise *What are you doing*? her frock was up over her head and off, her bra was undone and her over-generous breasts were exposed.

'No, no, you mustn't,' she murmured, her face as pink as if she were a virgin of fifteen.

'What a pair,' said Jacques, 'big as melons – the minute I met you I knew I'd got to have them out for a feel.'

He was kneeling over her on the bed, fondling them with both hands – he rolled them about, he squeezed them, he smacked them lightly to see them bounce. He put his head down and sucked the dark-red buds in turn. After a while he raised his head and asked if she was ready for it again. And when she gasped out *No* he grinned and said that was too bad because he was and she was going to have it, like it or not.

That was the way to talk to women – tell them. They knew what they had to do when a real man told them. Jacques straightened his back, straddling her on his knees – he had his stiff length out and he was holding it, his hand sliding up and down to show her how long and thick it was. Women opened their legs wide for him when they saw what he'd got, he'd proved that often enough.

'Take a good look at it,' he said boastfully, 'you haven't had one like mine up you before.'

Marie-Louise was staring at it as if bemused. She did nothing when he moved down her legs to the end of the bed and slid her knickers off. He pushed her legs apart unceremoniously to stare at her *joujou* and its neat little triangle of dark-brown curls. Not shaped in a heart like Odette's, he thought, but clipped to a small size – he wondered why some women wanted to change what was there by nature. As for himself, he liked a good thick bush between a woman's legs.

He got off the bed to remove the rest of his clothes. And now Marie-Louise saw that though he was thin the male part standing out in front of him was thick and long and heavy.

'I'm not at all sure I want you to do that to me again,' said she in muted voice.

'What a stupid thing to say!' Jacques said with an evil grin. His hand was back on his fifteen centimetres, stroking up and down. He flung himself on her, his hands gripped her and pushed her knees up and apart – *Oh*! she gasped as she felt his length of hard flesh slide into her.

'Feel the size of that, Loulou,' he said, 'all the way up!'

It excited him to know she was at his mercy, he was thrusting hard, ravaging her roughly in his desire for domination. Marie-Louise did what she always did when a man made love to her, she sighed and writhed and wriggled under him – and this time there was no pretence, she felt the sensations grow stronger and more insistent in her belly. To her amazement she was shrieking and clawing at Jacques. She raised her thighs to open herself wide and her body shook to the savagery of his thrusting. *Ah yes yes* she shrieked, clasping him to her hungrily.

It was no more than Jacques expected – women went mad when he got on top and slid it up them. Some of them made so much noise squealing and moaning close to his ear they nearly deafened him – sometimes they passed out under him. He was grinning while he stabbed into Marie-Louise, he'd really got this one going! She wasn't so quick about it this second time. The brute force with which he speared her made her jerk on the bed – but she didn't get her pleasure before he did, not this time.

He gave a long grunt of triumph and spurted into her, she let out a piercing shriek and wrapped her legs about his waist hard enough to break his back as her orgasm seized her. *More, more*! he heard her cry as he collapsed limp and sweating on her hard-straining belly.

He needed a rest after that – she had exhausted him more than was usual for him. He lay on his back for ten minutes or so and said nothing: in fact he hardly troubled to listen to whatever nonsense Marie-Louise was chattering – she sounded so cheerful. But he heard her suggestion that a little glass of cognac would revive them both – and off she went to get it, a satin negligée thrown carelessly round her naked body.

Jacques grinned when he was alone; comfortably spread out on the bed, hands under his head, he was congratulating himself. He had taught this rich snob of a woman a trick or two, he'd never doubted for a moment he could bring her to heel with his length of gristle – women respected it. She was his any time he wanted her now – he'd look in from time to time and she'd beg him down on her knees to do it to her. And she had plenty of money – he could touch her for a loan now and again, the sort of loan that never gets paid back.

She was back in a minute or two with a bottle and two glasses, a smile on her face, her big soft *nichons* bouncing out of the open negligée. Now she understood what sexual ecstasy was like, she intended to experience it again before she let Jacques go. After that, when she'd experienced all he could give, she never wanted to see him again. He was a guttersnipe, an untrustworthy type who would try to wheedle money out of her, she was certain of it. He'd served his purpose, being allowed to enjoy her body was payment enough.

Marie-Louise handed him a glass of cognac and sat down on the edge of the bed, her negligée open to let him see her breasts – that's what excited men. She reached out to take his dangler in her hand and lift it up to look at it closely – this thing that had caused a miracle to happen. It was *petit Jacques* now – not *Jacques-le-Grand*, but a little handling would make it grow hard and long again.

Now that she understood the purpose of love-making a question in her mind was whether Laurent could give her the same thrills as Jacques. He never had in the past, no one ever had. And upon reflection, Marie-Louise doubted if Laurent ever could. But she would give him the opportunity to try. Another idea came to her: the charming man she'd met that morning – Robert Dorville – how delicious if he could make her reach orgasm, now she understood what she wanted.

On the other hand, she thought, stroking Jacques's limp part, suppose this cheap salesman person is the only man who can make me do it? What a dreadful prospect – what a miserable trick of Fate that would be! It was necessary to proceed carefully till she knew what the true situation was.

Jacques stared down at his stiffening flesh in her hand, then up at her face – he grinned at her.

'You're like all the rest, you can't get enough of me,' he said in a most conceited way. 'You'll wear me out, Loulou.'

'Not you,' she said, handling him more briskly, 'you've got a big strong thing that never gets tired.'

To be truthful, now it was swelling in her hand and

attaining full-stretch, it was impressive. Although she was sure its size had not much to do with driving her half-insane with ecstasy: she thought Jacques' offhand roughness had somehow caused it to happen – the way he'd flung her face-down on the table and held the back of her neck as if he wanted to break it. But who could say? More practical research was needed. As soon as possible.

'Big and strong, that's right,' said Jacques, taken in by her flattering words, 'I'll have you on your back and bang you till your teeth rattle.'

Pauline Considers A New Career

On the evening that Laurent had met Pauline Joubert and danced with her in a small dark nightclub near the rue Monsieur-le-Prince, much of his time had been passed very pleasantly trying to look down the front of her frock. The neckline was braided, interestingly low-cut, and off the shoulder. It was impossible for Pauline to wear a bra with a frock like that – Laurent had had a view of white breasts swinging to the movement of her body.

He had slid his hands down her back to her waist, and lower still to grasp the cheeks of her bottom while they were dancing – but only when he'd been certain that Marie-Louise couldn't see what he was doing. The nightclub had been dark, the tiny dance-floor crowded with couples rubbing their bodies together – it had been fairly safe to indulge himself a little. Or so he thought.

Pauline had made it obvious that she was eager to be more closely acquainted – she had pressed her thighs and belly close to him, danced cheek to cheek. The fragrance of her perfume, so close, had excited a certain stiffness in his trousers that she must have felt against her belly. She had asked for his candid opinion of her figure – his professional opinion – did he believe she could be a model for a fashion illustrator of his eminence?

Laurent had already consumed most of a bottle of champagne by then and was generously disposed. He had given it as his expert view that she had a very good figure, certainly as excellent as most of the young women his agency sent to his studio to pose – and better than a good many of them. He had told Pauline this with all the sincerity of a man anxious to get her knickers down.

But, he'd gone on, his field of activity was, as she understood, exclusively confined to underwear. In the circumstances it was impossible to make a true decision from her charming appearance in an evening frock – it would be necessary to see her stripped to bra and knickers. No more was said on the subject by either, though they danced together closely entwined twice more before the evening ended – Laurent's hard flesh sliding maddeningly in his underwear against Pauline's hip until he was on the edge of spurting. It was a sweet torment he found delicious.

By next morning he had more or less forgotten the champagne-fuelled conversation with near-blonde Pauline. But she regarded it seriously and eventually she phoned him to remind him of his expert opinion that she had a good enough figure to be a model. And now here she was in his studio, undressing for his personal inspection!

She gave no evidence of unnecessary feelings of modesty, this near-blonde Pauline, she didn't conceal herself behind the red leather screen with the peacocks to undress herself. She smiled at Laurent and stood in full view beside the pink velvet chaise longue. She slipped out of her fine white woollen pullover with the rolltop neck, and her green-checkered skirt. She sat on the pink velvet to take off her shoes and slip down her stockings – and all the time she was smiling at Laurent.

Not a bold smile and not a challenging smile, not a come-and-get-me smile – it was far more provocative. It was a smile that asked for his approval and his assurance that her figure wasn't too impossible for an important illustrator to take seriously. Laurent was utterly charmed, he sat with legs apart on the high stool behind his drawing-board and stared in open appreciation.

Pauline wore a bra today – white lace and satin that matched her knickers. Laurent observed the pair of well-shaped handfuls that filled the bra cups, he thought they looked bigger than he recalled from the nightclub dance-floor when he saw them naked, but it was perhaps because the bra pushed them upward. He asked Pauline to stand up, to turn sideways, to turn her back to him, to bend over, to stretch her arms over her head – he took every advantage of the situation to study her body from all sides.

She had a long narrow belly and an attractive bottom, cheeks round and firm. On the dance-floor he'd squeezed them and knew they were delicious of texture. If she had a fault, this blonde Pauline, it was her thighs. Below the knees her legs were well-shaped, round of calf and slender of ankle. As pretty a pair of legs as a man would see below a hemline if he strolled the length of the Champs-Elysees from one end to the other.

But her thighs – it had to be admitted from an artistic point of view they were somewhat too full. Too fleshy between hip and knee. Thick would be an unkind description – but in his mind's eye Laurent compared them with Odette's long slender thighs and it was not to Pauline's advantage, this comparison.

Thinking of Odette's thighs immediately brought into his mind the image of the neatly-clipped *little heart* between them – his handiwork, his *chef-d'oeuvre*, the pretty source of his artistic inspiration. He alone had created this symbol of adoration from the thatch of dark brown curls Odette had allowed to grow wild, he alone had the right to touch her *little heart* and to feel it and open it wide and slide into it.

Or so he fondly believed – fortunately for his self-esteem he knew nothing of Jacques Brolin. Or Robert Dorville before him. And never guessing that the elegant Giselle Barras was as eager as he was himself to play with Odette's *joujou*. And capable of giving dearest Odette thrills of a different type, but no less marvellously gratifying. If poor Laurent had been aware of that he would have been miserably dejected. But what the eye doesn't see, the heart doesn't grieve over – and here was this pretty blonde stripping down to her underwear to please him.

On his high stool behind the tilted drawing-board, staring at Pauline in her satin and lace underwear, Laurent had undone his trousers. His stiff part thrust out and up, his hand clasped it firmly. The angle of the board shielded this from her sight but he was not even pretending to sketch. He asked Pauline put a foot up on the chaise-longue and stand sideways to him – it was to open her thighs, this position he required, so he could look at them more clearly.

So different from Odette's – those long slender thighs Odette wrapped round his naked waist when he laid her on her back and slid up into her. Different, yes, and exciting in their own way, Pauline's thighs had the fullness Odette's did not – no doubt they would grip him tightly if ever he got on top of her, but a more urgent thought in his mind was how pleasant it would be to put his face between those fleshier thighs and feel them press together. Feel them trapping his cheeks in their warm grip . . .

And under the thin satin strip between Pauline's thighs, what would he find if he took her knickers down? Not a neat-clipped *little heart* like Odette's, of course, and not a wild thatch of untrimmed curls either. In Laurent's experience blondes rarely had much body hair. Between Pauline's thighs he would expect to find no more than a thin covering of lightish-brown curls. Very very few women had blonde curls – except for those who bleached their little fur-coat to match the hair of their head.

While Laurent held his throbbing pride in his fingers to play with a little and think his vivid thoughts, Pauline reached the conclusion she'd had enough of this awkward pose with one foot up on the chaise-longue and one on the floor. If the object was to allow Laurent to look between her thighs, he'd had plenty of time for that. And why all this delay – surely he didn't think she was here just to pose for him?

She turned to face him and smiled. She sat on the pink velvet and crossed one knee over the other, her hands flat on the seat behind her, as she leaned back to show off her breasts in their smooth white satin cups.

'Laurent,' she said, her smile more confident than before, 'I know what you are doing behind that board.'

'What do you mean?' he gasped, his face turning red.

'Seeing me in my underwear has excited you,' she said calmly, 'you are touching yourself, Laurent, don't try to deny it. What would people say if they knew – what would Marie-Louise think? It is monstrous of you to amuse yourself while you keep me here balancing on one leg for you to stare at my body. It must stop. Come over here so we can discuss what ought to be done.'

While she said this Laurent was frantically stuffing his hard length into his trousers and zipping up. When he thought he was decent of appearance he slid off his tall stool and moved round the drawing-board towards her.

'I am amazed to hear you suggest such a thing!' he said in a tone that tried, with no great success, to be surprised, mildly offended and amused in a superior sort of way. But Pauline only smiled at the prominent bulge in his trousers and stretched out a long bare arm towards him. Whether it was to offer her hand or to point accusingly at his shame, he was too flustered to say – he walked stiff-legged to the chaise-longue and stared down at her. The view of her half-covered breasts was superb.

'The idea is ridiculous,' he said. 'I cannot begin to imagine how so insulting a thought could enter your head! After all, I am a professional illustrator – models have been coming to this studio for years. Do you suppose I sit at the drawing-board and touch myself every time a model poses in her knickers?'

'Yes,' she said, and smiled at him again. This time the smile was an invitation.

Poor Laurent was thrown in a fearful condition. He was highly aroused, of course – the vista of Pauline's near-naked breasts in a fragile satin bra and the graceful curve of her bare belly were intoxicating! But he was also in agony of mind about what to do next. He wanted desperately to push Pauline down flat on the pink velvet and take her underwear off and kiss and stroke her from head to toe. His stiff part was throbbing ominously in his trousers, demanding instant action. Yet to give way to this insistent desire would be to betray dearest Marie-Louise – and to betray her in the most blatant manner imaginable.

If only Odette had been there, no problem would have arisen. But he hadn't seen Odette for two days. She told him she'd been offered modelling work with a fashion-house, but she didn't say which one. What she did say was that she couldn't come to work for him at his studio every day in future.

She could give him two mornings each week, she informed him – from ten until midday, which was long enough for a few sketches for the magazines. And for whatever else he required. At first Laurent had been angry with her, he had protested vigorously at her proposed arrangements. He had shouted at her. He had seized her by the bare arm and shaken her to make her change her mind. She was wearing an almost transparent chiffon nightdress at the time – he was doing a page of illustrations for *Elle* magazine. Shaking her made her dark-brown hair fall about her pretty face and a shoulder-strap to slip down, exposing a charming breast.

Laurent stared at it as his shaking made the uncovered breast bob up and down – and he was lost. In an instant he was down on his knees, his hands up inside the chiffon nightdress to stroke her breasts while he pressed his cheek to her warm bare belly. Then he was kissing her *little heart*, his lips hot on the soft lips it framed – he was unable to resist pulling her down on to the studio floor and flipping her nightdress up round her neck to slide himself on top of her.

Afterwards, when the power of rational thought reawakened, he realised he was in no position to argue with her about anything at all. She knew too much. Doing delicious things to her wasn't a betrayal of Marie-Louise, Laurent was quite clear about that. It was necessary to his creative ability – as an artist he owed it to himself to do whatever his talents required. With Odette he could do it three times a day and feel not the least pang of conscience – what he did to her had no connection with his deep and enduring love for his fiancée.

But, but, but . . . with Pauline it was a different matter. This was not a question of artist and model and natural inspiration. Marie-Louise and Pauline were acquainted socially. Not closely, they were not exactly friends, but they'd met and they'd passed an evening of theatre and dinner together. With dancing, if the whole story were told – though Marie-Louise had been angry with him later because she'd seen him looking down Pauline's frock. Furthermore, Pauline Joubert was not a model – she had a job in an office. She had not come to pose for him.

While Laurent stood swaying on his feet, his mind in turmoil, Pauline reached up and unbuckled his belt – in a moment she had his trousers open and his stiffness in her hand.

'I don't think this is a good idea,' Laurent said doubtfully, but she smiled and didn't trouble herself to reply.

She parted her knees wide and pulled him in closer, using his throbbing part as a handle. Her lipstick was a dark red, he noted for the first time since she arrived it shone dully and gave her mouth a predatory look. He stared mesmerised while her lips opened and took in half of his jerking length of flesh. He gave a short stifled cry to feel her tongue lap repeatedly over the swollen purple head.

Her eyes were closed, her mouth seemed to be smiling while it sucked at him. Laurent moaned and sighed and swayed – delighted at what was being done to him, but at the same time appalled by it. He assured himself he was taking no active part in what was happening, but that was a poor consolation, a mere excuse – the truth he could not deny to himself was that he was involved in an act of gross infidelity to Marie-Louise. It was necessary to stop this woman and send her away before things went too far – before they got out of hand completely and something he would later regret was allowed to happen . . .

But the truth was that matters had already gone too far to be halted by a simple decision. Pauline took him very close to the moment of truth before she leaned back and slid her red-painted mouth off his wet and twitching part. This was his opportunity to escape, all he had to do was leap up and zip up his trousers and tell her to leave the studio. And never come back. It would not be difficult to appease his conscience over the question of a little stroking and licking.

Naturally, he did nothing of the sort. The moment she let go of him he fell to his knees on the floor and pushed her down on her back on the chaise-longue. His fingers scrabbled eagerly at her satin and lace knickers, to pull them down her legs.

She laughed aloud when he got them off and flung them away – she spread her knees and between her thickish thighs he saw she had a narrow strip of light-brown hair. Not the usual triangle, it was only a few centimetres wide, this charming little strip, a long narrow oblong of sparse curls.

'*Ah mon Dieu,*' he moaned, ducked his head and pressed hot kisses to the insides of Pauline's plump thighs, up where the skin was soft and smooth as satin.

He licked his tongue up into her soft groins, he licked along the full lips he had uncovered. He knew he could not stop now, not even if the ceiling fell on his head. There was nothing for it but to obey his shrieking body and let all considerations of infidelity and betrayal be submerged beneath waves of pleasure.

Pauline arched her back and slipped her hands under to unhook her bra – Laurent pulled it away and clenched his shaking hands on her breasts, their soft warmth sending him into paroxysms of urgent desire. In another moment he lay forward along her bare belly, his loins jerking in little spasms – he felt between her thighs to open her while wriggling his hips to find the way in. Then he was pushing deep inside her.

'Ah yes,' she said appreciatively, 'that's very good, *chéri* – be brutal to me, Laurent!'

He needed no encouragement – he was so frantic that he thrust into her hard and fast, gasping and crying out, until in a very short time he spurted violently. Pauline groaned in delight and squirmed underneath him. Through his wild and whirling thoughts he was vaguely surprised his orgasm had been so fast and yet so overwhelming. As good as he'd ever felt with Odette, he thought oddly, in so far as he was able to think during these instants of furious jerking and passionate spurting.

But marvellous though it was, five seconds later he wanted to get off Pauline as fast possible and send her away. The tremors of pleasure had faded to leave him a formidable sense of guilt. It had all come true, just as Odette had explained it to him on the first day she had come to pose for him. He'd invited a woman to his studio for reasons not connected with art – he'd kissed her and undressed her. He'd pushed her down on her back and got on top . . . he'd been flagrantly unfaithful to his fiancée.

Pauline was determined not to let him get rid of her quickly. She admired him as an artist and she liked him as a person. She had thoroughly enjoyed what he'd done to her, she wanted him to do it again. If the full truth were to be told, what she wanted was to take the place of Marie-Louise in Laurent's affections. And why not? Having met the fiancée, Pauline knew that she was better-looking than Marie-Louise. And she was much younger.

She put her arms round Laurent and persuaded him to lie down with her on the chaise-longue. She was naked, her bra lay under her and her satin knickers were halfway across the studio floor where he had flung them in his eagerness to caress her and kiss her. In contrast, Laurent was fully dressed, only his limp wet dangler was lolling out of his open trousers. Pauline touched his face and stroked it, she kissed his cheek, she told him how wonderful he was.

No man can resist that treatment; Laurent let himself relax a little and submitted to her flattery. She cuddled him close and murmured little endearments in his ear. His hand lay lightly on the bare cheeks of her bottom, but he didn't try to fondle her, he was busy with his conscience.

Odette had explained it all so well to him, ages ago when she first came to the studio. Making love to a model liberated the artistic nature, he was clear about that much. His work proved it beyond question. For the sake of art and culture he had done superb and fascinating things to Odette and everyone agreed his illustrations had improved.

Except Marie-Louise, who seemed to believe that he was having an *affaire* with someone else. She had gone so far as to accuse him to his face of it. Naturally, no woman could be expected to understand the needs of the artist. Her reaction to the simple truth would be rage, jealousy, shrieking – it was better not to even try to make Marie-Louise understand.

A very useful thought came into Laurent's head as he lay upon the pink velvet chaise-longue and Pauline held his limp and wet dangler in her warm hand. Perhaps it was her touch that did it, or perhaps the idea had been there from the start, hidden away and waiting for him to discover it. What occurred to Laurent at this interesting moment was that if, like Odette, Pauline was a model who posed for him to draw, the question of infidelity did not arise. It would be a straightforward artistic transaction – making love to her would be a normal requirement of his nature.

'Ah!' said Pauline as Laurent's limpness began to grow long and hard in her hand, 'I like that.'

'You came here to find out if you have the figure to become a model,' said Laurent, kissing her cheek lightly, 'and from what I have seen of you so far, I think you could. I'd like to make a few colour sketches of you, of the type demanded by *Vogue* and *Harper's Bazaar*.'

'In my underwear?' she asked with a smile, sitting up beside him. 'Certainly, Laurent, whatever you say.'

'As it happens,' he said, allowing his imagination free scope now he could see a strong possibility of an end to his guilty feelings, 'there is a set of underwear sent for illustration we could use for your debut as a model.'

'By all means,' said Pauline, standing up and stretching. The sight of her soft round breasts pulled upwards by the movement of her arms, and the smooth tautness of her belly as she leaned backward – his vision made Laurent sigh and touch himself for a moment.

Needless to say, the underwear he took from a drawer in a

low cabinet by the wall had not been sent for illustration – not by any fashion magazine. It was a set Laurent had bought in a shop in Pigalle one evening, the type of special shop where tourists buy books banned from sale in their own country and photographs of interesting acts committed by men and women together – or by women and women together. And various other ingenious items of merchandise, including underwear.

'*Oh la la*!' said Pauline when he handed the bra and knickers to her. As well she might – the entire set consisted of no more than three small triangles of shiny black satin, with the very thinnest of black strings to join them together.

'This for *Vogue*?' Pauline asked, her eyebrows rising up her forehead.

'It is a new style,' Laurent said untruthfully, 'they haven't decided whether to use my illustrations or not – it will depend on the result.'

Pauline stepped into the absurd knickers, though the word was not applicable to what was in reality only a *cache-sexe*, of the type seen at the Moulin Rouge and the Folies Bergère. Round her waist a narrowest possible string supported the little triangle and between her legs another string ran tightly up between the cheeks of her bare bottom. The bra, so-called, was not designed to support her breasts, nor to cover them, only their prominent buds were concealed under the shiny black triangles.

'Interesting,' said Laurent, unable to take his eyes off her. He was sitting in his favourite place, behind his drawing-board with his stiff part clasped in his hand. He truly meant to make drawings of Pauline – not for publication but for his own later entertainment, he had a thick black pencil in the other hand. Already he had a folder of private sketches of Odette.

Odette lying on her side on the chaise-longue – in black silk pyjamas, the jacket undone to show her pointed breasts. Odette in silk stockings and frilly white knickers, kicking up one leg like a cabaret dancer. Odette in a short pink slip bending over to show her bare bottom. The beginning of a collection, perhaps, to be extended now with drawings of Pauline in stage underwear.

In view of Laurent's continuing interest in underwear, it was not to be wondered at that he had explored the pleasures of the live shows for tourists in the streets around the Place Blanche and the Place Pigalle. He had paid his entrance fee and watched carefully as lithe young men stripped tiny transparent garments from the bodies of lithe young women and laid them down on beds and climbed on top.

Laurent's motives were clear and simple, commendable even. He was not a tourist looking for the thrill of voyeurism – he was an artist and it was necessary for his artistic development. He studied the absurd little undergarments that had been designed to be ripped off several times a day, he took note of what they were meant to conceal, if temporarily, and what was revealed.

In his heart Laurent compared himself with Henri de Toulouse-Lautrec. He too understood the allure of women's bodies partly clothed. He drew dancers at the Moulin Rouge kicking up their legs in the air to show their thighs. He drew the women of the famous brothel in the rue des Moulins, resting between clients in the sitting-room, wearing thin negligées easily removed – or raised – to display the bounties on offer.

All this Monsieur de Toulouse-Lautrec had observed and drawn, day after day and night after night, entranced by the vision of women's undressed bodies. *Ah, we have so much in common, he and I, so much we could have discussed over a glass of cognac*, said Laurent to himself very often. And though he never admitted it, there was the unegalitarian appeal of aristocracy. Count Henri spent his time in bars and music-halls and *maisons de tolerance* and who thought the worse of him for that? If Laurent had been of independent means, born titled and privileged... ah, what he would have done!

But he could take a step in the direction he secretly desired by marrying Marie-Louise de Beaucourt-Villiers. She had traits of character he disliked but that could be forgiven because she had, in his view, that *je-ne-sais-quoi* of aristocratic descent. The first time she had permitted Laurent to put his hand up her skirt and touch her *joujou* the enchantment had been so powerful he had spurted into his underwear.

To a less discerning lover it might seem to be an ordinary if charming *joujou*, ideally shaped to receive a length of hot hard male flesh – in Laurent's mind it possessed qualities far from ordinary. He dreamed of it for many nights afterwards and woke up stiff and throbbing in the dark.

Leaving that aside for the moment, a day would come, he firmly believed, when his work would be recognised for what it really was – true art, not merely illustrations of expensive underwear for fashion magazines. Then his sketches would be displayed in galleries, as the music-hall posters of Toulouse-Lautrec were, and people would arrive in their thousands to look at them. And to praise them, to compare his early work with his later work – to admire his insight and his brushwork.

'But you are adorable,' he said to Pauline, staring avidly at her over his drawing-board as she posed, her long pale body set off by the small black triangles of satin imposed on it. 'Put your raincoat on for a moment.'

Outside the sky was sullen and the pavements wet. Pauline had arrived wearing a long green raincoat tightly belted around her waist and the collar turned up at her neck. She shrugged at the suggestion and put it on, pulling the belt very close.

'And your shoes, chérie,' said Laurent, his pencil skittering over the white drawing-paper.

In high-heeled shoes Pauline struck an attitude, one foot up on the chaise-longue, the skirts of the raincoat falling away from her thighs to expose them, one arm up stretched in the air over her head. *Oh yes*, Laurent sighed, sketching rapidly, *two seconds more like that*!

She smiled and turned to face him, feet together on the floor and her knees slightly bent. She flicked open her belt, grasped the edges of her raincoat and opened it wide, holding it as a background to her naked body – though it was not entirely naked, that beautiful body, the three black triangles made her seem even more provocative. Laurent was breathing as heavily as if he were running up a flight of stairs instead of wielding a pencil.

'Pauline . . .' he sighed, at which she smiled and shrugged her shoulders, making her breasts sway. Laurent's simmering desire became too ardent to contain for even another second. He flung down his pencil and dashed across the studio to her, stiff part sticking out of his trousers and preceding him like a bowsprit on a yacht. His hands were on her waist, sliding over bare warm flesh, then up to her breasts to stroke them through the little black satin triangles.

In another instant he lifted her off her feet and turned her, she gave a little shriek of surprise as he spread her face-down over the pink velvet head-rest of the chaise-longue – bottom up in the air and her head and hands down on the seat. He flicked her raincoat up over her back and ripped the little black satin *cache-sexe* down her thighs.

'Ah, you are brutal, brutal!' she gasped now she understood what he intended to do to her. 'You are a savage, my Laurent!'

He said nothing in reply – for a moment or two he fondled the soft round cheeks of her bottom, then she felt the solid plunge of his fifteen centimetres of hard flesh into her.

'Brutal, brutal!' she moaned. '*Je t'adore, Laurent.*'

As for Laurent at that comical moment, his emotions were out of control. The sensations of sliding into her warm depths were enough to bring on his crisis. He slammed his belly against her and jabbed fiercely as he spurted his passion.

'Ah, ah, ah!' Pauline sobbed, her own belly clenching in the spasms of orgasm.

'*Chérie, chérie . . .*' Laurent was murmuring in content.

He had eased his conscience. He no longer felt guilty. There was no longer any question of being unfaithful to Marie-Louise. What had taken place was the normal artist-and-model agreement, a part of the creative process. In a moment he was going to ask Pauline to stay as she was while he fetched a pad and pencil to sketch her in this position – face-down over the chaise-longue, her beautiful pale-skinned bottom so excitingly displayed bare.

All that was left to decide was whether to pay her top rate – the same as he paid Odette – or just the ordinary rate, as this was the first time Pauline had posed for him.

Odette At Work

Odette's job in the haute-couture house of Jean-Luc Marigny was not greatly interesting. She was there from ten till four on three days a week to be a living display dummy when important clients came in to buy. Or sometimes they came just to look and not buy. These ladies were accompanied by a husband or lover; naturally he was a man with a cheque-book. Odette put on the frock or the costume that interested the client and twirled about to display the effect.

Few of these clients, it need hardly be said, had the slender figure and long legs that made Odette so alluring to men. Wives who came with their husbands were usually in their late thirties, or even their forties. They had produced heirs, that was a wife's job, but alas, a needlessly unforgiving Providence arranged matters so that their breasts and hips were never as attractive again. But that aside, they had earned the right to demand that their husbands spent money on whatever they demanded.

The young women who came to buy – those with the good figures and unlined faces – these were the pampered girlfriends of rich lovers. They were taken to couturiers and jewellers to be given treats, in return for treats they gave their rich boyfriends in bed. But even these women, to Odette's eye, were often a little too plump – a centimetre or two excess round the bottom, just a soupcon too full under the chin – it was the natural result of being taken to the best restaurants most days of the week.

They sat on gilt chairs, the clients and the accompanying men and the women stared haughtily at Odette as she paraded for them in Marigny's beautiful clothes. The men stared at her with more interest, imagining the smooth young body inside the expensive finery. Odette smiled and turned about, she strolled to and fro gracefully, amused by her own thoughts.

Ah Madame, she would say to herself as she cast an appraising glance at the client, your intimate friend in the dark suit and grey moustache sitting beside you is so devoted that he is here to spend a small fortune to please you – but what passes through his head when you take off your Marigny creation in the bedroom and he sees your body is not a quarter as desirable as mine?

And you, Madame, with the millionaire husband fidgeting there on the chair beside you – what do you suppose he would do if he were privileged to see the *little heart* between my thighs? It would be me sitting where you are now, Madame, me he bought the clothes for, the frocks, the fur coats, the silk underwear. And although he is fat, your millionaire, he would be on his knees begging me to let him take off the knickers he'd bought me and kiss my *little heart*.

Boring though the job was, Odette saw it as a step forward in her career. There was a certain *cachet*, an undeniable status, in being able to say that one was employed by Jean-Luc Marigny. And it had not escaped her attention that working here put her in the best possible place to be seen elegantly dressed by rich men. The married ones surely had young and pretty girlfriends – to amuse them in ways wives had forgotten or never learned. And unlike wives, girlfriends were replaceable at will.

And as for the unmarried men who came to spend money on their girlfriends, a time surely came when they too became bored with the spoiled and pouting beauties they maintained in luxury. And if they were a little restless at the moment, any of these men, the sight of Odette Charron, so vivacious, dark-haired, long of leg and slender of hip, Odette with the pretty breasts, Odette in a Marigny frock; well who could say? It might well stir a desire to become better acquainted with her. To get to know her well enough to take off her frock and caress what was inside.

In brief, Odette was not entirely set on a career as a fashion model; she was flexible – she had no objection to becoming the girlfriend of a rich man. A luxurious apartment in a good part of Paris, elegant clothes, jewellery, the best restaurants. The provider of these necessities dropping in three or four times a week for his pleasure . . . whatever he looked like, fat, plain or middle-aged, all three even – Odette would make it her business to pleasure him senseless.

Naturally, she kept these ideas to herself. Her face had only the most neutral of expressions as she turned about for clients to see the Marigny creations. But sometimes she allowed herself a tiny smile at selected men, when she was certain no one would see. Like the wife or girlfriend, for instance; that would give rise to outbursts of temper and near-hysteria, to demands she should be dismissed on the spot.

Even more important, Madame Barras must not be allowed to see her smile at a man. Giselle: sleek and dark-haired in stylish clothes, explaining to a client the secret of Jean-Luc's theory of the inverted triangle line for this season. Dear Giselle who was so taken by Odette that she had found a job for her at the couturier's – and insisted she stayed with her in her apartment four or five nights a week. When they had known each other only a week she wanted Odette to move in with her.

That was too much for Odette. It would be complete surrender, total domination by Giselle. Odette said no, and said it firmly in spite of icy temper tantrums. She kept her own apartment, or rather the apartment Laurent paid for, and maintained a degree of independence. After all, Giselle was not her final goal, she was a charming step along the road towards it. It was important to keep Laurent happy because he paid her as much in model fees as the house of Marigny paid her in salary.

Two, three times a week, it depended on her mood, Odette went to the studio apartment in the Boulevard Edgar-Quinet and posed for Laurent's underwear sketches for magazines. He worked even faster now than he ever had before, knowing that Odette was not minded to stay all day with him, as she used to do in the early days of their collaboration. He splashed water-colours on paper with reckless abandon; those who studied these things said that his style, had changed in a most interesting way, it had become looser and less tightly controlled. In effect, he gave himself thirty minutes to make the sketches he had formerly taken two hours or more to do – and then he stripped off whatever fine lingerie Odette had posed in and laid her down on the pink velvet of the chaise-longue to pleasure himself on her elegant body.

Every second or third time she went to his studio he took her to his bedroom at the other end of the apartment – attend to her curls with his manicure scissors and razor. The plain truth was that he was obsessed by this little creation of his between her thighs and he maintained it devotedly. Odette lay naked on the side of his bed, feet on the floor and well apart – Laurent knelt between her legs to shape her curls to perfection.

Familiarity never made the task boring for him, and his close attentions always aroused her. By the time he dropped the sharp implements of grooming and dabbed her dry with a soft towel she was sighing and trembling with excitement. And when, fascinated by his own handiwork, he put his face between her spread thighs and pressed a hot kiss on the long soft lips framed so expertly by the *little heart* – Odette experienced quaking sensations of delight that warned her she wouldn't last more than another few seconds!

Laurent knew this too – he had learned a lot about her in the few weeks of their acquaintance. When she posed for him in silk nightgowns or brief lace knickers he was a slave to her charms, he could sketch for only a limited time, his stiff male part in his hand, before he was compelled to abandon his work and cross to her side and stroke and kiss her body. It was different when he groomed and shaped her *little heart* – at this moment Laurent felt that he was in control. Not that he ever was, of course.

It was so satisfying to him, making her squirm and shudder to the touch of his tongue, to have her helpless and at his mercy. He exulted in the knowledge that he could flip her over the top into orgasm at the moment of his choice. And when she lay still again afterwards, her smooth flesh just a little shiny with the perspiration of ecstasy, her long slender thighs lolling apart, her eyes closed and a languid expression on her face – the fact was that she was still at his mercy. He felt strong and raging, he slithered forward over her belly and sank his hardness into her. And with fast hard strokes he raised her yet again to orgasm.

Dear Laurent, Odette thought fondly, he is addicted to me, as if he were taking drugs. Trimming my curls and making me climax like that gives him an inflated sense of his personality — like the effect of heroin. How absurd men are! But how very useful, to have him dependent and to be able to satisfy his craving in so simple a way — and reinforce his habit at the same time.

Three or four evenings of the week she was with Giselle. They went everywhere together like true lovers, to theatres, cinemas and restaurants — they held hands in the cinema and they kissed in taxis on the way home. They embraced naked in Giselle's bed, their thighs entwined, bellies touching and mouths meeting in a kiss, hands stroking each other. In these moments of intimacy Giselle's haughtiness disappeared — she rolled on her back in a languor of mind and body, as Odette kissed the pink buds of her breasts.

She opened her legs wide for Odette's fingers to brush across the clipped triangle of dark curls there, she murmured words of delight when Odette kissed the soft hairless lips beneath those neat brown curls. She squealed like a schoolgirl, the superior Madame Barras, when Odette's tongue ravished her and flung her into orgasm after orgasm. And afterwards she put her arms round Odette and asked, *Is Daniel Rocart still your boyfriend, chérie? You must tell me.*

'But of course not!' Odette assured her. 'He never was — how often must I tell you that before you believe me?'

'You must have nothing to do with him,' Giselle insisted, 'he has a dreadful reputation.'

'If you dislike him so much,' said Odette, 'why is he working for Jean-Luc Marigny? Why do you not terminate his services?'

'As to that, *chérie*, the truth is that he is very good at his job. Marigny trusts him. If I ended his contract for publicity, it would be necessary to justify my action to Jean-Luc himself. That would not be easy to do at present. I prefer to preserve a proper distance between professional life and private life – it is better so. You must stay away from him.'

'Daniel is not my boyfriend,' said Odette, stroking Giselle's breasts soothingly, 'he never was and he never will be.'

It wasn't true, of course. She met Daniel on evenings she was not with Giselle. Daniel was important, she judged, through him she'd found the position with Marigny, and she expected to gain other and even better favours from him in return for what he wanted – which was what all the men she knew wanted. And apart from that she liked him and found him amusing because to her surprise she recognised a certain similarity of outlook between him and her.

There was also the problem of Robert – Odette certainly meant him to be a boyfriend because he represented her fall-back, her final refuge. If her plans went wrong she proposed to move back into Robert's apartment and let him keep her in style until she was ready to take on the world once more. But she had been very occupied since leaving him – she had been back only once to let him take her to bed. And that was a fiasco. He had been in bed with a middle-aged woman with overdeveloped breasts!

Quelle horreur! Odette thought with a grin, handsome Robert pleasuring Madame with the enormous *nichons*, he must be missing me very badly – but how astounding to think he hasn't yet found a young and pretty girl to play with. It would be very foolish not to go there soon to let him rediscover the thrill of taking me to bed.

The woman, whoever she was, had been mortified to be found in the condition she was – the signs were clear to see on her body that Robert had just spurted between her huge heavy breasts. It was important, Odette told herself, to phone Robert and let him invite her to dinner – and then give him whatever he wanted all night afterwards. But when that would be she couldn't say. With Giselle and Daniel to satisfy – to say nothing of Laurent – her time was fully occupied. Robert would simply have to wait until there was a suitable gap in her social arrangements.

Whenever Daniel took her out he always joked about Giselle.

'Madame Barras is very attractive for a woman of forty,' he said with a grin. 'If she liked men in bed I would have become her lover. It would be partly for the pleasure of undressing her – she has an excellent body still – and naturally I would be keen to watch that haughty expression crack when I got on her belly and drove her to orgasm – what a delight that must be!'

'You will never know,' said Odette, grinning back at him.

'And also to make sure I never lose the Marigny contract,' he said, his hand stroking her knee under the table, 'but as things have worked out, you have the honour of causing her superiority to dissolve in shrieks of ecstasy and shudders and I share with her the delight of doing it to you, Odette *chérie*. I hope that my contract with Marigny is safe.'

'But of course,' said Odette with a charming smile, thinking it best not to tell him of Giselle's misgivings about him, 'you are held in high regard there.'

'As long as business is good,' he said, 'but if Marigny has a bad season because his designs fail to please the clients, then all will be blamed on the publicity and another company will be installed in place of mine. That's the way of it, *chérie*.'

Odette looked at him and shrugged. He was wearing a dark blue suit that evening and a lighter blue silk tie. He appeared very successful, self-assured, well-fed to the point of the little potbelly disguised by the cut of the suit.

'What makes you think you could ever have been Madame Barras' lover?' she asked. 'As you say, she is an attractive woman for her age. And because of her position, she is a powerful woman. If she wanted a man to make love to her she would surely choose a 25-year-old with film-star looks and a firm muscular body and endless stamina – and long dark eyelashes.'

'She would choose me,' said Daniel.

'But why?'

'Because I am charming.'

'*Oh la la*! The conceit of men!'

Daniel lived in some style in the Avenue Bosquet, between the Eiffel Tower and Les Invalides. It was a large apartment and it was furnished expensively and in good taste, but the first time he took Odette there she recognised at once it was not really a place for living in. It was where he gave parties for important people and clients and clients-to-be. The rooms had an ambience of being well-used for near-orgies, though there was no visible sign of it. The sitting-room had several large sofas and lights that could be turned down low on a switch and a large radiogram to provide appropriate music for men's hands to slip up skirts, after the dancing.

Each of the four bedrooms had a low double bed with beautiful lace-edged pillows and a silver champagne-cooler on the bedside table by a pink-shaded lamp and a crystal box of cigarettes. It was only a question of time, Odette guessed when she saw how he lived, before he would invite her to a party there and suggest she be particularly amiable to someone he wished to impress.

Not that she had the slightest intention of being available – Daniel didn't own her. But naturally, if she was asked to make herself amiable to one of his clients or contacts, she wouldn't refuse outright – it would depend on the possible usefulness to her of the person concerned how agreeable she was.

That was in the future. For the present Daniel was content to keep her to himself. Or to be exact, to share her with Giselle. And with Laurent, though he could never be sure whether she was Laurent's girlfriend or not. If Daniel asked, she denied it, as also did Laurent. She was a model, she declared, it was purely a business arrangement, she posed for him. And Laurent said the same. Daniel was in two minds – he half-believed her but he was inclined to be sceptical whether a man could remain for long on professional terms with a pretty young woman who stood about in silk underwear several hours a day for him to look at.

The question of parties came up one evening after he took her to dinner at La Coupole in Montparnasse. They ate and drank and sat watching the to-and-fro of the people intent on impressing each other. They talked and laughed at each other's witty remarks and held hands and Daniel touched her under the table from time to time, but he lacked his usual *joie-de-vivre* and appeared tired. Towards midnight a surly and unshaven taxi-driver conveyed them to the Avenue Bosquet. Ascending two floors in the lift Odette held on tight to Daniel's arm and balanced on one leg while she took off her left shoe and rubbed the heel.

Automatically he took advantage of her precarious position to reach under her skirt and clasp her *joujou* in his hand. *New shoes?* he asked sympathetically, fingers warm through the thin silk of her knickers. She nodded and slipped the shoe back on and stood upright. Daniel smiled and continued to stroke between her legs until the creeping lift reached his floor.

She dropped her chic new autumn coat on a side-table standing by the wall in the entrance hall of the apartment and followed him to the bedroom he slept in. To her it was indistinguishable from the other bedrooms in the apartment, except for a new copy of *Vogue* on the bedside table.

'What a day I've had,' said Daniel, flinging his jacket at a chair and missing. 'Three client meetings, an argument with the accountant, a crisis among the personnel in the office and two of them giving notice in sympathy with one who had been sacked. I'm exhausted by it all – if only I could leave it for a month or six weeks and go on vacation to somewhere the sun shines and the ocean is blue.'

'Poor Daniel,' said Odette dutifully, 'you work too hard.'

He grumbled away while he was stripping off his clothes as if she were not there in the room with him and he was going to bed only to sleep. Odette slipped out of her little black frock and stood carelessly posing as if he were not there to see her – in black satin underwear and black silk stockings. There was a big mirror she admired herself in, turning this way and that to see herself from all angles. Daniel's interest revived to

Marie-Claire Villefranche

the point of flinging himself naked on the bed and propping himself up on the pillows.

'Ah, you are adorable, Odette,' he said, although not with as much enthusiasm as she would have liked. 'Come here and make me forget what a terrible day it has been.'

She smiled encouragingly at him and took off her black bra to show her perfect little breasts. She cupped them with her hands and pretended to study them in the mirror – letting Daniel stew for a while before she went to him.

'Your *nichons* are marvellous,' he said. 'Come here and let me feel them.'

She smiled at him in the mirror and put her hand down between her slender thighs and stroked her *joujou* a little to tease him before she turned to face him. His body was smooth and pink all over, his chest absolutely hairless, his belly chubby from good living and famous restaurants. His thighs were apart and he was holding his male part in his hand – it was limp and small. *Poor little thing* she murmured as she climbed onto the bed and knelt between his parted legs. If it pleased him to play the role of the exhausted tycoon, she knew how to humour him in this game.

He sat with his back against the piled pillows, his male part hung forlorn between his plump thighs. She took it in her hand and squeezed it. He reached out to hold her breasts and stroke them and joggle them up and down. It did not take long for his flesh to stiffen in her fingers.

'Ah, you like that, don't you, Daniel?' she said, seeing his eyes grow dreamy. He nodded and sighed, content to leave it all in her hands. When he was at full stretch she let go while she removed her little black knickers. His eyes went at once to her neat heart-design and he smiled blissfully.

'*Je t'adore*, Odette,' he murmured, 'let me kiss you.'

He didn't mean her mouth, she knelt upright astride his legs, bringing belly on a level with his face – his lips brushed over her *little heart*.

'Poor Daniel,' she said, 'fatigued by a bad day in the office – what is to be done with him?'

She sank down to squat over his joined thighs and clasped his stiff part in her hand. 'I know what to do for him,' she said in a teasing voice as she held the pink-purple head against the long lips between her open thighs. Daniel stared into her green eyes with pleasure as her hand slid up and down firmly.

'*Voilà* Daniel!' she said, easing the unhooded head into her warm softness, 'there you have what you want – you are doing it to me *mon cher* without moving even one tired muscle. Or perhaps I am doing it to you – what do you think?'

'I think you are adorable,' he murmured and he slid his hands round her to sink his fingers into the flesh of her bare bottom and hold her fast. In the event, his body was not as exhausted as his mind – the sensations of pleasure wiped out his power of thought, he moaned and his body shook. '*Alors*!' said Odette with a sly smile. His hard part strained up through her clasped hand, he cried out and spurted wildly between the lips of her *joujou*.

After that exertion she thought he would want to lie down and go to sleep, but the sudden release of tension had the opposite effect. His normal avid appetite for life and love returned and he sent Odette to the kitchen to get a bottle of champagne from the refrigerator. This so-called kitchen had almost never seen any culinary activity during Daniel's tenancy apart from making coffee. It was more of a depot for his parties to entertain and involve those who could be of use to him, there were wine-racks filled with bottles, there were crates of cognac, champagne and imported spirits such as Scotch whisky and American bourbon.

He was lying comfortably propped on the pillows when she came back with the Veuve Cliquot and glasses. She stood naked by the bed holding a glass in each hand while Daniel opened the bottle and poured. 'To you, *chérie*,' he said, 'and your great future.'

'I have a great future, have I?' said Odette. 'Tell me about it if you know so much.'

'How do *you* see your future?' he countered.

'Perhaps with Jean-Luc Marigny,' she said, though she didn't really believe it herself. 'Madame Barras adores me and will do everything she can to keep me there at her side. There will be promotions, more money, more responsibility – and one day when she is ready to hand over to me, her job at the top.'

'Perhaps,' Daniel agreed with a shrug, 'but she's had several young and pretty friends like you in the three years I've been associated with Marigny. She adored every one of them. What can I say, *chérie*, the traffic through her bed is brisk. Not as helterskelter as the Place de la Concorde in the rush hour, but busy enough for there to be unexpected accidents and collisions and tears of disappointment.'

Odette put an expression of indifference on her face, she sat on the side of the bed and sipped her champagne.

'There was a Kiki before me, I believe,' she said as casually as she could, determined not to let Daniel think her naive.

'Ah yes,' he said appreciatively, 'Kiki with long blonde hair that descends straight and shining like a waterfall to the tips of her pretty little breasts. She is so Nordic in appearance – an Ice Maiden in manner. But when she is naked she turns into a tiger. Madame Barras was infatuated with her, she wanted to see where she was every minute of the day, she never let her out of her sight. And as for the nights, that one can only imagine and sigh over. Yet it is difficult to visualise so haughty a person as Giselle Barras in a frenzy of passion.'

'It sounds to me as if you had some experience of Kiki in bed yourself,' said Odette, opening her legs gracefully to give him a better view. No woman likes to hear another being praised by a man she has just obliged.

'It is true,' he confessed with a grin, 'but only twice, I am sorry to say. As charming as I am, it was not easy to persuade Kiki to give her jailer the slip and meet me for an hour or two – heaven alone knows what excuse she made for her absence when she returned to Madame's bed.'

Easy to see why Giselle doesn't trust Daniel, Odette thought, she suspects him of seducing her girlfriend away from her, even if the girlfriend left her for someone else. Or did she?

'What happened?' she asked Daniel. 'Did Giselle find out?'

'No, she never had the least suspicion of me,' he said with a confidence based on total ignorance of the facts. 'Kiki fell in love with a man called Jules Chasset, a writer of crime novels. And the same age as Kiki, twenty-two or twenty-three. It was instant attraction – she left Madame Barras' apartment and went to live with Chasset somewhere in Montparnasse. For weeks afterward our dear Giselle was like a scalded cat.'

'But Kiki still works as a model for Marigny,' Odette pointed out, 'I saw her at the show.'

'Jean-Luc likes her style,' said Daniel. 'He's not interested in women for the usual reason, of course, but admires a certain type of figure to show off his creations.'

'He beats her, this writer, and takes all the money she earns and while she is out working to keep him he goes with any woman who will take her clothes off for him,' said Odette earnestly.

Daniel laughed and said that must be Madame Barras' version – a story made up to soothe her own wounded pride that anyone she desired would dare to open her legs for a man.

'What would she say about you, I wonder, if she found out you were here in bed with me,' he asked, 'that you had gone insane and run off with a flea-bitten gipsy in a horse-drawn caravan? Some sort of face-saving story like that.'

Daniel had somewhat recovered from the annoyances of the day. He put his hand on Odette's thigh and stroked it – she put down her glass on the table and turned to lie facing him, arms about his neck loosely, waiting to see what he would do next. It was not probable, she considered, he would roll her on her back and get on top – he lacked the energy for that after his busy day.

But tired as he was, he couldn't leave her alone. His fingers roamed up between her legs to her *joujou* and opened it and slid inside to feel her moist warmth.

'Ah, the pleasure I am missing!' he murmured. 'I am frantic to have you, *chérie*, but I know I can't do it again tonight.'

Her long-fingered little hand gripped his drooping male part and massaged it lightly.

'Shall I say my prayers for you, Daniel?' she asked to tempt him with one of his favourite ways of pleasuring

BONJOUR AMOUR

himself on her while she knelt at the bedside and he took her from the rear.

'If I could, I would,' he sighed, 'but alas!'

'Then it must be like this again,' she announced and her hand glided up and down.

'Yes,' he agreed, 'just so, *chérie*.'

She excited him with nervous little strokes, knowing it would take some time to achieve what he wanted.

'Tell me how it is in bed with Giselle,' he said lazily. 'Does she hold you down and push your legs open and press her fingers into you? Do you find it exciting when she touches you?'

'The moment we arrive at her apartment she rushes me into her bedroom,' said Odette, with a complete disregard for the truth. 'She pulls my frock off and drags my knickers down my legs, she throws me on the bed on my back – she ravishes me, there can be no other word for it!'

In reality, Giselle concealed a certain diffidence in sexual encounters behind her haughty manner. She adored to see Odette naked, but it did not stir her to frenzies of passion, or if it did, she gave little sign of her emotions. She took the passive role in love-making – she was the one who lay upon her back and opened her legs to be caressed and kissed. By playing the more vigorous role Odette insinuated herself into Giselle's favour.

But this was not what Daniel wished to hear – it would surely spoil his hot little fantasy. In his mind Odette was a woman he undressed and stroked all over while she lay on her back on his bed – she was his to ravage to his delight and satisfaction. He pictured her similarly with Giselle, Odette lying naked beneath the other woman and being used for her pleasure. So Odette spun him a tale of how she was ravished time after time through long sultry nights by an insatiable Giselle.

Meanwhile her clasped hand slid up and down in medium tempo.

'What you say is amazing,' he sighed. 'I had no idea that she was so fiery in bed. How many times does she do it to you in a night – five, six? More?'

'More,' said Odette, 'many more – you have no idea how often; a man cannot understand how it is when two women make love. She exhausts me with caresses, she drives me to orgasm after orgasm until I lose consciousness and lie totally defeated before her. Even then I do not think she stops kissing and touching me . . . I think she keeps on doing it to my poor senseless body until she collapses exhausted herself.'

'*Bon Dieu*!' Daniel sighed, his stiff part throbbed furiously in Odette's massaging hand. '*C'est formidable*! When she throws you on the bed, does she kiss your charming little *nichons*?'

'She kisses them and licks them, as you do,' Odette told him, guessing what he wanted to hear. 'She sucks them until I am mad with desire and I plead with her to finish me off.'

'And then?' he gasped.

'She looks down at me with the haughty expression on her face and she ignores my plea – she can be cruel, cruel!'

'What I'd give to be treated like that by her just once!' he exclaimed, trembling from head to foot. 'To lie naked under her hand and at her mercy . . .'

'You would never survive it,' Odette said. 'A night in her bed is a night of being ravished to the very point of madness.'

Daniel began to babble and shake, she clenched her hand

BONJOUR AMOUR

round his fifteen centimetres firmly and jerked up and down fast. His body began to contract, his thick part straining up towards his chin, the contractions of his belly longer and harder each time. *Ahhh* he moaned, every muscle taut in an explosive climax of delight, spurting up into the air. That will keep him happy for tonight, Odette decided.

When he was tranquil again and ready to drift off to sleep he mentioned – sounding very casual about it – that he had invited a few good friends to dinner on Saturday evening and for drinks and conversation at his apartment afterwards. How very pleasant if Odette would be one of his guests on this occasion.

'Yes,' she said, keeping her voice as casual as his, 'I would like that, Daniel.'

'Good, it is arranged. You will enjoy the evening, I promise. There is someone I want you to meet – a charming man, extremely important. You'll like him.'

Odette Meets A Prude

There were six in Daniel's party on Saturday evening, three men and three women. Both male guests, it went without saying, were business contacts of Daniel's and Odette guessed the women were one-time girlfriends of his, pressed into service to entertain his important friends. Or could they be current part-time girlfriends, as she was herself? It was very possible; Daniel had a wide circle of acquaintances and he would never deny himself any of life's pleasures.

He took them to the Lido on the Champs Elysees for dinner and the show. He had reserved a table near the stage, naturally, to make sure his guests had a good view of the bare-breasted girls in feathers and spangles. The meal was not a gourmet's delight, that was not to be expected in these circumstances – but it was eatable and there was an endless supply of champagne to help it go down.

The important friend Daniel wanted Odette to meet was tallish and forty-something, his hair was an indeterminate shade of brown, his manner was polite and unassertive, his expression pleasant, but empty. In effect he made little impression at all. His name was Pierre Dubon, his significance to Daniel was that he owned, more or less, a large insurance business and believed he should spend extravagantly on publicity.

He was married, of course, and had three children – the facts were conveyed to Odette in advance by Daniel. He lived a quiet life, this Monsieur Dubon, he went to Mass on Sundays and was a benefactor of charitable causes. At some moment in the past a grateful administration had awarded him the Grand-Croix of the Legion d'Honour in recognition of – but who could say what services businessmen like him gave to political parties? Dubon was, in brief, a worthy but dull citizen.

As it happened, he liked the occasional night out with Daniel and his less civic-minded friends. Nothing scandalous – nothing too *outrée* – but a little outing to places he would never go to otherwise, an evening's entertainment of a more adult type than the normal scope of his life took in. Staid he might be, a very serious man, this Monsieur, but a man nonetheless with all that implied.

The Bluebells were the principal attraction of the Lido show, a stageful of beautiful young women with their hair piled up on top of their heads and adorned with imitation diamond coronets. Their breasts were modestly contained in pearl-studded bras and their pretty little belly-buttons left uncovered and delectable. There were more pearls and satin about their slim loins – not too much. But ah, their legs! The famous Bluebell long legs in black fishnet tights – the legs that kicked up nose-high in the unison of their dance.

Those sleek thighs! As each soared in the high-kick, such a glimpse was given of the thin strip of shiny satin between them – the strip that concealed so precariously a prize the men in the audience would give much to see. And to touch!

'Ah, yes, yes...' Pierre breathed. He had been seated next to Odette. 'They are daughters of English dukes and knights, these Bluebell young ladies, I read that in an illustrated magazine I bought to pass the time on a train journey. They are chosen not for beauty alone, though that is of supreme importance, but for their grace and their charm. They marry aristocrats after a few years on the stage, every one of them.'

'But of course,' said Odette, not wishing to disillusion him.

She was surprised to feel Pierre's hand brush over her knee. It was what men always did, of course, touch a girl under cover of a table, but she hadn't considered Pierre Dubon the type, he seemed too restrained. But then he apologised and she wondered if she'd misjudged him – perhaps he'd touched her by accident.

Don't be an idiot, she told herself with a mental grin, when a man touches a girl's thigh it's never an accident, he's making a statement. And what this strange bird is saying to me is that he'd like to get his hand up my skirt, if he dared. So there's nothing different about him.

Up on the stage twelve pairs of elegant Bluebell thighs moved and flashed to the music in perfect harmony. Down at the tables men stared in admiration and speculated how they could make the acquaintance of any one of the dancers.

'Every one of them a virgin,' said Daniel mischievously as he leaned across to tap Pierre on the arm. 'Think of it, all those lovely smooth young bodies stripped down to fishnet stockings – waiting for you in the rooms of a small hotel! Which would you go to first, *mon brave*?'

Pierre blushed, as if he was thinking something discreditable and Daniel had read his mind. Daniel laughed and patted him on the arm again. Between the two men sat a tall redhead with skin so creamy-white it looked almost unnatural – when Daniel leaned across her to make his remark, his shoulder brushed against her breasts. They were worth brushing against, full and prominent – and left very largely on display by the scooped neckline of her frock.

The redhead's name was Annette. She had known Daniel for some time, that was evident, and she was there specifically for him that evening. Odette had been assigned to Pierre, and the third woman, an indolent-looking beauty of nearly thirty in a black satin sheath and pearls that might just be genuine, had been attached by Daniel to the other man, a plump businessman of some sort or other from Dieppe.

Odette had decided on cerise for the occasion, it suited her green eyes. Cerise was an interesting colour, she decided when she first saw the frock in a shop-window, so clear and bright – eye-catching and suggestive, without appearing too obvious. But to make it more interesting, the close-fitting bodice was split down the front to the waist. But modestly. It revealed a narrow strip of satin-smooth skin, while completely hiding her perfect little breasts – and made it impossible to ignore them.

After the Bluebells there were other entertainers, comedians, singers, acrobats. Odette thought the comedians were not funny, but she had been told so often she had no sense of humour that she half-accepted it was her own failing if the jokes seemed to her idiotic. The acrobats threw various things up in the air at the same time and caught them coming down and threw them again. They balanced on metal ladders and one-wheel bicycles and threw and caught.

It was clever, of course, but excessively boring. If one were to drop the eight or nine hoops and daggers he was juggling and fall off his bicycle, that would be amusing. But they never did. A pretty singer warbled that she loved the man she loved. And a young man sang that the Seine flows forever through Paris – it was all pleasant enough to half-listen to.

There was a question in Odette's mind. Daniel expected her to be agreeable to this boring client of his, Pierre Dubon. So she did her best, she chatted to him, she smiled at him and flirted a little with him. It was slow going, but presented no problem. But later on, after they returned to Daniel's apartment – after a few more bottles of champagne, what then? Did Daniel really expect her to let this half-hearted man make love to her? Did Pierre himself expect her to get into bed with him?

If Daniel did expect it, if Pierre expected it too, then what was she to do? Five minutes of tedium on her back while Pierre sighed and moaned – that's all it would amount to, she thought, seeing the dull sort of man he was. Though no doubt there'd be ten minutes of groping her *nichons* before that, to work himself up to a proper condition of stiffness to be able to push it in. If she went through with it, which was by no means decided yet, it would be as a favour to Daniel in anticipation of favours to come from him. If only Pierre was a more interesting person, that would make the decision so much easier!

To end the show, lines of Bluebells danced onto the stage once more. They had changed their costumes, they had plumes of white ostrich feathers on their heads, glittering diamond necklaces – well, glass diamonds. Breasts and loins were delicately clad in lacy little garments studded with more glistening stones, slim arms were in white glacé gloves to above the elbow.

'Ah, see that,' Odette whispered to Pierre, indicating Daniel with a little inclination of her head. Both were staring at the stage in rapt attention, and Daniel's hand was up the redhead's skirt. Not just a little way up it, to stroke her knee or thigh – his arm was in to the elbow and her skirt had ridden up over her knees. His fingers were obviously in the redhead's knickers – if she had any on, Odette thought.

'Oh . . .' Pierre murmured faintly. He gripped Odette's leg just above the knee, through the cerise satin of her frock, as if he needed support. She decided she would tease him a little to see now he reacted.

'Annette never wears knickers,' she said, her mouth close to Pierre's ear so that he felt her warm breath, 'she adores to be touched by men.'

'Oh . . .' Pierre breathed again, as if the power of speech had deserted him. Odette became curious about him, she wondered if the spectacle of Daniel secretly stroking the redhead's *joujou* had any effect on this unemotional man. She dropped her hand on Pierre's lap lightly, intending to snatch it away instantly and make believe she had touched him by accident, as he had touched her knee earlier.

But now it was her turn to murmur *Oh* in surprise. There was a bulge in his black trousers of impressive length and thickness, he was not only aroused – he was rampant! Odette's hand stayed in his lap, her fingers slowly exploring the proportions of her discovery. Her sense of touch alone suggested there was a sight well worth seeing down between Pierre's thighs. He was blushing furiously – she could see the dark colour on his cheek and neck even with the house-lights dimmed while the Bluebell girls were prancing their sexy routine on stage.

Despite his evident embarrassment Pierre did something which made Odette think he was not quite the dull and torpid businessman he seemed – he dropped his discarded table napkin over his lap. Very casual the movement was – but it totally obscured what she was doing to him. She took a chance, she pulled his zipper down and slipped her hand in under his shirt – and there was a thick strong shaft of flesh that throbbed in her clasping hand.

Well, well, she thought in amazement, but who would ever have thought it! She could imagine lying on her back with her legs spread for that solid thickness to force its way deep into her. The feeling would be intense, it would stretch her wider than she had experienced with any man before – even Robert Dorville, and he was extremely well endowed.

She stroked it up and down a little, her fingertips gripping firm warm flesh. What a waste, she thought, a dry old bird like him to have a thing like this! She knew men in their twenties who would give ten years of their life to have one as strong and thick as this. Pierre sighed again, and he was not the only one – the redhead sitting on his other side was sighing to Daniel's eager touch between her thighs.

A last resounding chord from the band, and the charming Bluebell legs performed a culminating kick, the thighs of ivory gleaming beneath the stage-lights. The daughters of English dukes posed, arms stretched above their heads, smiles on their pretty faces. There was prolonged applause from the audience. Odette withdrew her hand from Pierre's trousers and zipped him up, leaving the napkin in position. He was too shy to meet her eyes, he looked fixedly at the stage and clapped the dancers taking a bow.

Before midnight they were in Daniel's apartment, dance

music on the radiogram and the lights turned low. Georgette, the indolent beauty in black satin and cultured pearls, was dancing cheek to cheek on the parquet of the sitting-room with the plump businessman from Dieppe. An unusual version of cheek to cheek this, she was some centimetres taller than him and she rested her cheek on his bald forehead – and his hand cupped the soft round cheeks of her bottom through her evening frock.

Daniel and the redhead Annette stood close together at one of the long windows, his arm round her waist. Because their backs were to the room it was not possible to see where his other arm was, but to Odette it was obvious his hand was plunged into the deep décolletage of her frock.

Pierre said he didn't dance when Odette suggested it. She sat with him on one of the many long sofas in the room, each with a glass of Daniel's champagne. Odette was still undecided, he had a formidable possession in his trousers, that was true, but she doubted if he knew how to use it to good advantage. And having three children proved nothing at all – except he'd made love to his wife three times in twenty years. Perhaps thirty seconds each time.

Pierre sipped at his champagne and looked away from Odette as he started to talk at last. He spoke apologetically. He said he knew women didn't find him interesting – it had always been so, he never knew what to do about it. Casual conversation was past him, he could never think of anything a woman wanted to hear.

He said clumsily he found Odette beautiful and attractive, he completely understood why she was a top model at Jean-Luc Marigny and in great demand for international fashion shows. He wished he was in the fashion business, not dreary old insurance – then he would be able to engage her services as a model for his shows. Odette looked thoughtfully at his expensive but ugly black suit and compared him to the elegant Jean-Luc Marigny fluttering his silk hankie and his eyelashes.

'I believe you would,' she said, smiling at the comparison.

'Let me fill your glass,' Pierre said, getting up hurriedly. He had embarrassed himself by being so open with her about his emotions. He came back with an open bottle of champagne and for a while fiddled about filling her glass and his own.

When he was composed enough at last to continue, he said that his dearest wish was to become her friend – a staunch friend to trust and rely on – though he knew it was impossible. Beautiful and charming young women like her moved in a different world to dull, everyday people like him. Odette said she was flattered by his kindness, she touched his hand, she leaned closer to him so that her expensive perfume would reach him.

While he was babbling incoherently she glanced around and saw the plump, little businessman from Dieppe had danced tall, svelte Georgette right out of the sitting-room, leaving her high heels discarded on the floor. No doubt he had danced her right into a bedroom and stripped off her black satin and was continuing the dance in a horizontal position on a bed. Daniel and the redhead were twined together in an armchair, she was sitting on his lap with her skirt well up her thighs and his hand in between them. And indeed, her hand was plunged down behind his belt.

Even as Odette watched, paying hardly any attention to Pierre and his half-hearted muttering, Daniel heaved the redhead on to her feet and stood up. She was gazing ardently into his face so far as Odette could make out in the dim lighting. He laughed as he slipped an arm round her waist to lead her to his bedroom, a very prominent bulge in the front of his trousers. The redhead was whispering into his ear. He winked at Odette as they passed her, a wink cynical and sly and friendly all at the same time.

The moment of decision had arrived. With the special type of logic women use for their dealings with men, Odette transferred the burden of choice on to Pierre.

'We are the last,' she said, her green eyes fixed on his in a thoughtful stare, 'we are alone. What will you do, Pierre, find a taxi to take me home – or ask me to stay with you tonight?'

'Oh, please don't go yet,' he said, not able to ask her to go to bed with him – a suggestion much too frank for his inhibited personality, 'it's not late. Another glass of champagne?'

Odette ignored the suggestion.

'Say what you mean,' she said, 'commit yourself – it's only a question of a few words. You want to undress me, is that it?'

Pierre's cheeks were pink as he nodded.

'At last!' she said. 'Where will you strip me naked, Pierre, here or in a bedroom?'

'Not here!' he said urgently. 'Someone might come in and see us – it would be a catastrophe!'

Odette smiled and stood up, holding a hand out to him.

'Then we will look for an unoccupied bedroom.'

'But suppose we burst in on someone . . .' he objected, his face pink again at the mere thought of interrupting either Daniel or the plump Dieppe businessman bouncing about on a naked woman.

'Come along,' said Odette, trying not to giggle as she hauled him to his feet and led him out of the sitting-room. She saw no necessity to tell Pierre she knew which bedroom

Daniel used for himself. She pressed her ear to the next door along the passage and thought she could hear the creak of bedsprings. At the next door she paused to smile at Pierre, who had an anxious look on his face. She turned the knob and pushed the door open – inside all was dark and still.

'Here we are,' she announced, switching on the light, 'come in and close the door. Now you can take off my clothes.'

'We can't leave the lights on all night in the sitting-room,' he said, 'and out in the passage. And I suppose Daniel left the light on in the kitchen – I'll go back and turn them all off.'

'If you do I won't be here when you get back,' said Odette as she slipped his jacket off his shoulders and let it fall to the floor. He would have bent down to pick it up – perhaps even looked for a hanger to put it on – but she prevented him with a sharp kick of her high-heel shoe to the shin.

'What are you doing!' he exclaimed, a look of acute agony on his face.

'Listen to me,' she said, undoing his tie, thick silk but of a design that was painfully dull, 'at this moment I am the most important consideration in your life – stop fussing over things that don't matter and concentrate on me. Do you understand? If I offer you the rare pleasure of seeing me naked the least that you can do is have the courtesy of showing some interest.'

'A thousand pardons,' he said, 'it was extremely rude of me.'

'Take my shoes off,' said Odette, giving him a radiant smile. He looked surprised, as if he'd never thought of taking off a woman's shoes before. He bent down to try to reach her foot and found he couldn't – after a moment or two's thought he lowered himself carefully to one knee and she set her foot on the other knee, as if on a foot-stool. The position raised the hem of her cerise evening frock – he had an excellent view of her thighs.

That ought to get him going, Odette said to herself. *He's been trying to see in the slit in my frock all evening to get a look at my nichons.*

He made a dramatic performance of removing her shoe, one hand behind the heel, on her stocking, the other beneath the instep. From Odette's point of view he was a deliciously comic sight, a dull red glow on his mild round face, a business tycoon in dark blue braces, down on his knees looking up her skirt!

He took her shoe off, she changed legs and put the other foot on his out-thrust knee for his attention, making sure her skirt rode well up to give him a good look. He had developed a glazed look in his neutral-brown eyes – instead of taking off her shoe he clasped her ankle lightly and stared as if mesmerised at her exposed thigh. No point trying to hurry him, Odette thought, he will get there by himself eventually.

She was right about that. After a time he began to stroke her raised leg slowly, from her slender ankle up to the back of her knee – and while he was doing so he stared up at her face as if begging permission to touch her.

'You like the feel of my stocking, Pierre?' she asked. 'They are nylon, not pure silk, but I don't suppose that you can tell the difference. And does it matter – when it is not my stocking you really want to stroke, but my thigh. Am I right?'

'Odette . . .' he whispered, seemingly dumbstruck by her words.

'You want to touch me above my stocking, yes?' she said with an encouraging smile. 'You enjoy stroking women's thighs? And why not? Slide your hand up to my ... well, slide it up and you can decide how far.'

From behind her knee his fingers moved cautiously beneath her cerise frock, gliding very lightly over the sleek nylon till he touched her bare flesh between her stocking and her little lace knickers. The expression on his face was indescribable. He gave a stifled moan as if tormented beyond all endurance and put his head under her skirt to press his wet lips to the inside of her thigh. At last, she thought, balancing on one leg, hands on his shoulders to steady herself.

He kissed the insides of her thighs twenty times at least, he kissed her knickers where they covered her *joujou*. She expected him to pull them down to kiss her bare – she felt sure he would be awestruck when he saw her *little heart*. She was certain he'd never seen one like it in his life – it would arouse him to the point of slavering insanity!

But he went on kissing her, he put both hands under her skirt and stroked her thighs and bottom, she could feel the warmth of his breath on her skin through her knickers. It was pleasurable – she began to consider what it would be like to feel that long thick thing of his sliding into her. And then he surprised her by pleading with her to let him wear her stockings.

'My stockings?' she said, eyebrows rising – she'd never been with a man who wanted to do that. Their normal interest was to get her stockings off, along with the rest of her underwear.

'Why not?' she said with a little shrug.

She was wondering whether this signified Pierre was a type of secret pervert, the wish to wear the stockings of a woman whose body was his to enjoy. If so, this might lead to an interesting situation – could he be made dependent on bizarre pleasures, as Laurent had become besotted about trimming her *little heart*?

'Take them off,' she murmured, stroking his mouse-brown hair.

She put both unshod feet firmly on the floor while his hands were trembling under her frock and fumbling with her suspenders – down came her stockings, he kissed her thighs again and eased the fragile nylons over her feet. How very useful it might turn out to be, Odette thought, seeing his evident excitement, if he became as addicted to pleasure with her as Laurent had – and as darling Giselle had. Pierre had so much more to offer.

To her surprise he stripped absolutely naked – a certain sign of the intensity of his excitement – and sat on the side of the bed for Odette to help him on with her stockings. They made her long slender legs look irresistible, of course, but on his there was not the same effect. His legs were thicker, his thighs were chubbier, but she smoothed them into place with her palms, from ankle to thigh. His waist was too large for her suspender-belt to go around, but so long as he remained on the bed and didn't stroll up and down the room the stockings would stay up.

She was hardly able, while she helped him with the stockings, to take her eyes off the stiff part standing up so boldly from the join of his thighs – it was formidable in its thickness and length. Her impression from feeling it at the Lido had prepared her for something out of the ordinary, but this was better than she had expected. She wanted to take it in her hand to feel its weight and strength – but she thought it better not to risk interrupting whatever bizarre fantasy was playing itself out in Pierre's head.

He stared down at his legs with dreaming eyes, he slid along the bed until he could see himself reflected in the big mirror. He stretched his legs out horizontally in front of him – Odette thought he looked faintly absurd, but evidently he enjoyed what he saw.

'*Très chic*,' he murmured, '*oui, chérie*?'

'Oh yes,' Odette agreed. It had suddenly occurred to her that the basis of his fantasy was the entertainment at the Lido, the beautiful Bluebell girls kicking up their long dancers' legs as high as their noses.

'Long strong thighs,' she said softly, stroking them for him.

'In sheer stockings,' he murmured, as if mesmerised.

'What a pity my knickers are too small for you,' Odette said, trying to ascertain how far she could extend his dreaming, 'but your hips are much wider than mine.'

'Wear your knickers?' Pierre gasped, his eyes bulging.

'Direct from my body to you,' she suggested, 'still warm from me – what do you think of that?'

While she was speaking she stroked his round belly, down from his deeply recessed belly-button to his nylon stockinged thighs – she sat beside him on the bed and pushed his knees well apart to trail her fingers in his hot groins.

'Wear your knickers as well as your stockings,' he mumbled in a shaky voice, 'I'd never dare . . .'

Odette realised he never would dare – not without coaxing and teasing for weeks to give him confidence in her and in himself. But the thought aroused him – it was worth continuing.

'You would have to caress me before I took them off, Pierre,' she said, 'to make me excited . . . very excited . . . so when you put them on you'd feel the warmth of my body against you . . . between the legs . . .'

She was delighted by his response – his upright part throbbed in her hand and he was moaning under his breath. She envisaged the possibilities of becoming his very special girlfriend – the one who helped him do things he'd never even heard about before in his boring life. The special friend who was richly rewarded.

'Yes, you'd like that, *chéri*,' she said, 'imagine us together – you in my knickers and stockings, me naked for you to touch.'

Pierre moaned and slipped off the bed, he turned on his knees to face her – his eager hands right up her cerise evening frock to grasp her little knickers and pull them down swiftly. He had them round her ankles and she opened her knees to let him catch his first glimpse of the perfect *little heart* between her legs.

'Oh!' he gasped, as if she had punched him in the belly. 'Oh!'

While he stared dumbfounded at the delight he'd uncovered she prised her knickers off one foot with the toes of the other and spread her legs. She folded her hands under her head and waited for Pierre to recover from his shock – it took him some moments before she felt his shaking hands on the insides of her thighs. His touch was tentative as he parted the lips of her *joujou* to reveal the pink bud inside.

'You are so very beautiful,' he said in a whisper.

'I know,' she said with a grin. 'I'm not just for looking at, you can do all sorts of marvellous things to me, you know.'

He sighed and slithered forward over her – creasing her frock up round her middle. But the position was not to his liking and he stood up to slip his hands under her armpits and

BONJOUR AMOUR

drag her up on the bed fully. The movement had pulled her skirt down and it covered her *little heart* – she hoisted it up with her own hands for him and he got a knee on the bed and an moment later he lay heavily on her again.

She held her breath when she felt the head of his thick solid part press against her *joujou* – she breathed out in a long sigh when she felt it pushing deep into her. So thick, so long – the sensation was of being filled full, of being stretched right to the limit. It was almost frightening, it was hugely arousing.

If Daniel or any of his guests had come into the bedroom they would have encountered a most comical sight – plump middle-aged Pierre stark naked, wearing flesh-tinted nylon stockings, lying on a slender young woman with her frock rucked up to her waist, his chubby bottom heaving up and down as he drove into her with accompanying moans. No one came into the bedroom, of course, he thumped away and moaned to his heart's content.

Odette had ceased to be an observer, a manipulator: the push of Pierre's stiffness had aroused her intensely – now she was a willing participant. Her emotions astonished her – it was as if she was being possessed for the first time, her body used for a man's selfish pleasure. She thought wildly that this was how it was when Jacques Brolin did it to her, when they were teenagers together in dreary streets by the railway yard, those days when Jacques could make her scream out aloud in ecstasy.

It was ludicrous to compare well-fed, soft-spoken Pierre Dubon with thin, sly Jacques Brolin of the cheap charm and unpleasing manners – utterly absurd! But the thought was in her mind and her body was responding in ways most unexpected. Her breath was coming in short gasps – it was impossible not to understand she was fast approaching an unforeseen orgasm.

'*Ah bon Dieu*,' she sighed, 'don't stop, *chéri* . . .'

The onset of her orgasm threw her into wild spasms of jerking belly and thrashing legs – she shrieked and arched her back and drummed her heels in a long noisy climax. The effect on Pierre was instant and dramatic, perhaps no woman had ever in his life responded so wildly to his attentions.

'Odette!' he gasped, his body flopped up and down rapidly on her, his long thick part ramming into her hot slipperiness. He shrieked – almost as shrilly as she had – and he spurted in her belly.

Not bad, Odette thought, but I'm sure my frock is so creased that it's ruined – but he can buy me another one. In fact, dear Pierre, though you do not know it, you have just become my loving *patron*, the man with the cheque-book who will keep me in style in return for my devotion and imagination in the bedroom.

He was covering her face with little kisses in the after-glow of his success and murmuring that he adored her.

So you should, she thought, smiling graciously at him, and it is only the beginning. In a month from now wearing my stockings will seem to you as nothing – wait till you see what I mean to do to you! For a start, I shall subject you to everything I've learned from Laurent, his games with knickers and silk pyjamas. And after that, *mon cher*, I shall become more inventive.

'Odette,' Pierre murmured, 'it was never like that before for me – I think I'm in love with you.'

'*Ah chéri*,' she said. She kissed his cheek warmly and ran her hand down his body to grasp the wet and softening part slipping out of her, 'how nice for both of us if you love me.'

I intend to turn your prudish little brain inside-out, Pierre chéri, she thought, much amused – *inside a month I shall teach this massive thick thing of yours to dominate your life, waking and sleeping. It will stand up stiff if I merely look at it and you will worship me on your knees.*

Odette Visits Friends

Odette in a stylish pink-and-white tweed coat and an ivory silk scarf over her brunette hair came up the steps from the Metro – on her way to visit Robert Dorville at last. The autumn streets gleamed with morning rain, but the sun had struggled through the overcast sky and it was a cheerful day, in keeping with her mood.

She liked the district where Robert lived. Opposite stood the church of the Madeleine, dominating the square with its columns and steps – a place of worship Odette had never been inside and never intended to enter. On those few occasions she felt it important to remind God of her existence, she preferred to say her prayers in a less grandly intimidating church.

But across from the church was the daily flower-market with a sprawl of colour, reds and yellows and blues and the greenery. Perhaps not so great a variety of flowers at this season of the year, but a pleasure to see. From the Place Madeleine there was a view down the broad rue Royale, to Place de la Concorde where the traffic surged round the obelisk and the jetting fountains.

Odette turned along the Boulevard de la Madeleine, crowded at three in the afternoon by shoppers and strollers. Boutiques and cafés, department stores, travel agents – all this was what she adored, the trappings of enjoyment, people there to spend money on themselves. Robert's apartment was in a quiet street off the Boulevard and very well placed for everything. To Odette's way of thinking Robert lived in an ideal location, one she envied.

This time she'd phoned in advance – it would be too absurd to catch him naked in bed a second time with the woman who had the lavishly oversize breasts. Naturally, he said it would give him the greatest pleasure to see Odette again – lunch, perhaps, or dinner? But Odette had a great many calls on her time – Robert knew nothing of her arrangements, of course – and she suggested dropping in at his apartment in the afternoon. Robert agreed at once, his prime concern being to get her clothes off.

That was Odette's intention too. Her visit was to give Robert the opportunity of stripping her naked and doing what he wanted to her. In her mind it was like paying an insurance premium; if disaster should strike, Robert would rescue her.

There was no hurry to get to him – she wandered along looking in shop windows, particularly at clothes. She could recall what she was wearing the first time she went to Robert's apartment – he'd taken her to dinner at a small restaurant nearby. It was a pink two-piece, close-fitting and belted in at the waist. She'd sat on a black leather sofa in Robert's apartment, with a glass of cognac in her hand – till he kissed her and felt down inside her jacket to fondle her. He tried to put his hand up her skirt between her thighs – but it was so tight that it frustrated his groping. That's why she remembered what she had worn that night.

In the bedroom he stripped her naked and launched them

into a night of passion she would never forget. He was like Jacques in this, he was able to give her orgasm after orgasm and never get tired. But unlike Jacques, he wasn't trying to dominate her and prove his masculinity. Robert had no doubts about himself, he simply showed her he adored her. And that was pleasing to know, not only at the time but as a comfort for the unknown future.

At the apartment door he greeted her with embraces and kisses until she was laughing and almost breathless. He took her coat, her head-scarf, hung them up and led her into his sifting-room. He was wearing no jacket, just an expensive pale blue shirt and dark blue trousers, a silk scarf round his neck and tucked down in the shirt. His initials, RD, were embroidered on the breast. They sat on the sofa of sleek black leather and exchanged news like old friends. Naturally, the news was carefully edited on both sides, Odette explained she was working now for the world famous couturier Jean-Luc Marigny, but she said nothing at all about sharing the bed of Giselle Barras.

The eyebrow-raising truth was that to her own surprise Odette had developed a certain taste for Giselle's style of love — but not to the exclusion of men, that was unthinkable. As a change from the usual, an interesting alternative to lying on her back with a long stiff thing sliding into her. A different route to pleasure. And, to be candid, love with Giselle was more than a diversion — it was very useful, a step forward in her career.

Robert enquired if she no longer modelled for that underwear artist Breville. Odette said only rarely, *Vogue* sometimes asked for her by name and this was so very flattering that she posed to oblige the editor, not the artist. There was a doubtful look on Robert's face at that, he had his own views on Odette's arrangements with Breville. He was not likely to forget that it was after her first visit to Breville's studio that the thicket of walnut-brown curls between her thighs had turned into a clipped heart-shape.

He naturally made no mention at all of the two or three women who had consoled him since Odette's departure with her suitcase from his apartment. Certainly he made no reference to the older woman with big pink balloons on her chest Odette had seen in his bed on the occasion of her unexpected arrival. And Robert being Robert it was not long before he had an arm around Odette's shoulders, a hand on her knee, words of endearment on his lips. He raised an eyebrow in comic style as he asked his next question:

'Now you hardly ever pose for the underwear artist, have you considered letting your little fur-coat grow back to its state of nature, *chérie*, or do you still trim it to a heart?'

'I'm very fond of my *little heart*,' she told him with a grin, 'and so are you, Robert – every time you see me you want to get your hands on it.'

She saw no point in informing him it was Laurent Breville who kept it so neatly trimmed – it would annoy Robert to know that. His hand slid under her skirt and up her leg – no problems with a tight skirt today, she had planned for this visit by putting on a green and cream striped frock. It had a swirling skirt and the bodice had big buttons down to the waist. Buttons like that excited men, Odette knew – the moment they saw buttons they had an urgent desire to undo them.

Buttons on women's clothes were an aphrodisiac for men – ns failed totally to have the same effect. It would be amusing to discuss this with Laurent and see if he became inspired to draw women's underwear with buttons. Perhaps he could create a new style from his fantasies!

For the same reason that she was wearing a frock with a loose skirt to visit Robert, Odette had knickers which allowed a hand to enter the lace-edged legs without struggle or groping about. As Robert's hand did now, with practised ease – his fingertips traced sensitively round the edges of her neat *little heart*.

'You know I adore you,' he said, smoothing a single fingertip over the soft lips between her thighs, 'what you do to yourself here is *très chic* – I am sure illustrators for magazines think it is the *dernier cri*. Perhaps I am a little old-fashioned, but for me the wild brown thatch you used to have was very exciting – it was so *sauvage*. You remember when you lived here with me, I could never leave it alone – night and day I had to touch it, and stroke it – and ride it.'

'Dear Robert,' said Odette, moving her legs apart to make it easier for him to feel her, 'between good friends what do a few curls matter? How is my old companion *Jean Jeudi*?'

He smiled at the childish name for it, his smile became wider as she ran his zipper down and slid a hand into his trousers to clasp *Jean Jeudi* and bring him into the light of day.

'Hard as a steel bar,' she said, 'as ever!'

She swung her legs up on the sofa and lay full-length upon it with her head in Robert's lap. His fingers had lost touch with her *joujou* when she changed position, he undid the buttons down her bodice and put his hand down the top of her slip to caress her elegant little breasts.

'Odette – why not move back into my apartment?' he said.

She was staring at close quarters at the stiffness rearing up out of his open trousers, formidable in its size and power, the only one that could compete with Jacques' in giving pleasure . . . but Jacques was a shadow from the past, a person to avoid being involved with. Her hand slid up and down fondly, recalling the advantages Robert had to offer.

'Perhaps I will,' she murmured, 'but not now – I want to find out if I can succeed on my own.'

And it was true – Odette intended to make a career by her own ability, though it was not true in the way Robert was meant to understand it. Before he could continue his attempt to persuade her to move back into his apartment, she slid her head and neck forward on his lap and took his upstanding part into her mouth.

What happened was inevitable – the application of her tongue to the head of his pulsating shaft aroused him fiercely. It was only moments before he slid from under her and twisted himself around in an acrobatic contortion and was lying on her.

'Odette, Odette . . .' he was moaning.

As best she could, under his eagerly shaking body, she pulled her frock up her thighs and eased the loose leg of her knickers to the side. The arrangement was not ideal but Robert was in no condition to wait while she took them off. His hands fumbled at her thighs, his rapid breathing warned her his crisis was about to manifest itself. He moaned as he slid *Jean Jeudi* all the way into her with a single strong push – and then three strokes was all it took before he convulsed and spurted his desire.

For Odette it was too fast, of course, and he knew that. When he regained his breath he kissed her face a score of times and took her in his arms to carry her into the bedroom. He took her frock off, the bodice unbuttoned already, the skirt creased by lying on it. He removed her slip and stockings and knickers, he arranged her on the bed with her legs slightly apart – in order to show off her neat *little heart* to best advantage.

She lay at ease, with arms folded under her head to watch him undress. When she had lived with him she'd adored observing him naked – he had a strong and well-shaped body, broad in the shoulders, flat-bellied, taut of backside, muscular of thigh – he was the fittest man she knew. He had a regime of daily exercise to keep himself strong and healthy, he lifted big weights, he did push-ups and knee-bends, he used a hugely-sprung chest-expander – it was a pleasure to lie lazily in bed and watch Robert exercising every morning.

Not that he was exercising now – at least, only horizontally. He slid himself onto Odette's belly, her legs parted, her knees rose to welcome him. She gave a moan of pleasure when she felt him push up into her, her climax had been delayed too long. He made amends with vigorous thrusts, she panted and sighed to his strong rhythm. Her fingers clawed down his spine and her teeth bit his shoulder as a violent orgasm overwhelmed her.

'Robert, yes!' she groaned, not caring whether he spurted or not. But he carried on after her spasms of ecstasy finished and she opened her beautiful green eyes wide to stare into his face – his lips were drawn back in a grimace that was almost a snarl and his eyes were fixed and unseeing.

'You want me – more than anything in the world, Robert,' she whispered sharply, 'admit it!'

'Oh yes, yes,' he gasped, '*je t'adore*, Odette, *je t'adore*.'

An instant later his loins bucked and he squirted his passion into her. Odette hugged him close and pressed her hot mouth to his, she forced her tongue deep into his mouth, in the same way he forced his spurting male part into her belly. *Ah yes, Robert*, she was thinking, *it's not always convenient to come round and let you do it to me, but I'll make sure you never get rid of me – the day may arrive when I need you.*

Later on, while they were resting, Robert was content and affectionate. She raised the question that was in her mind. Who was the woman with the absurdly big nichons she had seen him in bed with?

'But surely you know,' he said, caressing her elegant breasts with a tender hand.

'If I knew, I wouldn't ask. But how could I know her?'

Robert laughed at that.

'She is Mademoiselle de Beaucourt-Villiers,' he said. 'She is the fiancée of that underwear artist you pose for.'

'What? Impossible!' Odette exclaimed.

'But true, I assure you. She was here because she thought you lived with me. She believes that you are having an *affaire* with Breville – she came here in a rage to confront you and threaten you. Perhaps she would have scratched your eyes out and pulled your hair, who knows?'

'If she came here in a rage to assault me, why was she in bed with you?'

'I'm not entirely sure,' said Robert with a shrug of his broad shoulders, 'it happened because she wanted it to happen – maybe she had some confused thought of spiting you.'

It was Odette's turn to laugh, her breasts swayed deliciously and tremors ran across her smooth little belly. Robert observed this in delight, his hand stroking her long slender thighs.

'*Ah la vache*!' she said, grinning wickedly, 'I wonder if she will be able to explain to Laurent Breville why she let another man do it between those floppy pink cushions on her chest? Not an easy thing to justify to an outraged fiancé!'

'You saw that?' said Robert with a grin. 'You were spying on me through the keyhole, *chérie*?'

'But of course not! There was still a trickle down her chest when I came into the room expecting to find you alone and eager to see me. Did you do it to her *nichons* before or after you did it between her legs?'

'As we are being so very frank with each other, after,' said Robert, 'the moment you left the room she jumped out of bed and got dressed. And that was the end of it.'

'My poor Robert, I shall make it up to you now. I can't offer you a pair of balloons like hers to ravage, but I'm certain I'm better in bed than she is. She ran off in a state of panic, did she? Let's hope she's calmed down enough by now to dream up a convincing tale to tell Laurent!'

'But surely you do not propose to inform the underwear artist that you saw her in bed with me?' Robert asked with a frown of disapproval.

'I don't think it will be necessary to do that.'

'Then what? You can't mean to blackmail her?'

Odette was certain she understood why Laurent wanted to marry Marie-Louise and it had little to do with love. But she was far from clear why Marie-Louise wanted to marry the fashion artist, a man sexually obsessed by silk knickers. But evidently she had her reasons, which raised possibilities in Odette's agile mind. Nothing so indiscreet as blackmail, naturally, perhaps a little persuasion. There had to be some way in which so well-placed a person as Mademoiselle de

Beaucourt-Villiers could be of use to Odette's career.

'No, no no,' she assured Robert, 'how could you think such a terrible thing! I intend to become her friend, as soon as the misunderstanding between us is resolved. She did me the honour of calling here, although it was the wrong address, and I shall return the compliment by calling on her. Do you know where she lives?'

'No,' said Robert, shaking his head. 'Try asking Breville the next time you pose in your underwear for him.'

Odette rolled over on her side facing Robert and caressed the inside of his thigh with a slender, perfectly-manicured hand.

'No need for you to be jealous, *chéri*,' she murmured into his ear, 'I'm not having an *affaire* with Laurent, how many times do I have to tell you that before you believe me?'

'I remember when you told me Breville was left-handed. Yet he is engaged to be married. As I have good reason to know because his fiancée turned up on my doorstep out of the blue!'

'I was mistaken,' Odette said sincerely, 'it was an easy error to make, men in the fashion business usually are. But he has no interest in me – now I know him better I can assure you that he is absolutely devoted to his fiancée. He adores her insanely – has no eyes for other women.'

'She doesn't think so,' Robert said, 'she is convinced he is deceiving her. With you.'

'Another little misunderstanding to clear up, then. I shall go to see her tomorrow without fail. Her address is sure to be in the telephone directory.'

'More to the point,' said Robert, 'where do *you* live now?'

'Didn't I tell you? When I started work at Jean-Luc Marigny

I made friends with a *vendeuse* there and she asked if I'd share her apartment – it's too big for one person, you see.'

'What is her name, this friend?' Robert asked suspiciously.

'Giselle Barras. She has a nice apartment, it's near the Parc Monceau.'

This was a fabrication – for Robert's benefit, of course. She did not live with Giselle, she spent two or three nights a week in her apartment. But it calmed, for the moment, his suspicions that she was being kept by Laurent Breville. As for Laurent, he believed she lived in the little apartment he paid for near the rue Mouffetard. He'd never been there, she made sure he had all he wanted of her when she went to his studio to pose.

She was at Daniel's apartment at least two nights a week, and often three – depending on other engagements. Most often at his parties – he entertained clients and contacts continuously – but Odette had insisted on an understanding with him that she would not be expected to go to bed with anyone but Pierre Dubon or if he was not present, Daniel himself. Unless someone was present she found particularly interesting.

Because Monsieur Dubon was so attracted to her, Daniel agreed to her stipulation. Dubon's business was worth a lot of money – he had no intention of annoying so very important a person over the services of a young woman. He suggested to Odette she ought to give Dubon the impression that she was his girlfriend alone, and certainly not let him suspect she got into bed with Daniel. Odette followed his advice – for one thing it gave her a hold over Daniel, to have influence with his most important client.

With all these diversions and entertainments and

amusements, it was a pity her own little apartment was empty so often – and so she sublet it to a nineteen-year-old striptease artist named Suzi. It seemed a logical and advantageous course of action.

This Suzi did not restrict her professional activity entirely to taking off her clothes to music in public. Her smooth chubby body had a considerable attraction for men – some of these were worthy of closer friendship, and Suzi entertained these special admirers in private, one at a time. For this purpose she needed a suitable place. Odette set the rent high and put the money in her savings account.

When she had a night free, so to speak, and nowhere to sleep, she took a room in a cheap hotel in the Boulevard St Germain. She never stayed the night with Laurent – he never asked her to because it would make him feel guilty, it would transform their artist-and-model arrangement and turn them into something like lovers. Or so his muddled thinking ran. If he had asked her to stay she would have refused anyway. It was by being his model in lace knickers that she controlled him.

She could have stayed with Robert any night, of course, but he had the inconvenient habit of asking questions. Perhaps in the future she would call him, to be taken out to dinner and bedded for the night, now that he thought she shared an apartment with another woman. Perhaps.

For the next month or so the problem of whose bed to sleep in was not going to arise. Pierre Dubon was planning to extend his insurance business abroad and on Friday he was sailing for Rio de Janeiro by luxury liner to discuss the various possibilities with businessmen there. By now he had allowed himself to become fascinated by Odette and he asked her to accompany him. It went without saying that his wife knew nothing of this.

At the time of the invitation to share his journey Pierre was flat on his back – wearing black fishnet stockings and women's black satin knickers, with ivory lace edging. Odette had bought them for him as a present – he blushed crimson when he realised what she wanted him to do and stammered objections. But he knew in his heart that he wanted to wear them and eventually he took his clothes off and put the knickers and stockings on. And then stared at himself in a mirror with tremulous pride.

'I've never dared to dream...' he said, almost to himself.

Odette smiled encouragingly and patted his cheek. She made him lie on his back on the bed – the setting for this comical scene was a suite in the Grand Hotel. There was a smile of content on Pierre's round face as he obeyed. How convenient for a prude to be persuaded by someone else to do what he wanted to do.

It was only a moment or two before Odette was naked herself – except for a thick gold necklace Pierre had bought for her. She got on to the bed and knelt over his astounded face, and she rubbed her trim, neatly-clipped *joujou* against his mouth. He made soft gurgling noises – shock, delight, dismay, arousal – only he was able to distinguish his own emotions. But it did not take long before his plump legs kicked up off the bed and he went into an involuntary orgasm. Odette rode his face faster and harder, and grinned to see a wet stain spread across the front of his satin knickers.

She rose from his gasping mouth and lay beside him, a hand on his chest. She knew what to expect when he recovered. He'd roll her on her back and lick her body centimetre by centimetre from her chin to her toes. There was no doubt about it – for a prude he had learned a tremendous amount since he first met Odette at Daniel's party. And she congratulated herself on how well she'd carried out her secret promise to turn his mind inside-out.

Eventually he'd take the black knickers off and lie on her to do it the usual way – if it could be called usual for him to be wearing fishnet stockings. But to her surprise, no sooner had she dismounted from his face to lie beside him than he told her about his intended voyage to South America and asked her to go with him. Luxury class, pampered all the way.

She thought it over for one whole second before she accepted. It was almost too good to be true. A month uninterrupted to use her charms on Pierre – she was confident she could teach him in that time to spurt in his underwear if she touched his hand. As for raising her skirt to let him glimpse her thighs, that would send him into ecstasies of rolling on the floor by the time she had trained him properly.

And various other tricks to keep him in a condition of happy dependency – he would shower her with jewels to be permitted to kiss her *little heart.* When they returned to Paris he would be so completely under her spell he would be delighted to find her a luxury apartment in a prestige district and furnish it to her taste. An apartment not too close to Giselle, not too far from Robert, both of whom she intended to keep as reliable friends.

There was the little matter of explaining to Giselle that she would be away from Paris for some weeks and that she wanted her job back at Jean-Luc Marigny when she returned. A way had to be found of persuading Giselle that there was no question of going away with a man – that would make her bitterly jealous and end their friendship.

The next evening found Odette at Giselle's apartment, smiling and affectionate. Giselle's accomplishments included impressive skill in the kitchen and she produced an exquisite dinner. They sat on the sofa in the sitting-room afterwards, with coffee and cognac, talking and occasionally kissing gently.

When the glasses were empty Giselle slowly undid the front of Odette's frock and slipped a hand inside to stroke her elegant little breasts – she never wore a bra when she was at Giselle's because experience showed it to be an inconvenience. She rested her head on Giselle's shoulder, held close by the arm round her waist, and let Giselle kiss her cheek and caress her breasts.

After a long and delicious time she felt her friend's fingers feeling up her thighs above her stockings. Fingers slid easily into her knickers, long thin fingers that knew how to thrill.

'Odette,' she heard Giselle murmuring, 'you are so beautiful, *je t'aime, chérie, je t'aime.*'

Soon she was pulling Odette's tiny silk knickers down to look at her little heart and stroke it – she parted the warm lips in the neat brown curls and pressed a fingertip to the bud she had exposed. She leaned down to kiss it tenderly – to Odette with her eyes closed it felt much the same as if Robert was doing it to her. Or did it? Was there a subtle difference in the caress of a woman – or was it in the mind that the quality was changed to something more nurturing and less demanding? Who could say, and did it matter, when the end result was the same ecstasy?

Ça va, she said to herself, *I came here to explain why I shall be away from Paris for a few weeks and dear Giselle is falling in love with me – or says she is. It won't be too hard to tell her I am going to stay with my widowed sister in Anjou, because she is seriously ill and needs help with her three children.*

Needless to say, neither of Odette's sisters lived in Anjou – or anywhere else outside Paris. Or were widows. One sister had married a railway worker and lived in the same street they had grown up in. The other sister, the one with the three children, lived only a ten-minute walk away and had never troubled to marry the fathers of any of her children. But that was not for Giselle to know or guess.

'No, I want to see you do it first,' said Odette and she took Giselle's slim wrist to pull her hand away. She pressed Giselle to lie on the sofa with her knees up and sat between them. She bent down, hands on bare skin above her stockings, and breathed hotly on the thin silk between her open thighs. Giselle sighed and murmured and wriggled at the warm intangible touch upon her skin and said they should go into the bedroom and undress.

And there they were, naked and beautiful together. Giselle on her back, still with a model's figure at forty – small pear-shaped breasts with pink tips, flat belly and long slim thighs. Odette stroked her belly and the thin lips under a little triangle of dark-brown curls.

'*Je t'aime,* Odette, *je t'aime* . . .' Giselle murmured again as her belly quivered and Odette's tongue touched her exposed pink bud tenderly.

Odette ravished her gently at first, she made her shiver and sigh – then more insistently as Giselle's excitement grew, then fiercely until Giselle was shrieking and arching her back. Soon enough she was sobbing with delight and unable to

10c. (styles) hardboiled / humorous / hardcore / ironic / romantic / realistic?

10d. Are there any other ingredients that particularly appeal to you?

11. We try to create a cover appearance that is suitable for each title. Do you consider them to be successful?

12. Would you prefer them to be less explicit / more explicit?

13. We would be interested to hear of your other reading habits. What other types of books do you read?

14. Who are your favourite authors?

15. Which newspapers do you read?

16. Which magazines?

17 Do you have any other comments or suggestions to make?

If you would like to receive a free erotic novel of the Editor's choice (available only to UK residents), together with an up-to-date listing of Headline Delta titles, please supply your name and address. Please allow 28 days for delivery.

Name ....

Address ....

....

....

Headline Delta Erotic Survey

In order to provide the kind of books you like to read – and to qualify for a free erotic novel of the Editor's choice – we would appreciate it if you would complete the following survey and send your answers, together with any further comments, to:

> Headline Book Publishing
> FREEPOST (WD 4984)
> London
> NW1 0YR

1. Are you male or female?
2. Age? Under 20 / 20 to 30 / 30 to 40 / 40 to 50 / 50 to 60 / 60 to 70 / over
3. At what age did you leave full-time education?
4. Where do you live? (Main geographical area)
5. Are you a regular erotic book buyer / a regular book buyer in general / both?
6. How much approximately do you spend a year on erotic books / on books in general?
7. How did you come by this book?
7a. If you bought it, did you purchase from: a national bookchain / a high street store / a newsagent / a motorway station / an airport / a railway station / other . . .
8. Do you find erotic books easy / hard to come by?
8a. Do you find Headline Delta erotic books easy / hard to come by?
9. Which are the best / worst erotic books you have ever read?
9a. Which are the best / worst Headline Delta erotic books you have ever read?
10. Within the erotic genre there are many periods, subjects and literary styles. Which of the following do you prefer:
10a. (period) historical / Victorian / C20th / contemporary / future?
10b. (subject) nuns / whores & whorehouses / Continental frolics / s&m / vampires / modern realism / escapist fantasy / science fiction?

male part, but for a few moments he was confused about the woman he was holding.

'Ah, ah, ah . . .' he sighed as he rubbed himself against a warm soft belly. She bent her knees and drew them up and gripped his narrow hips between them.

'Do it, Laurent,' she whispered, 'Do it, *chéri.*'

He wailed and convulsed in quick little spasms – and she felt a sudden wet warmth soak through the thin silk to her skin. She stroked his head while he became calm.

'See,' she whispered close to his ear, 'it was perfectly all right to do that, because I am your model and what you do to me is for art and culture.'

'Odette,' he said, certain again now which woman he was with.

'When you are ready, Laurent,' she said, 'you must take me to your bedroom – my *little heart* needs your expert attention.'

'Yes,' he said, his interest reviving, 'yes, *chérie.*'

And after that, she thought, *when you have been on top of me, I shall tell you about my visit to Anjou to care for my sister. And you will insist on giving me money for the journey and for food and medicine and whatever for her while I am there. When I return to Paris you will be so happy to see me that you will do anything I ask,* chéri, *to promote my career.*

'Let's go to the bedroom,' he murmured, 'we must take off the knickers I have spoiled and then I will pay my respects to your adorable *little heart*. You like me to do that.'

'Yes, Laurent,' she said, 'of course, *chéri.*'

a woman who has every right to demand your complete fidelity.'

'Yes,' he sighed pitifully, 'it is inexcusable,' and his arms were round Odette, holding her close, his flushed cheek against hers. He was hard and thick in her hand. She smiled to herself over his shoulder and pressed his jumping part against the soft silk of her knickers, just above her little heart.

'My poor Laurent,' she murmured, 'shall I take them off?'

'Not yet,' he gasped, furiously aroused by her underwear – as she had known he would be. He slid his throbbing hardness up and down against the silk, his hands were scrabbling under her slip to undo the cream bra and stroke her elegant little breasts.

In his emotional confusion he remembered how he had made love to Marie-Louise in her ancestral chateau. The night she let him do it to her three times on her old and creaking wooden bed. At dawn he woke up ready again – but she wanted him to go back to his own room. He rolled her on her back and was on top of her, trying to push her legs apart with his knees. But she resisted, he was too aroused to stop – he slid his throbbing stiffness up and down on her belly, rubbing against her chiffon night-dress, until he cried frantically and Marie-Louise felt a warm wetness soak through the chiffon to her belly.

Perhaps it was because he'd just been talking to Marie-Louise on the phone and he'd become excited by her invitation to visit her apartment that evening and stay with her all night. Perhaps down in his unconscious some instinctive part of him understood that she was concealing her own sexual arousal while she talked to him disjointedly – and someone was with her doing things to her . . . perhaps it was the rub of silk on his and long in her hand, 'do not ask me about Pauline, I implore you.'

'Her name is Pauline, is it? We are making progress now. And you are too ashamed to speak of her for the simple reason that you betrayed your fiancée, Mademoiselle de Beaucourt-Villiers, with this Pauline with the fat thighs.'

'I couldn't help myself,' he sighed, no longer denying it, 'I have missed you so much, Odette, since you stopped coming every day to pose for me. What could I do?'

'So you did precisely what I warned you against,' Odette said with a sad expression, 'evidently Mademoiselle Pauline and your fiancée are acquainted. You did the wrong thing, you know that. You were deliberately unfaithful to the woman who loves you and she will never forgive that if she finds out.'

'No, it was not like that,' Laurent protested, attempting to justify himself. 'I paid Pauline the proper fee for posing – it was all done professionally.'

'Of course it was,' said Odette, her hand sliding up and down his stiff part, 'it was highly professional to ask her to pull the nightdress up to her waist and show you her *joujou* – and it was even more professional when you got this out and slid it up her. There is no point in trying to deceive yourself, Laurent – giving her money afterwards cannot change the facts.'

While she was speaking she slid forward on the high stool and pulled the cream silk slip she was wearing up round her hips. A tug on Laurent's hard part drew him in close between her parted thighs.

'*Ah, mon Dieu!*' he moaned. 'If only I'd waited for you! But you come here so rarely now, Odette . . .'

'There is no possible excuse,' she said, 'you have betrayed

BONJOUR AMOUR

'Ah, a friend,' she said, 'but isn't that dangerous?'

Laurent came round the drawing-board to take the sketches and shuffle them haphazardly into the folder. Odette held on to the chiffon nightdress picture and stabbed at it with one long thin finger to illustrate her point.

'But the pose is so obvious,' she said, 'there she is on your chaise-longue, with her legs apart and naked below the waist to let you see her charms and excite you. Don't try to deceive me, Laurent, I know you too well for that.'

'Certainly not,' he insisted, 'no such thing took place – and since you are so interested, I can tell you she never actually posed like that for me. I drew this from memory and imagination after she'd gone, for my own amusement. That is the truth.'

'But that isn't how you like to do things,' said Odette, 'you like to sit here behind your drawing-board stroking yourself as a woman poses in silk underwear for you. It was hardly a secret – Madame Drouet hinted as much. And you were giving yourself a little thrill the first time I came here to work for you – if I hadn't caught you at it you would have squirted into your hand. We are good friends now, Laurent, we have no need for lies.'

Laurent stared at her open-mouthed, not knowing what to say. She dropped the sketch on the drawing-board and slid the zip of his black linen trousers down.

'We must have only the truth between us,' she said seriously, and she reached inside his trousers to grasp his limp part.

'So *this*,' she said, giving it a squeeze, 'was never in *this*, is that what you want me to believe?'

At the second *this* she prodded with a stiff forefinger at the narrow strip of curls between the thighs of the woman sketched.

'Odette . . .' Laurent breathed, as his male part grew stiff

277

conscience. She lay on the chaise-longue in another sketch – wearing the flimsiest nightdress – one knee up, the other leg dangling over the side, a pout on her face. The nightdress was shown casually pulled up to her waist to the part men were mainly interested in.

Odette saw that the model did not have a *little heart* between her spread thighs – she had a narrow strip of light-brown hair, only a few centimetres across, not the usual triangle. At least she had no neat heart shape when Laurent made the sketch of her – but perhaps afterwards he had taken her to his bedroom to use his little scissors and razor.

Impossible, Odette decided, it was not possible to turn that upright strip into a heart. For that it was necessary to have a broad fleece like her own natural growth before Laurent decided to improve it. And apart from that, surely he'd never dare attempt to repeat the unique charm he had created for Odette? Ah yes, my poor Laurent, she thought, you are still besotted by me – the blonde with the thick thighs is merely a substitute when I am too busy to visit you and let you play with me.

Footsteps at the door: Laurent had returned while Odette was looking at the drawings. She made no attempt to hide them – she sat on his high stool and spread them out on his drawing-board. Laurent came into the studio and stopped dead, his face turning red when he saw what she was looking at.

'You've found another model,' Odette said with a knowing grin that made his flushed face turn pale. 'Did Madame Drouet at the agency choose her for you, *chéri*?'

'No, she is not from the agency,' he said, and then wished he hadn't when he saw Odette's grin expand further.

– to her it was evident that Marie-Louise had gone into orgasm at the moment she stopped talking. To hear Laurent babble on about having her three times that night was meaningless. She wondered if it was Robert who was doing it to Marie-Louise as she spoke to her fiancé – something to ask him when she returned from her trip to Rio de Janeiro. If it was Robert, he would tell her and make a joke of it.

She put the phone down silently on Laurent's foolish babbling and drifted round the studio looking in filing cabinets, an ear open for the sound of his return. Her search was rewarded – she found a green folder that held nine or ten sketches. Three were of herself and she had seen them before, they were made for his own pleasure, not for publication.

He had sketched her standing in ivory lace knickers, breasts cupped in her hands. And another of her reclining on the chaise longue in a black chiffon nightdress, her charms very visible.

Far more interesting were the sketches of a blondish woman – she looked to be in her late twenties, too old really to be a model. She had a long slim body and good posture. But her thighs were much too thick. *Really*, Odette said to herself with the composure of a woman with perfect thighs, *how could Laurent even think about using her as his model*. But then, it was not a question here of illustrations for a fashion magazine. The woman stood naked, a smile on her face and her hands on her hips. Naked that is, for most practical purposes – she wore three little triangles of a shiny black material.

Though Odette couldn't know it, the model was Pauline Joubert and she had visited Laurent's studio more than once. Though not to pose, except as an excuse for his uneasy

Jacques was not to be deterred. He was on his knees to slide his hands underneath Marie-Louise's hips and lift her bottom up off the bed. She wriggled and tried to escape his grip without any indication of her struggle appearing in her voice, but she could not shake free from him.

'I am alone, I assure you, *chérie*,' said Laurent feebly.

Jacques had Marie-Louise on her knees now, her bare bottom in the air and her face down on the bed with the phone pressed to her mouth. She very nearly shrieked and betrayed her plight to Laurent when she felt Jacques press the head of his stiff part between her thighs – it slid into the soft warmth of her *joujou* and he was doing it to her again!

Fortunately, Laurent had no inkling of this. He sensed Marie-Louise's agitation, how could he not, when a man was mounted on her back and thrusting ruthlessly into her? But he thought she was annoyed with him because she suspected he was lying when he said he was alone.

'Laurent – I want you here this evening,' she gasped into the phone, her belly shaking with spasms of delight. 'You are to be here at seven, not later! And you will stay here all night, do you understand me?'

Hastily Marie-Louise turned the phone away from her mouth and pressed it down hard into the bed to block out her long shrieks of ecstasy as Jacques' ferocious mauling drove her to a climax.

'Yes, *chérie*, I shall be with you this evening on time,' said Laurent, 'for dinner, yes? And then?'

But there was only silence from her end of the line, and this he interpreted as an invitation to tell her what he intended to do to her all night.

Odette had heard all she wanted to hear of the conversation

his thin face had sneered down into hers, his lips drawn back and teeth bared – she had experienced the orgasm twice before he spurted.

He was crushing her breasts in his hands again – her mind was in a turmoil. Without knowing why, she reached for the bedside phone and dialled Laurent's number. Her breathing was not back to normal, she struggled to control her voice and be calm while she wished Laurent *Bonjour*. She could not speak about what was uppermost in her mind, she chattered on about nothing much, and Laurent responded awkwardly.

It was not for her to know that he was riddled by feelings of guilt – because as he was talking to his fiancée he was looking at Odette sitting on the chaise-longue, in a pair of white silk knickers. His male part was standing up boldly in his trousers, and that added to his moral discomfort and shame.

In Marie-Louise's bedroom, Jacques continued his caresses. He kissed her thighs, he slid a hand under her bottom and tickled between the soft cheeks. She tried to drag his hand away while talking normally to Laurent – but Jacques' impudent tongue was between her legs, lapping at her *joujou*. She clutched the phone to her ear and rolled over, face-down, to protect herself from these infuriating and deliciously exciting attentions.

'Are you working, Laurent?' she asked, her voice sounding a trifle shrill. 'Is there a naked model in your studio? Are you aroused sexually – tell me the truth!'

'But of course not!' he protested, thankful that he had left the studio to speak on the sitting-room extension and was able to say he was alone with complete truth. 'I am alone here and I am attending to my business correspondence.'

'The truth, Laurent. I insist – is anyone there with you?'

was not a question Marie-Louise had asked herself. While he did, what was the point of asking? Or worrying? His reasons might not be to her liking, she was intelligent enough to know that. He thought she was rich, the answer was no doubt to be found in that.

Meanwhile, he was there in her bed and he had just had her. A warm glow of happiness pervaded her – he had slipped out of her and was lying on his back smoking a cigarette, but it was as if she still felt the solidity of his stiff part inside her belly. He didn't say much when he was pleasuring her, he was hardly an intellectual – he called her Loulou and he groaned in the final moments. None of which mattered in the least, because he alone knew the trick of sending her into a spine-bending orgasm.

He stubbed out his cigarette and began to fondle her massive breasts, his long thin naked body pressed hard against her warm fleshiness. His touch made her body shake. He had taken her so fiercely, ten minutes ago, so savagely – as if he meant to kill her! This was how Marie-Louise imagined it had been during the Revolution, when a mob from the gutter vented its blind rage on a helpless aristo . . . so brutal, so exciting.

She lay on her back in semi-exhaustion, waiting for his touch to arouse her body into new frenzies. He was naked but she was not – almost contemptuously he had pulled her nightdress up to her waist to bare her for his furious lunging, and the top was deliberately torn open to expose her breasts to his handling; those oversize breasts she had been slightly ashamed of – until she met Jacques.

While he was ravaging her body so bestially, his strong hands had been clamped round her throat as if to choke her, phone to listen, and her guess was confirmed, it was Marie-Louise on the line.

To Odette's discerning ear there was a curious note in Marie-Louise's voice – as if talking to Laurent had aroused her – but surely not! Odette listened carefully to the silences as well as the words, and reached the conclusion that someone else was present at the other end of the line. And that it was a man and he was touching Marie-Louise in a way that excited her.

It was a shrewd guess. In simple truth Marie-Louise was still in bed at eleven in the morning and there with her was Odette's childhood friend, Jacques Brolin. Since the day he had demonstrated the true purpose of sexual activity to her, Marie-Louise wanted to experience that unfamiliar but ecstatic sensation very often indeed – she had years of lost time to make up for! Other men ought to be able to take her to orgasm, but her experiments so far had been disappointing – Laurent had produced only the mild feelings of pleasure she had known before.

But Jacques; whatever his social shortcomings he scored every time – every arrow from his bow hit the gold dead centre of the target. Until Marie-Louise could find a more suitable lover who could make her feel the same sensations, Jacques would have to do. She had arranged for him to come to her apartment every day straight from the train that brought him from the suburbs – and his young wife – and he was in her bed by nine each morning. It had been necessary to reorganise the maid's hours – she arrived at midday now – by which time Jacques had thrilled Marie-Louise and gone.

Why this working-class young man should fall in with her wish and spend his weekday mornings in bed with her – this no longer believed Laurent was having an *affaire* with Odette, it was Madame Drouet at the model agency and her insinuations that were responsible for misleading her, she explained.

The Drouet woman was malicious and a spiteful gossip with her hints of shameful practices, to say nothing of perversity, when the truth was that every one who knew Laurent knew what a sweet and sincere man he was, candid and goodhearted.

Odette agreed completely about Madame Drouet – the woman was unreliable – and Odette had long ago determined to have nothing more to do with her. She agreed with Marie-Louise that Laurent was a sweet and sincere man – during the time she had posed for him she had never heard him utter the least suggestive word. He was completely professional in his work, totally trustworthy. She posed for hours in underwear while he sketched and he had never made the slightest approach to her – the idea was ridiculous!

And Odette assured Marie-Louise that though she had found her naked in bed with a good friend of hers, Robert Dorville, there was obviously a perfectly reasonable explanation. Marie-Louise sounded a little strained as she agreed and declared her belief that so sympathetic a friend as Odette would never say even one word about the incident. And Marie-Louise felt no necessity to mention that she'd met another friend of Odette's by chance – a tall, thinnish man named Jacques Brolin, who had done remarkable things to her. And was still doing them, every weekday.

Laurent's phone conversation became more involved. He said to his caller and to Odette that he'd continue on the phone in his sitting-room, and off he went, leaving her alone in the studio. She waited a few moments before picking up the leather screen to change. This posing for Laurent was only a formality, an excuse to ease his conscience – she and he knew why she was there. Whatever the cause of his anxiety, it would vanish when he was at his drawing-board, staring at her body in scanty silk underwear, his paint brush in one hand and his stiff male part in the other.

The underwear she was to model was pretty enough – a matching set of short slip, bra and knickers in cream. But it was for an older woman, she decided. Suitable for someone in her thirties or perhaps her forties. Someone with a body less exciting than Odette's. But this was the game Laurent wanted to play, so why not? She undressed and put the set on, emerged from behind the screen and stood waiting while Laurent looked at her.

'Imagine you have just got up and are dressing to go out,' he said. 'You are inspecting yourself in a mirror, one hand on the back of your head pushing your hair up.'

Odette thought it banal, but that was not important – in five minutes he would be bored with his pretence of drawing and want to lie on the chaise longue with her. But he had hardly begun – there were not more than three brushfuls of water-colour on the paper – when the phone rang. He abandoned his drawing-board to answer – it was fixed to the wall like a public telephone.

Odette sat down on the pink velvet chaise-longue until he was ready to start again. But it turned into a long conversation and he glanced uneasily from time to time over his shoulder at her – a certain giveaway that it was his fiancée on the line!

Odette smiled secretly to herself. She had paid her respects to Mademoiselle de Beaucourt-Villiers and after some antagonism they had reached an understanding. Marie-Louise to be prepared. He too would have the honour of meeting *Suzi Charron*, the younger sister of his favourite model. If he did, Odette's guess was that he would be so enchanted by the wrap clinging to Suzi's naked body that he would want to sketch her. And pay her a model fee.

The underground train was slowing, the next stop was Odette's and she stood up. The man sitting opposite her had lowered his newspaper until the bottom edge touched his thighs and hid what he had been so willing to display. Now it was his face on show, over the top of the morning paper — a full face under the brim of his hat, a face with a vacant expression. He was holding the newspaper awkwardly, Odette observed, then she realised that he was holding it one-handed. His other hand was behind it, and no great imagination was required to guess what he was doing.

The train ran out of the tunnel into the lit station and Odette moved along the carriage towards the door. As she passed the man with the newspaper he stared up at her, his mouth open, his expression so intent that she knew he had reached the very moment of climax and was spurting into his hand. She gave him a mocking grin as she went past him and murmured, *Vive le sport*!

Dear Laurent was looking just a little harassed that morning, she noted when she reached his studio. His clothes were casual, but stylish as ever — a sleeveless suede jacket that was dove-grey and soft to the touch, open over a bright yellow shirt and dramatically black trousers. He kissed Odette's cheek and said he was pleased to see her, and he had an elegant and beautiful set of underwear for a drawing for *Vogue*. But she felt that he was slightly worried.

It was eleven in the morning; she went behind the red

BONJOUR AMOUR

She would make certain he had nothing to pray for after that. When she returned she wanted to take up with him where she had left off, his contacts could be very useful to her.

Ah, but there was something else to remember – Daniel knew of Odette's little apartment. And he was a good friend of Laurent. There could be unfortunate results if he gossiped. To make sure Daniel had something to occupy his thoughts besides the redhead with the plump *nichons* – Annette Colombes, over whom Odette had no influence – and to prevent her getting too close to Daniel while Odette was away, she had devised a little stratagem.

She was going to tell Daniel that in her absence her younger sister would be living in her apartment. Daniel was predatory – and inquisitive. He would surely go there when he had nothing else to do. And he would find Suzi, a pretty nineteen-year-old blonde with a happy smile and very well-developed *nichons*.

Odette had told Suzi about Daniel – the stripper was ready to present herself as Odette's sister, and flash her body about in the skimpy wrap that seemed to be all she wore at home. Daniel would find that of interest and he would surely decide he must have her at once – he was like that. Suzi would let him, though not for nothing. She was a girl with a living to earn.

And Daniel would devise a way of using a girl of her talents to assist him to entertain his business clients, of that Odette was certain. She might become another on offer to clients being wined and dined – perhaps do her striptease dance to gramophone music in Daniel's apartment.

Odette had also warned Suzi about Laurent – she doubted if he would visit the apartment in her absence, but it was best

The next time she looked at the man, there below the edge of his newspaper his trousers were undone at the waist, as if his zipper was slipping down by accident. A few centimetres of his white shirt could be seen, nothing more. She saw his face fully when he lowered the paper to turn a page – it was not a face of much interest and he was careful not to meet her eyes. And when he raised the newspaper and read on the zip had slipped all the way down and the white shirt was pulled up.

Something was revealed that stood upright, something that had a pale-purple head. Odette shrugged slightly, men had an absurd belief that they had only to bring out *Jean Jeudi* in a state of erection and every woman who saw it would be struck speechless with admiration. At night-time the dark corners and doorways of Paris contained lurking men with trousers undone, prepared for a quick display to any passing female. *Put it away idiot*, Odette said in her mind, *the only ones I play with belong to important men who adore me and help me with my career – go to the nearest bar, mon ami, and you will find a girl who will gladly join in your game for a few francs.*

She ignored the man and resumed her previous train of thought – there was no reason to tell Daniel the story of the sister in Anjou because he knew his important client Dubon was sailing for South America and would not be surprised to hear Odette was going with him. Daniel was such a cynic that it was possible to be truthful with him. He had a great many women friends – and a casual attitude to them. If one of them vanished for a while it was of no great significance.

But before she left on Friday with Pierre, Odette intended to have a night of saying her prayers on her knees for Daniel.

Odette Makes Her Arrangements

There were arrangements to be made about Daniel, Odette thought on the Metro journey to Laurent's studio on the morning after her passionate night with Giselle. The rush-hour was long past and there were not many people in the carriage rattling through the tunnel south under the Seine towards the Edgar-Quinet stop.

There was a man sitting opposite her, a man in a brown trilby hat and a brown-checked overcoat. He held an open newspaper up in front of him as if reading the daily account of murder, wars abroad, political chicanery, provincial stupidity and the other irritations of normal existence. But Odette saw how he glanced at her legs every few seconds over the top of his newspaper. It did not surprise her in the least, her legs were very beautiful – long and sleek in sheer nylon stockings.

The man's overcoat was unbuttoned, he wore a dark brown suit and a jade green tie. His shoes were well-polished – not a poor man, thought Odette, not a rich man. Approaching forty, from what she could see of his face over the newspaper and under the brim of his hat. She crossed her legs the other way, gracefully and slowly, affording the merest glimpse, for a quarter of a second and no more, of pretty knees and four centimetres of thigh.

tolerate any more sensation but no escape from it was permitted – Odette was determined to make herself remembered.

When at long last Giselle's racking ecstasy was completed the two women lay embraced in each other's arms, face to face, mouth to mouth, breasts to breasts, belly to belly, their slim thighs enlaced. *Je t'aime, chérie*, Giselle whispered yet again and it seemed a good time to tell her about a sick and widowed sister in Anjou. And then do it to her again.

It was a long and passionate night – of ecstasy and sighs and tears and gasps and laughter, kisses and caresses and savagery and tenderness and eternal declarations. And when they let each other go to sleep towards dawn Giselle believed the story about Anjou and Odette knew she had a reliable and influential friend – for as long as she let herself be adored.